THE LIFE OF
A SIMPLE MAN

Emile Guillaumin

Edited and introduced by Eugen Weber
Revised translation by Margaret Crosland

University Press of New England
Hanover and London

Published by University Press of New England
One Court Street, Lebanon, NH 03766
www.upne.com

© 1943 Editions Stock
This translation © 1982 Sinclair Browne Limited
Editorial matter © 1982 Eugen Weber

First published in the USA in 1983 by University Press of New England.
This edition first published in Great Britain in 1983 by Sinclair Browne Limited,
10 Archway Close, London N19 3TD England.
Originally published in France in 1904 as *La Vie d'un Simple*. Revised edition
published 1943 by Editions Stock.

Printed in the United States of America 10 9 8

ISBNs for the paperback edition:
   ISBN-13: 978-0-87451-246-5
   ISBN-10: 0-87451-246-8

LIBRARY OF CONGRESS CATALOGING IN PUBLICATION DATA
Guillaumin, Emile, 1873–1951.
The Life of a Simple Man.
Translation of *La Vie d'un Simple*.
Includes bibliographical references.
I. Weber, Eugen Joseph., 1925– . II. Title.
PQ2613.U43V55   1982   843´.912   82-40339
            ISBN 0-87451-247-6
            ISBN 0-87451-246-8 (pbk.)

THE LIFE OF
A SIMPLE MAN

CONTENTS

v

INTRODUCTION

1. *THE TIMES*

*The strange is not always to be found in a strange land;
one could make vast discoveries at home; one would obtain
unusual results if one learned to look on the familiar scene
with unfamiliar eyes ...*

Charles Peguy

A MAN BORN in France in 1823, as was Etienne Bertin, the simple
man this story is about, and dying, as we must presume, sometime
in the early twentieth century, would have lived through five
distinct political regimes. He would have seen the reigns of three
contrasting kings, one Emperor, and several presidents of two
different republics. The three quarters of a century of his life-span
witnessed two revolutions (1830, 1848) and several *coups d'état*. Not
the least of these was the one in December 1851 which put paid to
the second Republic before it was four years old, and the one which,
in September 1870, brushed away Napoleon III's Second Empire,
broken by the Prussian armies.

A man born in the 1820s would know people who had lived
under Louis XVI, under that *Ancien Régime* of which the monarchy
restored in 1814 was only a pale reflection; he would know more
people who had lived through the revolutions of the 1790s and
through the Napoleonic wars. Great things had happened in the
two-score years before his birth: the last surviving feudal rights
had been abolished, along with tithes, corvées, and aristocratic
privileges. The country had one code of laws, one administration,
one constitution (at a time); and, under these constitutions – which
changed, of course, as political régimes changed – a growing
electorate and representative assemblies. The French were no
longer subjects but citizens. By 1830, their king recognized that he
was no longer ruler 'of France', but 'of the French'. By 1848, all

male citizens had been enfranchised. This did not mean that all retained the franchise or that, when they did, they bothered to vote; but whatever the practice, the principle of universal (male) suffrage was never challenged again.

While political liberties advanced, the economy also surged. Between 1847 and 1867 foreign trade trebled, urban population grew from a quarter to a third of the country's total, ironworks like Le Creusot which turned out 18,000 tons a year in 1847 were producing seven times as much twenty years later. The French economy passed from the artisan to the industrial plane, although new factories still lived side by side with workshops and home industries. The value of industrial production doubled, that of trade quadrupled, so did the number of shops using steam engines, while the horsepower in them grew fivefold. New banks mobilized capital, pulling small savings into investment and speculation. The railway network grew from 3,600 to 18,000 kilometres and railway personnel from about 30,000 to about 140,000. Living standards improved and the Second Empire would see consumption of wheat rising 20 per cent, sugar 50 per cent, potatoes 80 per cent, wine 200 per cent, coffee 300 per cent.

Not everything was rosy, but many had reason to be satisfied. France was growing richer, and its wealth was being more widely distributed. Without the tax burden being raised, revenue from taxes increased from 42 to 57 francs per inhabitant between 1851 and 1861. In 1849, 730,000 persons had 97 million francs in savings banks deposits; in 1869, 2.5 million had eight times as much. Investments grew and turned increasingly from land to stocks, to the kind of deals best carried out with someone else's money, until (in the words of a novelist) the Stock Exchange became for this generation what the cathedral had been for the Middle Ages, and the habit of investment or speculation spread to the lowest classes – with Ferdinand de Lesseps of the Suez Company being told by a cab driver: 'I am one of your stockholders'. To have money invested in stocks and a *rente* – a yearly income from them – became the crux of comfort and every Frenchman's aim: what an estate or office had been under the old régime. In 1800 the sum of annuity interest paid out in the country was 713 million francs; in 1870 it was 12 billion, and 36 billion in 1895. In this last year, state bonds alone accounted for 80 billion owned by 3 million bondholders, while almost 9 million persons had savings accounts totalling over 4,000 billion francs.

A war fought and lost in 1870–71, the German annexation of Alsace and Lorraine on France's eastern border, made little economic difference in the long term. Despite serious recessions, the years from 1870 to 1914 were quite prosperous. The great depression that affected Europe in the late 1870s, the 80s, and the early 90s, hit France far less than more industrially developed and hence more vulnerable countries. Agriculture faced serious difficulties, but these were largely remedied by protective tariffs which permitted farmers to vegetate without fear of competition. Population continued to shift from agriculture to industry, but it did so slowly and, in 1914, nearly half the French still drew their living from the land. Between 1870 and 1914 industrial output tripled, the national income doubled, real wages in industry went up by fifty per cent. In 1870 a third of the peasantry was still illiterate. By 1914 illiteracy had almost been wiped out. Schools, trains, bicycles, newspapers, all spread political awareness through the land. France was a country of small men content to be independent on small profits, and a German proverb described the good life as living like God in France.

The interesting thing is how little these events and these statistics had to do with the lives of people like Etienne Bertin. Agricultural profits, quite real at least during the three decades after 1850, affected mostly those who disposed of a negotiable surplus, and they were only a small fraction of those who worked the land. For three-fourths of the peasantry, access to the market was limited to the weekly sale of some eggs or vegetables. Such people remained largely unconcerned by the ups and downs of the national – let alone the international – market. Their conditions of life improved over time, but long persisted in the closed circuit of near-subsistence. Their awareness of the wider world, beyond the market town, grew just as slowly.

This is why *The Life of a Simple Man* is so important: it places the history that we learn and teach in a new and different light, revealing the perspective of those invisible folk around whom historical developments seem to swirl, on whose backs history is often made, but whose voice seldom reaches beyond hamlet or village or field, when it is raised at all.

2. THE BOOK

I can find little to admire in this whole class of men, whose talk and dreams are of things of the soil, and who knows of nothing save the regular interchange of summer and winter with their unvarying tasks and rewards. None save Cincinnatus ... can be ennobled by the spade.

Norman Douglas

IN ONE OF his letters, Emile Guillaumin says that what he wanted to do was 'to show the gents of Moulins, of Paris and elsewhere just what a sharecropper's life is like'. Surely, he has succeeded. His book is history – very good history, the sort that comes alive. And it helps to solve one of the great problems the historian faces when he ventures beyond his desk within the city walls: the problem of evidence, of sources.

The evidence historians draw on is provided (mostly) by literate people. Literacy, like its carriers, is urban. As is only normal, the literate look at others – especially at rural people, who are twice removed – from their own point of view. But different experiences, expectations, codes of behaviour and of values, even different speech, are scarcely grounds for sympathetic understanding. And as one tries to advance beyond what one already knows, there is little to go on: illiteracy is opaque. An illiterate who learns to write is a turncoat more likely to express the prejudices of the camp he has joined than the views of the world he has so painfully abandoned. That is why the life of Etienne Bertin, born in October 1823, just fifty years and one month before his creator, remains the best thing a peasant has ever written about peasants. It is also (I think) the best description of *these particular* peasants' lives from the inside, based on memory and familiarity and personal experience. Emile Guillaumin never deserted, never rejected the world and the people he describes, and that is why his descriptions and judgments are valuable, always remembering that reality is diversity and that the world of Tiennon (and of Emile) is that of particular people in a particular place and time.

Right through the nineteenth century, most of the French population were peasants, or close neighbours of peasants, or peasants only recently come to town.[1] But only a minority of these were sharecroppers: 344,000 according to statistics in 1892. If you count families, that must have accounted for something like 1½ million souls, most of whom toiled, it seems, in central France, not far from old Tiennon.

Sharecropping is an association between a peasant who does not have the capital to buy or rent his land *or* to set himself up with the equipment, horses, cattle and seed that he will need to work it, and a landowner who will furnish stock and seed in return for a share of his tenant's products. Each party's share is established by a contract, generally imposed by the *propriétaire* on a lessee who cannot read or write. Contracts vary, of course (Tiennon indicates that they became more demanding as the years went on), but all stipulate that, before the division of produce, the tenant owes the lessor a host of goods and services, including milk, butter, fowl, and that precious commodity, time; and also an annual cash payment, a sort of minor rent to be subtracted from his share of the proceeds.

Sharecropping has been praised as making for close relationships and mutual confidence between owner and tenant; it has been criticized as an association on poor land of slow labour and timid capital. Guillaumin suggests that the former view is largely false, and that the latter may be a caricature based on reality. But it is well to remember that, even if the number of *métayers* was not over large, and even if conditions and relations with the lessors varied, the picture Guillaumin paints holds good for a far greater proportion of the French peasantry than just the sharecropper. the Bertins' way of life reflecting in a general way that of millions of others. What, then, do we learn from it?

The countryside might look charming to roving townspeople, it might bear beauty even to native eyes, but it was not the friendliest or easiest place to dwell. Life there was hard, uncomfortable. The home farm was a mess: crowded, untidy, dark, the earthen floor almost impossible to keep clean, dirt inescapable when lanes, stables and yard were a mass of mud, of muck, gluey and degrading, clinging to clogs and clothes, trailing into the house, denying all hope of freedom from dirt for the house or for oneself.

In this house – essentially one room oriented to the fire, chief source of heat and light, where the cooking was done and to which you sat as close as you could – the family, sometimes the servants too, slept several to a bed, sick and well together. Only the very ill, those with a disgusting ailment or taking their time to die, were somehow segregated; even then not far enough to keep them from

XI

hearing their kin's expressed impatience to be rid of them. The peasant world respects health (and men); it scorns the sick (and women). The pretence we sometimes put up, that our affections and our care for others are stronger than the inconvenience they create, relies on certain material conditions, like privacy, without which our needs crowd in too thick upon us to allow much heed of others.

Material conditions could scarcely be described as favourable. Hunger hugged the threshold, when it didn't cross it. The food of humans was scarcely better than that of their beasts, and not so different either in its vegetarian mass: rough rye bread, soot-coloured and gritty as if it had sand inside; vegetable soup with lard added only in the summer (when work was hardest) and at feasts; potatoes, beans, and doughy fritters so clammy the teeth could hardly move. White bread was for the sick or for a great occasion. On another farm, jam on a piece of bread was a delicacy one tasted after one's First Communion and remembered all one's life. Tiennon knew no such treat. The suit or dress that one wore to be married was put away, came out for the great occasions once or twice a year. Finally, one was buried in it. Shoes too, if any – more likely boots, if that – were put to use once or twice a year. For a family photograph taken at the beginning of the 1914 war, the photographer has to touch up his print because two brothers owned only one pair between them. Those who could bear the hardships (of course, taken for granted!) performed strangely impressive feats: in Corrèze, not very far away, pregnant Jeanneton returned from the fair at la Groslière, delivered her child behind a hedge, cut the umbilical cord, put the baby in a sack and walked back home with it.[2]

From all this there was no hope of escape, and no thought of it: 'Everyone lived resigned, obedient, carrying out his share of the bounden task according to the seasons'.[3]

Havens in a threatening world, the household, the family, were themselves a battleground where each preyed on all he could, subject only to the pecking order of some kind of power: physical force, wealth, productivity or, sometimes, a sharp tongue. In this pecking order, children came lowest, serfs of the serfs, exploited by their exploited elders when they were not ignored. The child was given the meanest tasks and, when his elders weren't using him, they jeered at him. Tiennon is put to work at seven years and, after that, he never stops. Like his elders but far more than them, he is a prisoner of fear: of the dark and the unknown, of animals, of strangers, of punishment, of dread accidents as when his unguarded sheep gorge on forbidden clover and threaten ruin. A friend of Guillaumin's was thirteen (older than many!) when he began to guard cattle at night, on the wild and lonely moor, with wolves all around. He had two dogs, a rosary on which he prayed the Virgin for protection against ghosts, phantoms and wild beasts, and a straw torch which he learnt to plait and which he lit when the wolves came too near and his flint managed to strike a spark.

Tiennon learns very soon that every pleasure must be paid for – in vexation. He also learns to evaluate his kith and kin quite coolly. In an article of the *Travailleur rural* (Nov. 1906) Guillaumin, no doubt thinking of his father's lot, denounces large patriarchal families as, above all, a formidable machine for the exploitation of children by their parents. 'Have we heard them sing its praises . . . ?' And yet, 'seen from nearby it is a mass of suffering, deprivation, bullying and a civil war of every day. Married children got bed and board and were supposed to get 100 francs a year that they generally didn't. Unmarried children got a 2-franc piece on their Sundays off'. Echoes of Tiennon, confirmed by the fact that in this case the writer writes for fellow-peasants who know whereof he speaks.

These merciless exploiters, the grownups, are in turn quite wrung and fleeced by others, masters or strangers especially from town, who despise and (they believe) exploit them. Also, as the years pass, they get their deserts from their offspring, now grown up, whom they have taught their own ruthless utilitarianism: if you're no use, you're not wanted.

Affection, all in all, plays a very small part in Guillaumin's pages. Family relations, at best, seem based on resolution or stabilization of tensions (those who live together come to terms or leave the household); eventually, on habit and exhaustion. Tiennon reports no affectionate gestures from his parents and none from him to his small children or his wife. His own kindnesses are mostly ascribed to duty, to doing what should be done, at least until he becomes a grandfather – in a slightly more comfortable world – and can indulge the luxury of now indulging someone else. With that sort of exception, the dominant family sentiments seem to be envy, the concern that sibling or in-law might get more than their share, and resentment which comes out, for example, when Tiennon leaves home.

Resentment is not reserved for family. Its favourite objects, of course, are masters and their stewards. But masters are of many kinds, and so is servitude. A good friend of Guillaumin, who later became a syndicalist, was nine years old when orphaned and entrusted to a neighbouring family of sharecroppers who lived, eighteen of them, in one room with five beds. Their young slept four or five to one cot, so the orphan was put in the stable, on a bed of bracken, where rats sometimes ran over his face and where his only comfort (and, in winter, heat) came from his neighbour, the ox Bruno. He slept there for twenty-five years.

Tiennon is a master too; he drives his servants hard. Victoire, his wife, is just as exacting, and sullen to boot; their household gets an undesirable reputation. Sometimes Tiennon can feel the servants leagued against him by resentment, sense the hostility, glimpse the hatred in their eyes, and tries to overcome it. But, as when he was a child, fear dogs his steps and spurs him on. He trembles all winter with the fear of being in want at the end of the season. He is afraid to displease Mademoiselle Julie, Gorlier's cook-mistress; he is afraid of cocks crowing after sunset; he is afraid of temptations, the 'debauchery' that would make him spend money he should scrimp and save; he is afraid of calamities, like the dreadful hail, that can destroy a year's work in a few minutes. Yet such experiences do not inflect or qualify the judgment that he passes on the *propriétaires*. Quite the contrary.

Tiennon has suffered a lot. He has had many bad years and only a few good hours, and he has found no reason to like his masters. It is not impossible to happen on a good master – his one-time friend Boulois is lucky – but they are few, and of those few none has come his way. Tiennon has no luck with masters or their stewards. They exploit him, humiliate him, rook him, refuse to let him work as he thinks best. He finally turns against them, against their rapacity, their tyranny, their insolence, which he fends off only by silence and hypocrisy.

Masters are *other*. They live in a different world, one of comfort, hygiene, leisure and manners (though these are scarcely used to deal with their inferiors) which make one ill at ease, not only because they are alien, but also because they are inappropriate to the peasant's lot. When Tiennon enters the landowner's great house he is uncomfortable, of course; but he has time to reflect that the beautiful room he sits in contains, in fact, only useless things. And he goes on to wonder if it is just that some should live so well and others, like himself, so badly. On this score his creator had already drawn certain harsh conclusions. In May 1897, fire had broken out in an aristocratic charity sale (the *Bazar de la Charité*) held annually in Paris. The flames swept through the premises, fed on the silks and laces of the fashionable crowd and, in the panic and stampede they caused, left 125 dead and hundreds injured. Guillaumin, 23, doing his military service at Aurillac (Cantal) read accounts of the disaster in the papers, which, he reported, were full of it. A letter to his parents (May 12) gave his personal view: '... of course, it is a great calamity. But when a mining accident kills two or three hundred miners it is even worse, for they found their death earning their bread and now leave misery behind them [for their dependants], whilst, after all, these noble ladies were about their pleasure. Their families will suffer morally, but not materially'.[4]

Tiennon, of course, keeps critical reflections to himself, as he does at home most of the time; unlike the masters who can afford to treat him as a yokel, a buffoon or, simply, as a curious object deserving some minutes' observation and a few notes, his safety lies in that 'art of dissimulation so necessary in life', which his father, to his cost, had never learnt. 'The poor ought to know how to keep their thoughts to themselves.' The master assumes him to be a primitive being, not quite a personality; as Norman Douglas has it, a 'shifty, retrogressive and ungenerous brood, which lives like the beasts of the field and has learned all too much of their logic'. For the master that is enough to know, especially since these creatures 'have a beast-virtue ... contentment in adversity'.

Well, yes and no. It depends what you mean. Rather, they come to terms with need, acknowledge necessity, resign themselves when there is nothing else to do, give vent to the accumulated frustration and bile when an occasion offers – what George Sand once described as 'a spirit of blind submission in perpetual struggle with a spirit of savage revolt'.[5]

Again, that is as seen from the outside: apparent apathy mixed with real violence, that eases the choler in the breast, the bitterness that swells behind the not-so-blind submission whose mask permits men to survive and endure. The violence is generally limited, accidental, soon regretted when prank or momentary rage lead to bloodshed. The uncle who had skewered an enemy on his bayonet is looked upon with awe. Tiennon's own adventure in this realm is a horrid tragedy, not easily forgotten. When one discounts the cuffs and clouts that come the way of children, the picture Guillaumin paints is strangely pacific, perhaps in reaction to Emile Zola's sensational exaggerations in *La Terre* (1887) whose peasants are savage brutes. Tiennon's folk and his neighbours may well be rough, but they are not savage. They are truculent but not callous. Hostility itself is often ritualistic and fits into the pattern of conflict with 'the others'. Hence the friction between peasant 'louts' and village artisans who mimic city gents, and the recurring fights between their gangs. For, if masters live in a different world – where the spoilt, tormenting children are only the untamed image of their sires – urban working men do so too. The brother-in-law who is a glassblower 'expected good food, meat and wine every day', exceptional fare for Tiennon and Victoire, touchstone of difference between herbivorous country and carnivorous town. Years after that difficult man has gone to push up the daisies, the nephews from Paris are more alien still. The least one can say is that to be rid of such folk is a relief.

For Guillaumin, his fellow-peasants held themselves too cheap, self-scorn their greatest drawback. In 1912 he explained the failure of their syndical efforts by what today we should describe as a whopping inferiority complex. 'I show that the peasant is considered an inferior being, that he himself tends to think of himself as such, and that most of his ills stem from that.'[6] Out of his element or exposed to interlocutors from beyond his ken the peasant is ill at ease, what the French call *mal dans sa peau*, uncomfortable in his skin. This is how he feels when he goes to market, this is how he feels when he goes to town. His clothes look odd, heavy and out of date. The homespun's weight makes his gestures stiff. His clumsy clogs make him walk awkwardly on city streets, even when he wears unaccustomed shoes. He cannot figure, hence cannot keep accounts. He cannot speak correctly and finds it hard to express himself because at home he speaks the local dialect and French does not come naturally,[7] especially the French of those who have been to school.

Tiennon wanted his son to go to school: he could have helped with the accounts, above all the accounts, and it's a nuisance too to have recourse to others for your letters. At any rate, it was not to be: he asked for help from his then master (whom else could he have asked?) when it was not in the master's interest to help. At least, when Tiennon was old and his grandson of an age to read (after 1882, all children went to school free) it became clear that print provided more than just a measure of emancipation. It offered entertainment beyond the limited hoard of tales and riddles a memory could hold. It was fun to have the paper read, even though there were things in it one did not understand. But before then more serious interests had been jeopardized by this built-in awkwardness and isolation and their concomitant: ignorance of the world's ways. Tiennon's savings were lost because he had no way to invest them securely, or even to bank them as he would do with reluctance many years later. Banks were rare, especially rare in the countryside, and scarcely interested in the small saver. No wonder lots of money stayed in mattresses, or pots, or on top of a chest, in danger of ferreting and loss.

In any case, this is a world where money is rare, where cash is scarce, where most of the coins, scrounged together out of the petty profits of the market, would go on rent and taxes and a mortgage, and the rest be hoarded for a rainy day or, if the sun shone, to buy a piece of land. There was not much money in circulation, partly because the owners who had it (at least, who had more of it than their tenants) did not like to invest. They might build new stables because it would help the stock and raise their profits; they might be persuaded to buy fertilizer, though not in every case; but they would not spend to improve the tenants' living quarters: there was no profit there. These last would remain decrepit, dank and sombre until the century turned, and a good while after that.

When landowners took the initiative in improvements, things generally went no better. Some tried to introduce novelties like drainage, fodder, selective breeding, new seeds or ploughs. Others (or the same) insisted on improving the diet of their tenants, lest their productivity should suffer; and there were those who even furnished flour, lard or wine against the peasants' will, in order to be sure that they would be consumed, and charged them for it.[8] The peasants resented the hours of free labour they were asked to invest in 'improvements' and mistrusted assurances that these would result in a higher productivity whose benefits they would share; they feared changes which, if they should fail (as in the case of Sebert's 'scientific farming') would impoverish them further; and they preferred to stay with their routines, which worked well enough most of the time.

It is well to remember that improved land, more crops, meant harder work and longer hours. More important, the costs of proposed improvements were shared equally, but the improved land or stock lay at the landlord's mercy. Every few years, sometimes every year, the contract was renewed, and then the rent could be raised or the tenant evicted. The peasants were well aware of this, and their ill will ensured the failure of ventures, many of which would probably have come a cropper anyway, but also confirmed their image as mulish reactionaries, stuck in their ruts, their mud, their mindless inertia. Encouraged by a law of 1889, that gave them absolute freedom to set the terms of lease, the more determined landlords imposed ever more stringent, more detailed, more exacting contracts, focused less on the division of produce and more on forcing their tenants to carry out their will.

Of such stuff is the class war made: not epic clash but petty nagging, a history of stinginess and mutual demurrers in which the peasant is as grudging and unforthcoming as his master. Each has learned to mistrust and play against the other. And much the same might be said of politics and religion, both concerned with the advancement or preservation of material interests, both generally disappointing. Religion is a contract with God: the peasant respects the rituals, God preserves and provides. Antoine Bertin is 'far from accepting everything priests say'. But he never misses the ceremonies on which successful crops depend, always goes to Mass on Palm Sunday, attends the procession of St Mark, sprinkles the hayloft with holy water . . . One never knows: it may work, and what is there to lose?[9] On the other hand, he and his folk disliked being forced into religious practices of no interest and of which they had lost the habit. They also saw quite clearly the discrepancy between professed beliefs of the devout and their behaviour.

Just so in politics, which show a similar break between promise and performance. Politics, in any case, are a nebulous and woolly realm, the national image blurred and out of focus. Vague, distant figures come and go in Paris, governments change, even régimes, but 'in the country we do not bother with those things. Whether Peter or Paul is at the head, we still have to cope with the same tasks', the really serious matters like sowing in March, mowing in June, harvesting in August or grinding the winter fodder in October. The regularities of the natural liturgy are only interrupted by the accidents of national history – of little consequence, as in 1848 (there is no mention of 1851), or equally irrelevant but far more tragic as in 1870 and 1914. Guillaumin's own letters from the front lines, where he spent almost all that war, reflect a peasant's acceptance of the unavoidable, but also rising anger at the awful waste not only of lives and time that could be spent on useful labour but, also, as he writes in 1916, 'to see a fine stretch of clover lost under the grapeshot'.[10]

For Tiennon, the war of 1870 is the conscription of his sons. What he remembers of the Republic set up in 1848 is that it removed the tax on salt. He knows it also introduced suffrage, and 'workmen in the towns' thought that very important. He did not think much of it, he heard a lot of contradictory assertions from all sides, he voted first for the Republic, then a few months later for its enemy, Louis-Napoleon, because it was alleged that the Republicans would have brought down the price of grain. In any case, how free were Tiennon's kind to choose how they would vote? Long after 1848 and after Louis-Napoleon, his reactionary master, M. Noris, throws Fauconnet's Republican pamphlets in the fire and tells him exactly how to vote: the gamekeeper will give him the ballot he is to put into the ballot-box.

As for Dr Fauconnet, though a man of the Left, his contracts were as harsh as those of other landowners. As stingy as his political enemies, his political views do not prevent his wringing as much money as he can out of the people that he claims to love. Patriotism is no better, no stronger than other illusions: the National Guard of Bourbon dissolves when more pressing interests call; and military service, of course, is viewed as a disaster.

'What a difference always between words and deeds!' Repeatedly verified, such surreptitious comparisons, subversive of public hypocrisies, soon lead to scepticism. Tiennon (and Guillaumin) do not believe in religion or fatherland or humanity. Selfishness and avarice remain the moving forces of men's lives (of women's even more!) and hard labour continues to fill their monotonous days with no particular aim except to make ends meet. Guillaumin's book, like Tiennon's life which it depicts, is about work. Work is the hero of the story, the most alive of all experiences depicted there.

Hard obstinate work and parsimony mark the daily struggle, accumulate gains and sometimes achieve victories, as when M. Frédéric agrees to buy lime to marl the fields. Despite accidents and tragedies, life gets a little better: the earthen floor gives way to flagstones, the black and branny loaf to one that is white and tastes much better (hence the obstinate resistance of Victoire who foresaw that one would eat more of it!). The roads improve and the oxcart or the packhorse give way to carriages, even for peasants;[11] a railway runs past, though Tiennon muses that it is not made for the likes of him, until he discovers after the drought of 1893 that it has its uses. Grumbles go on but the style of life changes and so does the well-being: 'Think of how much more comfort we have today,' Tiennon reminds old Daumier. And a modest conclusion: we are a little less enslaved.

How much less? And how? A study of sharecropping in the Bourbonnais, published as late as 1898, speaks clearly: 'Where the master has expressed his will, the tenant must obey'.[12] And yet by then this splendid rule was falling out of date. Part of the peasant's subjection stemmed from an absence of alternatives. Overpopulation meant underemployment: too many candidates for every job, for every farm, for every strip of land put on the market. The 1890 census is when the rural areas reached their highest population. Thereafter they would shrink; and this depopulation (which had begun here and there in the 1860s, but only very slowly) meant better opportunities for employment, higher wages, and more self-respect for those who stayed on the land.

Despite avaricious landlords and mistrustful, reluctant tenants, productivity increased and so did its demands on the peasants' time. Children, growing up in family communities which kept but scarcely paid them, realized that the family's profits were rising and wanted their share of them. This was the more so, since 'luxury' was spreading into the countryside: city clothes, city ways like smoking or playing billiards, the sort of 'debauchery' Tiennon had sought to avoid. If the father refused their demands, they left the home that not long before they could not do without, for now they knew they could quite easily find work, pay, food elsewhere.

Some found these in the towns: they were, of course, those who contributed most to rural depopulation. When these migrants or their children came back for a visit, they brought with them extraordinary notions (and examples) of diet, fashion, comfort, and as an army officer deplored, 'those dissolute ways that sap the family, that scoffing tone which destroys the most sacred things'.[13]

But even those who stayed behind knew more about the world. They went to school, saw pictures and maps of the world, were taught about the duties they owed France.[14] They went on military service and they came back different. They picked up new ideas. They got used to speaking the French they had been taught at school. They got into the habit of drinking a bowl of coffee in the morning instead of spooning the farm breakfast of cabbage soup with bacon; they asked for coffee when they got home. Like the fresher baker's bread they had also come to expect, this meant less work for the womenfolk.

They even learnt to take an interest in elections if not in politics, because of the activity elections brought, arguments, meetings; their entertainment value was high when entertainment was very scarce indeed.[15] Despite one's scepticism there were even possible gains to be derived from them. Although Tiennon tells us that 'the elections were quickly forgotten', he who presumably voted as old Noris told him in 1881, and without demur, had his own candidate and political views in 1893. By that date, some men would even join unions, some of which flared briefly in the 1890s whilst others appeared around 1905. These also failed after a few years, but clearly some peasants at least no longer considered themselves to be inferior beings, and fewer outsiders still thought of them as such.

When, in 1936, Guillaumin himself looked back on this evolution since 1875, he concluded that the grandson of a peasant of 1850 stood further from his grandsire than the latter would from some distant ancestor, contemporary of Henry IV or Louis XIII. More had changed in the half-century since 1850 than in the two or three centuries preceding it.[16] Today that sort of observation is a platitude. But old Tiennon had actually seen and *felt* the changes, and knew they were for the best.

Notes

1. For a detailed account of the French rural world of the 19th century and how it changed, see my *Peasants Into Frenchmen* (Stanford, 1976).

2. Those details not drawn from the book come from Françoise Raison-Jourde, *La Colonie auvergnate de Paris* (Paris, 1976) p. 368 and *passim*. Incidentally, Tiennon does not mention washing, a subject of minor concern at the time, in town as well as in the countryside. The Bertins at least had a well by the house; but think of the woodcutters who had to trudge a long way for a bucket of water, a situation not unknown to many farmers too.

3. Emile Guillaumin, *Panorama de l'évolution paysanne, 1875–1935* (Paris, 1936) p. 13. A student of the Haute-Loire confirms this from the manuscript notes of a local priest writing in 1860: at mid-century, '... chacun reste encore à sa place ... les uns commandent, les autres s'inclinent'. Jean Merley, *La Haute-Loire de la fin de l'ancien Régime aux débuts de la troisième République* (Le Puy, 1974) pp. 424–25.

4. Letter of May 12, 1897, in Roger Mathé, ed., *Cent dix-neuf lettres d'Emile Guillaumin* (Paris, 1969) p. 34.

5. George Sand, *Le Marquis de Villemer* (1860 – Verviers, 1962) p. 59. See also Merley, *op. cit.*, pp. 460–61.

6. *Le Syndicat de Baugignoux* (Paris, 1912) p. 181.

7. The present translation gives little hint of the language problem that most peasants faced (and many continued to face into the 20th century) because the occasional passages in local *patois* have been translated into English. In any case, Guillaumin uses the local idiom sparingly, partly because it was hard for the reader to understand it, partly because he disapproved of the device. But he is also describing a part of France where the speech of Paris was more readily and more easily assimilated. The situation to the south, where the speech of Oc (the *langue d'Oc*) predominated, was quite different. For detailed treatment see my *Peasants Into Frenchmen*, ch. 6.

8. Camille Gagnon, *Ygrande* (Moulins, 1973) I, pp. 55, 46–52.

9. If religious observances were utilitarian and animistic, church attendance was utilitarian and social: the one occasion to meet others . . . and to be entertained. As a local official wrote about Sunday Mass at the beginning of the century: 'C'est le lieu de leurs rendez-vous. C'est leur opéra . . . c'est là où ils traitent souvent de leurs affaires'. Merley, *op. cit.*, p. 475.

10. Letter of June 12, 1916 and other letters cited by Jean Gaulmier in *Le Centenaire d'Emile Guillaumin* (Paris, 1975) p. 38.

11. Ygrande was a progressive village. As early as 1878 the municipal council had installed half a dozen lampposts on the main street, with petrol lamps that were lit at dusk and snuffed out at 9 p.m. Acetylene lamps followed in 1910. In 1925 it was decided to keep these lit all night in winter on the days of major fairs, to help the drovers driving their cattle to market. Gagnon, *op. cit.*, II, p. 370.

12. Martin Desboudet, *Le Métayage en Bourbonnais* (Paris, 1898) p. 36. The syndical activity Guillaumin helped to spark attracted unusual attention both to peasant syndicalism and to sharecropping in the region, with books, articles and dissertations devoted to the subject. A good general treatment, though biased to the conservative viewpoint, can be found in Auguste Souchon, *La Crise de la main-d'oeuvre agricole en France* (Paris, 1914), esp. p. 253 *et seq.*

13. Gabriel Boscary, *Evolution agricole et condition des cultivateurs de l'Aveyron pendant le XIXe siècle* (Montpellier, 1909) p. 186.

14. At the little village school of Mérilheu 'the inculcation of patriotism had a privileged place'. But when one day the little boy came home announcing his discovery that he had two mothers, his own and the fatherland (*la patrie*), he met little enthusiasm. Every morning the children had their hands, neck, ears inspected to see that they had washed. Hair was to be cut very short – a sensible way of keeping down fleas, and even lice. Despite all this, 'French was still a foreign tongue'. The old hardly understood it and answered only in *patois*. Men returning from their military service used it awkwardly, when it could not be avoided. Pierre Manse, *Mérilheu de mon enfance* (Pau, 1971), pp. 14, 15, 19.

15. A contemporary novel describes village reaction to an election campaign: 'Les paysans se passionèrent aux élections législatives. Ils voulurent participer à l'agitation des villes, amener dans leur solitude le feu des assemblées, des banquets et des fêtes, réclamer surtout l'argent de l'Etat et des préfectures . . .'; George Baume, *Une race* (Paris, 1892), p. 98.

16. Guillaumin, *Panorama* (*cit.* note 3) p. 11.

3. THE AUTHOR

When Guillaumin died, his neighbours turned out to see him off. They set out, in groups, all meaning to accompany to his grave [the man] who had told their lives in a book which all had read. Paper that does not lie: the man who had achieved that deserved the gift of a working day. They gave it.

Daniel Halévy

EMILE GUILLAUMIN WAS born late in 1873, on a lonely farm, Neverdière, about two miles from the village of Ygrande (Allier) in central France: population 2145 in 1881, 1695 in 1911. From Neverdière, a low building, one vast room with a large fireplace and curtained beds in every corner, only a rough sunken lane led to the road. Around it were fields, hedges, copses, the *bocage* country of northern Bourbonnais, a land of hedge-enclosed, isolated farms hidden in clumps of trees.

The tenants of Neverdière were Guillaumin's grandparents on his mother's side. They had come from Burgundy, about 100 miles northeast, twenty years before, in 1853, because their large family farm had become overcrowded, and had brought with them a sense of orderliness and comfort unknown in the poorer Bourbonnais. Above all, they could both read and write, something exceptional in those days. Their daughter married a local lad who came to live in his in-law's house as was the custom, all found and 120 francs a year: less than a farm servant got, because he was a member of the family. In 1892, after twenty years of this, the grandfather retired on a very small holding and Gilbert Guillaumin, Emile's father, set up by himself on a piece of land bought with his own savings. Until this move Emile, then 19, had spent all his life at Neverdière.

The household was relatively well off. He was born in November; by spring his mother would be taking the baby out into the fields where she would leave him in a sheltered corner on a piece of sacking, while she worked. But the little boy would know advantages few local children enjoyed. Because he did not like the staple *soupe au lard*, his mother made milk soup specially for him. When his grandfather returned from a fair he would bring him a piece of white bread, even a lump of sugar. The grandfather also taught him his first letters, by the fireside, at the evening *veillées*.

Then, at seven, school: six kilometres a day, bad weather or good, like the other children. Emile belonged to the first generation to enjoy free, compulsory schooling introduced at the beginning of the 1880s; and he benefited from a teacher of that first generation, too, for whom teaching was less a job than a calling. M. Beaune, himself born in a village not far away, expected children in his class to really know their grammar, but also spoke seriously to them about serious things: patriotism, human solidarity, the failures and the hopes of humankind. He turned out twelve years' worth of young peasants marked by solid knowledge and by the will to learn more. His influence persisted into the twentieth century, when we find Ygrande quicker to light its high street, to found mutual aid societies, or libraries, or educational groups than any neighbouring village.

Emile was M. Beaune's star pupil. In 1886, at twelve, he graduated, first in the district. The teacher and the local priest both suggested that he should go on with his studies. Instead, he decided to remain a peasant: guarding the sheep, driving the cattle, ploughing, hoeing, sixteen hours a day, up in the dark, in the wet and the cold. In this second school, more demanding than the first, Emile was just as successful. He became a real farmer, yet with a difference. He wanted to go on learning, he pored over books, his family worried at his studiousness and attributed his bizarre behaviour to a bad fall out of the hayloft ... on his head.

All his life, Emile Guillaumin would live on two levels: in the daytime a peasant; at night he turned to the world of books. He read everything he could lay hands on: novels (Balzac, Dickens, George Sand), poetry (Lamartine), history and natural history (Bouffon), and the works that the local papers published in instalments (notably Pierre Loti's *Pêcheurs d'Islande*, his first great inspiration). He began to buy his own books. He learned much of Lamartine by heart and declaimed *Le Lac* aloud as he drove his waggon from the fields at nightfall. He ordered a treatise on rhyming from Paris, and a rhyming dictionary. In 1891, he wrote his first poem. In 1894 a local newspaper printed his verse. He went on writing throughout his military service, which he hated, from 1894 to 1897 – sometimes a sonnet a day. During his service he would rhyme little ditties for his comrades' girl-friends.

But poems proved no more for him than schoolish learning.

Romantic poetry with its love, death and despair, was too far from reality. He wanted to tell about the world in which he lived, the drama of the apparently insignificant lives that went on around him. As he would write a decade later: 'the sorrow of a peasant who loses his cow, swollen on too much clover, can be as poignant as the despair of a fine gent betrayed by his mistress'.[2] Besides, it was 1899, it was 1900, the cities of France were torn by the Dreyfus Affair, and this countryman who read the city papers was a *Dreyfusard*.

Half a century before, an urban working man, also self-taught, remarked that 'nearly all workmen who like to read come to pay attention to politics ...'.[3] Guillaumin's versifying, what was left of it, would be placed in the service of new causes. His poems now attacked 'arrogant little bourgeois and those with the big bellies'; praised 'the shrewd Reds, who avoid Mass and don't think much of squires'; tried to speak for the peasant in untranslatable lines:

> Voué quand mêm' trist, dépis l'bas âge,
> D'trimer tout l'temps pus d'son chien d'saoûl,
> D'passer sa vie en esclavage,
> D'vieillir malh'reux, d'mourir sans l'sou![4]

But, like the rest of his life, and though he declared himself a socialist, Guillaumin's politics would never be quite like those of anybody else. Their essence consisted of trying to teach his fellow-peasants to help themselves and, in the process, to reveal them to themselves – and to those others who had no idea what peasants really are.

Peasants were not unknown in the literature of the nineteenth century, but their figures and lives were drawn from the outside. Sometimes the resulting images were tinged with fear (Balzac), sometimes with affection (George Sand), sometimes – most recently – they appeared as playthings of natural forces (Zola) or as misled creatures in flight from the land (Bazin). For Guillaumin, the bucolic convention and the naturalist description were both wrong. Zola, who sends a character of *La Terre* to mow the alfalfa on a rainy February afternoon, does not understand anything about farming; Bazin views his yokels from the terrace of a country house; and those who prettify or ennoble peasants forget the harsh realities of peasant life that forge harsh, none too attractive, personalities. The fact is that 'there are no general truths, only a mosaic of local realities, often contradictory'.[5]

Guillaumin dreams of trying to illustrate this, of writing a novel that will present 'the peasants' life as told by one of them ... a sharecropper's existence as told by himself'.[6] He yokes himself to the task in 1901 and completes it in a year. Then he has to find a publisher. In spring 1903 he is still looking; so, at the beginning of May, after the oats and the potatoes have been sown, he takes off for Paris with his manuscript in a brown paper parcel (which he forgets in a café and breathlessly recovers) to persuade a liberal editor and notorious *dreyfusard* to take it on.[7] He only manages this by agreeing to pay half the costs and, in 1904, *La Vie d'un simple* appears.

The reader will decide how well it fulfilled the author's intention. At any rate, in Paris, it was a success and its admirers put it up for what was then a new literary prize: the *Prix Goncourt*. Guillaumin did not get that,[8] but he was awarded another, lesser, one. With its proceeds and with his share of the royalties he was able to buy 3 hectares (7½ acres) of land just outside the village of Ygrande and build a house on it. That was where he lived henceforth, farming his own land by day, writing by night, his shoulders covered with a goatskin for warmth (the fireplace long continued in the main room only!) and that was where he turned out the rest of his life's work.

He continued a lonely man and one whom his first-chosen public, his fellow-peasants, never quite understood. As a young man, having written a story, 'The Old Mower', he tried to read it to his family of an evening, by the hearth, only to be laughed at. That may be why, in 1899, he wrote to a friend to say that he could not both write and work: 'I shall try to think only of my farming and abandon literature completely'. He couldn't. He continued a moralist and a moralizer, and his neighbours continued unheeding. In 1901 he was complaining once more: 'I had dreamed to draw country people out of their apathetic thoughtlessness ... but I really think it's practically impossible.... It is my fate to be always different, always misunderstood'.[9]

As with all the best, disillusion never prevented action. A few years after this, Emile had plunged into the syndical enterprise, another dismal failure, which he recounts in cathartic clear-eyed detail in *Le Syndicat de Baugignoux* (1912). The sharecroppers' unions he worked so hard to set up soon folded.[10] The village libraries the syndicates had founded were little used. The young farmers showed little interest in *Le Travailleur rural*, the quarterly he edited for six years single-handed: it struck them as too austere, too set on edifying, not nearly lively enough. 'You are a peasant, you are a countryman, but you don't know how to speak to peasants, to country people,' one young correspondent complained in 1911. 'You make [us] suspicious when you talk to [us] of solidarity, of frankness, of raising the moral standards. All this doesn't mean much to [us] young peasants.'[11]

Guillaumin should have known better. Reading his works and his letters, what stands out is his realistic scepticism. Neither his characters nor he himself believe much (or at all) in goodness, or intelligence, or the sincerity of social interchanges. Both he and they appreciate hard work, persistence, a modicum of material security and comfort, a rather parsimonious moderation in all things. Once again the two souls in his breast clashed, struggled, and brought forth a body of work remarkable both in its measure and its tragic colour: over twenty books or pamphlets, of which six were novels, and well over one thousand articles by 1940.

Guillaumin died in 1951, never having ceased to write. All this time he worked, raised a family, tried hard (but failed) to make a success of the first peasant unions in France (1905–1912), never abandoned either his modesty or his estate. In 1912, offered the editorship of a local paper, he refused: partly because he did not think he could bend with the political compromises it would involve, partly because he was about to buy a third cow and could not handle the additional work on two fronts at once.

He made little money. He lived in his little house, where he lit his own fire in the grate, fetched water from the well, sawed the firewood and tended the cows. In 1932, at 59, he described himself as 'a poor devil, still more or less needy'. A few years later, visiting Paris to see the Exhibition of 1937, he was knocked down by a truck while crossing the street, badly hurt, and taken to hospital where he registered as *Emile Guillaumin, cultivateur, Ygrande* and was placed in the public ward as just another simple farmer.[12]

In his collected works, *The Life of A Simple Man* seems almost an accident: its spontaneous, natural tone influenced by reading two bourgeois novels: Eugène Le Roy's *Jacquou le Croquant*, the tale of a rebellious peasant of the 1820s, and Antonin Lavergne's *De Jean Coste*, the story of an unhappy and tormented village teacher told by a village teacher. Even in *The Life* we find passages, mercifully few, of fine writing, as when a peasant compares the dew to pearls. But the straightforward speech of Père Tiennon, the simple man, would be abandoned almost at once for stylistic 'improvements' and 'refinements' that Guillaumin hoped would bring him closer to real literary style and to the highbrow recognition that he also sought. His later novels, though not his articles, carry too much 'fine writing', too much of that borrowed, artificial style that threatens all autodidacts impressed by their cultural superiors. All of them, and especially *Albert Manceau, adjudant* (1906) about a peasant's army career, *Rose et sa parisienne* (1908) about a village woman who takes in and raises an orphan from the town, and *Le Syndicat de Baugignoux* (reprinted in 1960), are wonderful documents of village life and ways. But none ever reached the honesty – or the greatness – of his first book.

*   *   *

A word about the translation, made by Margaret Holden several years before the First World War. In 1912, a letter from Guillaumin to Valéry Larbaud mentions that Duckworth, the English publisher, had refused Holden's translation, despite the strong support of Edward Garnett. A foreword by the latter would introduce the English edition when this was finally published in 1919. He praises its candour, the intimacy and justness of its vision, the absorbing effect of what most books about 'a life' rarely are and this one is: a work of art. To a friend who had stayed up half the night reading it, he can suggest only two comparable books, but none as good 'for the completeness and finality of the whole picture of a peasant farmer's life'.

I agree. Which is why I very much wanted it to be available, once more, to English-language readers. The Holden translation is very imperfect; it has here been thoroughly revised and corrected so that old Tiennon can at last speak for himself in English.

E.W.

Notes

1. I want to thank the Rockefeller foundation for the opportunity to edit *The Life of a Simple Man* and write my comments around it in the peace and comfort of its Villa Serbelloni at Bellagio.

2. Dedication to Charles-Louis Philippe in a presentation copy of *La Peine aux Chaumières* (Nevers, 1909).

THE LIFE OF A SIMPLE MAN

3. Sébastien Commissaire, *Mémoires et Souvenirs* (Lyon, 1888), I, pp. 76–77. He goes on: 'When we knew one thing we wanted to know another, and thus, by slow degrees, we were led to concern ourselves with public affairs'.

4. 'Cri d'esclave', written in 1902, printed in *Ma Cueillette* (Moulins, 1903):

    It's sad all the same, from the earliest days
    To toil all the time, and well past your fill;
    To spend all your life a slave of these ways;
    To grow old in want, and die broke and ill.

5. Quoted by Françine Masson in *Le Centenaire d'Emile Guillaumin* (Paris, 1975) p. 93.

6. Letter of July 1901 to Charles Guieysse, reprinted in Roger Mathé, ed., *Cent dix-neuf lettres d'Emile Guillaumin* (Paris, 1969) p. 44.

7. Joseph Voisin, *Le vrai visage d'Emile Guillaumin* (Moulins, 1953) pp. 105–109.

8. Another social novel did: Leon Frapié's sentimental *La Maternelle*.

9. *Mathé, op. cit.*, p. 82, note 6.

10. Mathé, *op. cit.*, p. 254. This is what he had to say about it, looking back from 1943: 'Sur l'idée syndicale à Ygrande, mieux vaut ne pas insister. Le syndicat des ouvriers agricoles n'a pas vécu, le trésorier ayant plus ou moins *barboté* les quelques fonds en caisse. Et celui des metáyers n'obtint pas plus qu'ailleurs *un franc succès*. Feu de paille! De même le groupe d'études sociales'.

11. *Le Travailleur rural*, December 1911.

12. Letter to Louis Lanoizelée, February 18, 1932. Louis Lanoizelée, *Emile Guillaumin* (1952) pp. 35, 20.

BRIEF BIBLIOGRAPHY

Those who want to read more about changing conditions of life in the French countryside can refer to a few works in English:

Jacques Beauroy *et al.*, eds., *The Wolf and the Lamb: Popular Culture in France* (Saratoga, 1976).

Pierre Jakez Hélias, *The Horse of Pride: Life in a Breton Village* (New Haven, 1978).

Henri Mendras, *The Vanishing Peasant; Innovation and Change in French Agriculture* (Cambridge, Massachusetts, 1970).

Edgar Morin, *The Red and the White; Report from a French Village* (New York, 1970).

Roger Thabault, *Education and Change in a Village Community: Mazières-en-Gâtine* (New York, 1971).

Eugen Weber, *Peasants into Frenchmen: The Modernization of Rural France, 1870–1914* (Stanford, 1976).

Gordon Wright, *Rural Revolution in France* (Stanford, 1968).

Laurence Wylie, *Village in the Vaucluse* (Cambridge, Massachusetts, 1957).

Theodore Zeldin, *France, 1848–1945*, 2 volumes (Oxford, 1973, 1977).

TRANSLATOR'S NOTE

La Vie d'un simple, The Life of a Simple Man, was first published in London in 1919 by Selwyn and Blount, translated by Margaret Holden, a writer on country life who contributed articles to *The Manchester Guardian* and has remained known for her book about birds, *Near Neighbours* (1930). Edward Garnett wrote a foreword to the Guillaumin novel in which he considered the author in relation to the English writers Cobbett, Clare, Richard Jefferies and Crabbe, while the translator pointed out the failure of many better-known French novelists to deal with the realities of country life.

In 1932, when the French publishers Stock brought out a new edition of the novel, the author wrote an introduction describing what he had learnt as a self-taught writer:

'When a manual worker, with no basic education, tries to write for the public, he doesn't know what he's letting himself in for. I can confirm this from personal experience, and also from the work of several comrades who have done me the honour of submitting their efforts to me.

You take risks: boldly you describe the awakening of spring, the babbling brook, the golden ocean-swell of the harvest, the falling of the leaves, the snow in the fields, the young loves of Pierre and Fanchon, imagining you are doing something new. What you do not know does not exist. So on you go, battling against the winds and the tides! On the way you pick up clichés and commonplace expressions. The honest desire to include everything drives you to spin things out in exaggerated fashion. The memory of some chance reading which once delighted you leads you into pale imitation. Sometimes the search for effect produces a diffuse style and rhetoric in the worst taste. Discoveries of which you are proud appear disarmingly naive when exposed to critical examination.

All in all, because of his ignorance and temerity the self-taught writer is too easily satisfied and insufficiently concerned about possible ridicule. It is therefore a painful experience for the self-taught writer to re-read what he wrote much earlier, because the experience one has acquired makes one see inadequacy and weakness all too clearly.

When this book was published by Editions Nelson in the spring of 1922 I felt I had to revise each page thoroughly, in order to say the same things with greater precision, by correcting stylistic negligence and by seeking out the right expression.

Some people assured me that the result was worth the trouble. I valued their opinion, particularly because of a different verdict given by other equally reliable friends: "This work was certainly commendable but not necessary. The book, which was very good in its original form, has lost something of its character. You were writing then with the means you possessed at the time, and they fitted in well with the subject matter."

This argument, justifiable when all is said and done, leads me to accept the offer from the Librairie Stock to republish *The Life of a Simple Man* in the original text.

In it there is a résumé of what a receptive youthful brain can accumulate about the family scene: direct impressions, things seen, stories heard. I hope the total sincerity of these pages will compensate to some extent for their clumsiness. ...'

Guillaumin's experiences as an autodidact were not over, and in 1943, when the book was again reprinted, he added two more paragraphs to his introduction:

'A further decade has passed: a second is in progress. Forty years after the publication of this book the favourable attitude of the reading public continues to earn it an increasing success. I have pondered deeply over the problem set out above and I am convinced that it is the duty of the author to search for the best in his writing as long as he is capable of doing so. Since many details in the original text no longer satisfied me I have therefore decided to include in it once again the major part of the corrections included in the Nelson edition, excluding however those which did not seem to me entirely justified. For in all circumstances and in all spheres elementary wisdom consists in retaining from differing opinions whatever experience shows to be the most reasonable.

I hope therefore that this account of peasant life in a French province during the second half of the 19th century will long retain, in its now definitive form, the valued approval which so many thousands of readers have bestowed upon it so far....'

The version of the book presented here is based largely on Margaret Holden's translation of the original French edition. It has been found necessary to make substantial alterations because of in-accuracies and stylistic peculiarities in the original English version, and also because it was considered right to incorporate the major part of the revisions which the author describes above. Thus, in the main the text here presented now follows the definitive edition of 1943; however we have been unable to resist the temptation to follow Guillaumin's example and, because we found them so fresh and vivid, we have left in some passages which he had decided to leave out in 1943.

The term *métayer*, which Eugen Weber has explained in his introduction, and other words from such varied spheres as local administration and cookery, have been left in French.

M.C.

TO THE READER

Old Tiennon is my neighbour: he is a dear old fellow, all bent with age, unable to walk without the help of his hazel stick. He has a thin fringe of white beard, rather red eyes, and a wart at the side of his nose; like his beard, the skin of his face is white, but spotted and flaky. Except in the summer months he wears a big cotton smock with a leather belt round the waist, baggy blue trousers, a woollen cap turned down over his ears, a cotton handkerchief loosely tied round his neck, and sabots *of beechwood bound with iron hoops.*

I often meet Old Tiennon in the lane which connects the farm where he lives and the one I occupy to the main road, and we always have a chat. Old people like to have attention paid to them, and are often disappointed over this. But during the little leisure that I have I provide old Tiennon with a willing listener.

Having had a long life, he remembers many things, and he tells them vividly, adding his personal comments, which are sometimes very shrewd and often unexpected.

In this way he has told me the story of his life in fragments; it contains nothing very remarkable; it has been the poor, monotonous life of a peasant, like many other lives.

Old Tiennon has had his hours of pleasure; he has had days of trouble; he has worked hard; he has suffered from the elements, from men, and from uncontrollable fate; at times he has been selfish and at times a good fellow − like you, reader, and like me.

I said to myself: "People know so little about peasants; if I put together old Tiennon's stories to make a book of them ..." One day I told him about my idea. He replied with an astonished smile:

"What good will that do you, my poor boy?"

"But it would show the gentlemen of Moulins and Paris and elsewhere what the life of a métayer *really is − they don't know; and also it would prove that peasants aren't as stupid as they imagine; for, in the way you tell things there is a touch of that 'philosophy' they make so much of."*

"If it amuses you, do it, but you can't write things as I say them: I speak too badly, the gentlemen of Paris wouldn't understand."

'That's true: I shall write in plain French so that they can understand without trouble: but I shall follow your thinking as it

I

were, translate your phrases; like that the story will really be yours."

"All right, that's settled: begin when you like."

The poor old man has come to see me many times, in conscience-stricken mood, to tell me things he had forgotten, or even things he had vowed never to divulge.

"Since I'm relating my life through you, I ought to tell all, you see, the good and the bad. It's a general confession." He has done his best to satisfy me, and I have tried to do the same by him, but perhaps here and there, I have put in more of myself than I should have done. However, I read him each chapter as soon as it was written, retouching where he indicated, repairing little deviations from the truth, changing the sense of thoughts that I had not quite grasped at first.

When it was complete I read the whole thing through to him again; he found this story of his life accurate; he seemed satisfied. Readers, may you also be satisfied.

Emile Guillaumin

THE LIFE OF
A SIMPLE MAN

MY NAME IS Etienne Bertin, but I've always been called "Tiennon."
I was born in October 1823, at a farm in the Commune of Agonges,
near Bourbon-l'Archambault. My father was a *métayer* on the farm
in partnership with his eldest brother, my uncle Antoine, called
"Toinot." My father's name was Gilbert, shortened to "Bérot": it
was the custom at that time to distort everybody's name.

My father and his brother did not get on very well. Uncle Toinot
had been a soldier under Napoleon: he had been in the Russian
campaign, returning with frost-bitten feet and pains in every part
of his body. After his return his health had improved, but any sharp
change of temperature revived his pains badly enough to prevent
him from working. Even when he was not in pain, rather than
attend to his own work he preferred to go to the fairs, carry the
ploughshares to the farrier, or walk in the fields, his bag of tools on
his shoulder, on pretext of repairing the gaps in the hedges.

His life in the army had spoiled his appetite for work, and given
him a taste for lounging and spending money. He constantly
smoked a very short black clay pipe, swallowed a drop of brandy
when he woke up and could never go to Bourbon without loitering
at the tavern. In short, he was ready to exploit any situation for his
own benefit. I relate these things not because I had any direct
knowledge of them, or was able to understand them myself, but
because I often heard them talked over at our house.

At last my father decided to break with him. At Meillers, on the
border of the forest of Gros-Bois, he took, in *métayage*, a property
called Le Garibier, which was under the management of a Bourbon
farmer, Monsieur Fauconnet.

At the time of the removal there were painful discussions as to
the sharing of the tools, furniture, linen and household utensils. My
grandmother was to accompany us, and that complicated things still
more. My aunt, who disagreed with her the most, wrangled with
her about what she ought to take, and snatched sheets and towels

out of her hands. My father had a very calm temperament and sought to avoid these disputes, but my mother, quick and impetuous, sided constantly with my grandmother against the others. It used to terrify me to hear them shouting so loudly and shaking their fists with menacing gestures as though about to strike each other.

On Martinmas Day they hoisted me for the journey onto the top of a cart drawn by two dark red oxen, of the Salers or Mauriac breed. I sat between the frame used for drying cheeses (in which they had placed some fowls) and a basket piled up with crockery. Everywhere the roads were potholed and muddy. Lumps of sticky earth caked on the wheels, then fell to the ground with a dull thud.

As we passed through Bourbon I opened my eyes as wide as I could to see the fine town houses and the tall grey towers of the old château. I was interested also in the proceedings of a gang of workmen busy metalling the great road to Moulins which was in course of construction.

All this exhausted me and as a result, as soon as our procession had again reached the open country, I went to sleep without anyone noticing, resting against the cage of fowls, and rocked by the continual rolling of the vehicle. But an extra sharp jolt turned the cage over and made it tumble to the ground, so of course I followed pretty quickly. The fowls began to squawk and I to cry. They rushed forward to rescue us. It appears they had some trouble in comforting me after this rude awakening, although I was not hurt, the mud into which I had rolled having broken my fall.

This meant that I did the rest of the journey on foot, except for one little ride on the shoulders of my brother Baptiste, who was also my godfather.

On our arrival my mother put me to bed on a heap of old clothes in a 'corner of the bakehouse, and I found in another sleep, very peaceful this time, the true remedy for the excitements of the journey.

Much later I was awakened by my sister Catherine, who called me into the big room. The furniture was all in place round the walls, and the clock was striking midnight.

Some neighbouring drovers, who had helped us to move, had just finished their dinner and were talking loudly, laughing and singing. My father pressed them to drink, the glasses clinked noisily, the wine they had spilled reddened the white tablecloth. Everybody seemed extraordinarily gay: great bursts of laughter shook their excited faces. They gave me some scraps of meat, *galette* and *brioche* to eat; then an old man I didn't know gave me a gallop on his knee: so I had my share in the general merriment.

But the next day I heard my mother say in a vexed tone to my father that moving house was a pretty expensive business. My father replied:

"That's true. Fortunately it's not something one does often."

"We would soon be ruined," my mother concluded, "if we had to make a fresh start often...."

I was then nearly five; these episodes of the move form part of my earliest memories.

II

Alongside the wood our farm possessed a strip of virgin soil, which had always been fallow land. It was covered with heather, broom, brambles and bracken and in some places great grey stones protruded from the ground.

That part of the property was known as La Breure, and served as pasture for the sheep for most of the year. My sister Catherine, who was ten years old, took care of the sheep, and I often went with her. Thus La Breure soon became familiar to me. There we came across all kinds of animals, there were endless birds and reptiles, and sometimes we saw wild animals from the forest. One day I saw a whole family of great black pigs running across the lower part of the pasture: wild boars, my sister said. Another time there were a couple of roe-deer busily browsing on the green shoots of the hedge, just as our goats did. I ran towards them, but they quickly scampered away.

There were also wolves in the forest. Towards the end of the winter, one of our lambs disappeared without trace. Rightly or wrongly a wolf was blamed for this mysterious disappearance. My sister did not want to go alone again to La Breure as she was terrified at the idea of the wolf reappearing; so they made me stay with her all the time, and I must say that neither of us was particularly reassured by this arrangement. We talked only about the wolf, and we made it into a frightful monster capable of every crime. However, we never had occasion to compare a real wolf with the creature of our imagination.

Much less rare were the rabbits; we saw many of them running about every day. Our dog Médor chased them, and sometimes managed to catch one, but he thought it better not to show it to us: he hid behind the hedge of a neighbouring field, or went into the wood to eat his meal without the risk of being disturbed: he would return later, looking very sheepish, with hair and blood in his grey beard, and wagging his tail with an air of asking pardon.

To tell the truth, it was quite excusable that the poor dog should be so voracious when chance provided him with any extra food. Nowadays dogs are treated like people; they are given good soup and bread. But at that time they were only allowed to poke about in the trough which contained the pigs' swill, which was very thin stuff. To supplement this we used to dry in the oven a quantity of little sour crab apples which grew wild in the hedges. Dogs were considered capable of providing for themselves by hunting. When Médor returned from the fields apparently famished, and at meal times prowled round the table seeking crusts, my father would ask Catherine:

"Hasn't he caught any rats then?"

When my sister replied "No", my father would say:

"He's a lazybones; if he was hungry he should have caught a rat: anyhow, give him a crab."

Catherine would then go into the bakehouse adjoining the house, which also served as a lumber room, and would take from an old dusty basket one or two little wizened apples and offer them to Médor, who would go into the yard and munch them on the rushes where he used to sleep. On such diet he was lean and his hair rough: it would have been easy to count his ribs.

Truth to tell our own fare was hardly more appetizing. We ate bread as black as the chimney and as gritty as if it contained a good dose of thick sand from the river; it was made of coarse-ground rye, with all the husk left in and mixed with the flour; they said it was nourishing. Some wheat was also ground but that was for fritters and pastries, tarts and *galettes*, which were cooked along with the bread. They also usually kneaded out of this flour a little round white loaf which smelt good, with a golden crust and white crumb. But this small loaf, the *ribate*, was saved to go into the soup for my little sister Marinette, who was the youngest, and for my grandmother, on the days when she suffered from her stomach complaint.

Sometimes, however, when my mother was in a good mood, she

would cut me a tiny piece, which I devoured with as much pleasure as if it had been the finest cake. But that happened seldom, for the poor woman was mean with her little wheat loaf.

Soup was our chief fare; onion soup morning and evening, and at midday potato soup with haricot beans or pumpkin, and tiny dots of butter. Bacon was reserved for the summer, and for feast days; with that we had *beignets* (dumplings), indigestible and doughy, which stuck to our teeth, baked potatoes, and beans cooked in water slightly whitened with milk.

We regaled ourselves on baking days, because then we had pies and *galette*, but those extras were quickly exhausted. Ah, good things were not plentiful!

III

It was as a shepherd in La Breure that I began to make myself useful.

The third summer after our move to Le Garbier, Catherine, having reached her twelfth birthday, had to take the place of the servant whom my mother had employed until then. Catherine gave up the sheep in order to busy herself with domestic concerns and to share the work in the fields. I was almost seven years old by then, and they entrusted me with the care of the flock.

Before five o'clock in the morning my mother pulled me out of bed, and I set off, my eyes heavy with sleep. A little lane, sunken and winding, led to the pasture. On each side enormous hedges grew on the banks, along with pollarded oaks, and elms with black exposed roots and thick, leafy branches. As a result the sunken lane was always dark and mysterious – an ill-defined fear always gripped me when I passed along it. I would even call Médor, who was yelping conscientiously at the freshly-sheared sheep, obliging him to keep very close to me, and I would put my hand on his back for reassurance.

When I arrived at La Breure I breathed more freely. Towards the east and south the view extended beyond a wide and fertile valley to a bare hillock covered with rust-coloured grass, which rose in front of the Messarges wood. A few cultivated fields could be seen on the north side, while to the west lay the majestic forest of tall firs, with pungent resin oozing from their trunks.

But La Breure itself was vast enough, and in fine weather when I arrived there in the early morning it was magnificent: the dew sparkled in the caressing rays of the sun and sprinkled with diamonds the great bushes of broom whose vigorous blooms formed a golden nimbus on the sombre greenery; it hung from the ferns and the tufts of white daisies disdained by the sheep; it masked with a uniform mist the fine grass in the clearings and the grey heather studded with rosy flowerets. From the surrounding hedges came trills, scales, chirpings and warblings, the whole enchanting concert of a summer dawn.

In cracked, shapeless *sabots*, my legs bare to the knees, I wandered about my domain, whistling in unison with the birds. The dew from the bushes soaked my smock and my cotton trousers and dripped down onto my frozen legs. But this daily bath did not hurt me, and the sun quickly dried me off. I feared the brambles more; they spread treacherously at ground level and were hidden by the heather, and I was often tripped up and cruelly scratched by them. The lower parts of my legs were always covered with fresh or half-healed wounds.

I carried in my pocket a piece of hard bread and a little bit of cheese, and I used to eat this sitting on one of the grey stones which pushed up amongst the flowers. At that moment a cheeky little blackheaded lamb never failed to come to me, and I would give him morsels of my bread; but the others noticed this, and a second one would get into the habit of coming, then a third, then still more, so many that they would easily have eaten all my provisions if I had allowed them; to say nothing of Médor, who, when he was not hunting, would come too and ask for his share: he even drove off the poor lambs (without hurting them, however) so that he alone might gaze at me with his big, gentle, pleading eyes. I would throw some little bits far off to send him away, and then the sheep would quickly take the opportunity to gobble up from my hand what I felt like giving them.

That amused me, as did many other incidents of less importance. I watched the doves in flight and the rabbits scampering about. I toured the domain, following the hedges to find nests. In the grass I caught black crickets or green grasshoppers and tortured them pitilessly: or I could pick up one of those little creatures with red backs spotted with black, ladybirds (gentlemen call them "the beasts of the good God"; here we call them *marivoles*), and sing to it the song Catherine had taught me:

8

Marivole, vole, vole;
Ton mari est à l'école,
Qui t'achète une belle robe.

The poor little creature did well to fly away as quickly as possible, for it risked being reduced to a most wretched condition.

In spite of all this I sometimes found the day very long. I was instructed to return between eight and nine o'clock, when, because of the heat, the sheep refused to eat and huddled together in a shady corner, lowering their heads.

If I returned too early I was scolded and even beaten by my mother, who never laughed, and gave a slap more readily than a caress. I forced myself, therefore, to stay till the appointed time. So I stayed until the shadow of the oak at the right of the entrance fell perpendicularly across the fence, and I knew it was eight o'clock.

But how hard it was to wait till then! And in the evenings how hard to wait alone for nightfall. Sometimes, overcome by fear and misery, I wept, wept without reason and for a long time. A sudden rustling in the wood, the scuttling of a mouse through the grass, the cry of a bird unfamiliar to me, those were enough in my hours of weariness to make my tears flow.

My first great fright occurred after several weeks. It was during a warm afternoon, when the air was heavy with the soporific buzzing of insects. I was walking along drowsily with my eyes half-closed, when I saw, at the edge of the ditch which ran alongside the wood, a great black creeping reptile, as thick as the handle of a hay-fork and nearly as long. It must have been an adder. Never having seen anything but lizards or slow-worms, and having heard of vipers as particularly dangerous evil beasts, I believed that I saw before me an enormous black viper. I began to make off, then returned rather cautiously, wanting to see it again, but it had disappeared.

A quarter of an hour later, having already forgotten this incident, I was sitting some way off, preparing to cut a branch of broom with my little knife, when suddenly I again saw the black viper gliding among the heather, and approaching me very quickly. Instinctively I started running towards the sheep. Alas! I had not reckoned with the trailing brambles. Before I had run twenty yards one of them tripped me up, and I fell. I was terrified, sobbing and trembling so much that at first I had no power to move. Then I felt a strange touch on my bare legs, something cool skimmed over the back of my head. I thought the black viper had caught up with me and was worming itself over my body. In a panic of fear I sprang up at one bound. No aggressive reptile was near, only two friends who had come to show their sympathy and lavish their caresses upon me. It was good old Médor who had licked my legs, and the little black-headed lamb who had poked his nose into my neck. I recovered a little from my great terror, but when I returned home as usual in the gathering dusk, the tears were still running down my cheeks, and I was convulsed with sobs.

To console me, my mother cut me a piece of the wheaten loaf and gave me some Saint-Jean pears which she had found under the peartree in the hemp field. But I had a wakeful feverish night with a frightful nightmare and my parents had to get up several times to calm me.

The next morning they allowed me to sleep later, and as the haymaking was almost finished, my grandmother took my place with the sheep for a few days.

When the rye was ripe, I had to go back to my work again, only to receive another shock, perhaps even more violent.

I was busy making a bouquet of flowers blending with the sweet-smelling honeysuckle and the glowing colours of the golden broom, some white daisies and pink heather, when Médor's warning yelps made me look up quickly. Coming out from the wood and advancing towards me I saw a great black-bearded fellow, who carried on his shoulder a keg at the end of a stick.

Since our farm was so isolated, I rarely had any occasion to see strangers, except from the neighbouring farms: the Simons of Suippière, the Parnières of La Bourdrie, and sometimes the Lafonts of L'Errain. When I saw a big dark person, who was neither from Suippière, nor La Bourdrie, nor L'Errain, I was terror-stricken.

He called out: "Hullo little man, come here." But into my mind came the tales of malefactors and brigands, which I had heard during the winter evenings. Without answering or waiting to hear more, I started running towards the gate. I found myself in the sunken lane, running towards the house. But the man with the black beard called after me:

"Why are you running away, little man? I won't hurt you."

He laughed, following me still and, though only at his normal pace, gained on me.

Every time I managed to cast behind me a terrified glance, I saw he was getting nearer; and when at last I turned into the farm, he was only a few paces away. No matter, I felt I was safe now that I could rush into the house. But to my surprise the door was locked. Too exhausted to run any more, I crouched down in the doorway, screaming as though I was being murdered. The man from the wood came up. He was very gentle.

"Why are you crying, my little friend? I am not wicked; on the contrary I am fond of little children."

He patted my cheeks, and in spite of my tears, I noticed that he had horny hands, a thin face and kind, gentle eyes under thick black eyebrows. He repeated his first words:

"I won't hurt you," and then he said, "where are your parents then?"

His accent was not that of our district; he pronounced his words separately. This puzzled me a great deal. Naturally I did not answer, but only wept and screamed more loudly. To my astonishment he did not try to seize me and carry me off, but spoke gently, and patted me. We remained thus a little while, he very embarrassed and not venturing to say anything, and I choked with fear. At last my grandmother returned. She had been taking the cows to a distant pasture and had come hurrying back on hearing my screams. To keep up with her, my little sister Marinette, who was holding her hand, had had to move her short legs much more quickly than usual.

The man went towards them, apologizing for having unintentionally frightened me, and explained why he was there. He was a long-sawyer from Auvergne, who was working in the forest with a gang of workmen. Their timber-yard had been set up the previous evening in a clearing near to our La Breure, and he had been sent to fetch some water.

My grandmother showed him the spring which was common to the two farms of Le Garibier and Suippière and which rose in the meadow belonging to the Simons, beyond our own Chaumat. The man went at once to fill his keg, and on his return he came into the house to thank us. I crouched down between the cupboard and my parents' bed, and obstinately refused to look at him, still more to go back with him to the pasture, as he suggested.

My grandmother had some difficulty afterwards in persuading me to return to the flock. She only succeeded by going with me halfway along the sunken lane, and assuring me that the Auvergnat was not hiding anywhere, and that he had really disappeared.

However, this man finally won my confidence. I saw him again the next day and, although his presence caused me to make an instinctive movement of fear, I did not run away. I even raised my old hat in greeting when I saw him approach. Then he began to talk to me gently, and gave me some pretty branches of strawberry plant covered with little strawberries that he had gathered in the wood especially for me. The following day when I saw him appear with his keg, I ran to meet him, and went with him across La Breure, then into the sunken lane and half the way from our house. I did this for a whole week.

One morning he suggested that I should go with him to his timber pit. My mother had strictly forbidden me to go into the forest, for fear of snakes and I had obeyed her, more or less, especially since the incident of the viper. Nevertheless, I readily consented to follow my friend the Auvergnat, particularly as he had promised to find me some more strawberries, and to give me some scraps of wood, out of which I could carve little men and various implements, that being how I liked to occupy my time.

First we had to cross the belt of firs; the ground was strewn with their fine dry needles, and some of the previous year's fir-cones with their gaping, distorted scales. After that we came to birches and oaks, many of their sturdy trunks marked with a red circle which announced their forthcoming execution. Next we came to some very thick underwood where walking was difficult; however, being little, I followed quite easily in the wake of my companion, who was not making rapid progress himself. Once he let go too soon of a flexible branch, which he had held back for me and it lashed my face painfully. I was brave enough not to show how it hurt. The presence of strangers puts us on our mettle!

It took about twenty minutes to get to the timber pit. Three men were working there in the midst of giant oaks which had been felled. They had long beards and long hair, and wielded long axes with their long arms. Some planks were already cut, and some beams and rafters. An enormous log was held on a saw-bench by great chains. Four black camp kettles sat side by side on a heap of grey ashes. A pot without a lid lay near their hut. This hut was made of branches and turf, and its roof reached down to the ground. The sky was luminous and the sun shone brightly upon that little clearing, that space momentarily withdrawn from the great surrounding mystery. Wagtails and swallows were chasing the huge swarms of midges.

The workmen stopped their cutting and after questioning their comrade about me, they declared, laughing, that they would make a long-sawyer of me. Then each took his can and sat on a log to eat.

"Sawyers' soup, you see, little man," said my friend. "The spoon should stand up in it."

In fact, he stuck the spoon right in the middle and it didn't budge, for it was a thick paste without a trace of gravy. He used another phrase which made me laugh, and which I have not forgotten.

"It's got body in it, this soup; it's better than what you have in your house ..."

When each of the four men had emptied his can of soup, the oldest, who had a grey beard, pushed aside some wood chips and uncovered a saucepan; in it was a large piece of rancid bacon which he divided up. Each took his portion on a slice of black bread, which did not seem much better than ours, although it came from a baker in Bourbon. When they had finished eating they refreshed themselves in turn from the keg, which they held suspended at arm's length above their mouths, and I could hear the water gurgling down their throats.

After he had finished, the youngest wiped his mouth with the back of his sleeve and said:

"King Louis-Philippe has probably not dined as well as I have."

The evening before, he had gone to get some tools that were being repaired at Bourbon, and he had heard that Paris was in revolt, that they had driven out the old king, and that the white flag with the *fleur-de-lis* had been replaced by the tricolour flag, and finally that the new king was called Louis-Philippe.

The foreman, the sawyer with the grey beard, had his own opinion:

"If they wanted a change, it is little Napoleon they should have sent for."

"Yes, that he might kill people and devastate countries as his father did," said another ironically.

"I should have liked a good Republic," said the young man; "a good Republic to annoy the priests and the bourgeoisie."

"Let's go and look for strawberries," said my friend to me. We went off round the glade between the fallen giants. He found a strawberry plant whose fruit had not been picked and I regaled myself at my ease. I liked that better than listening to the others talking about the flag and the King.

They resumed their work, and I waited a moment to watch them, interested above all in the continual movement of the great saw, worked at the head of the log by the old Napoleonite, and at the foot by the young Republican.

I rolled in the sawdust, and amused myself by filling my pockets with it, then I selected a stock of chips; and finally said timidly that I wanted to go back.

My friend kindly led me back to the belt of firs, and before leaving me, he touched both my cheeks with his bearded face.

I arrived without hindrance at the edge of the wood, and was glad to see my pasture again, with its rosy heather and golden broom, which looked pale in the bright sunlight.

Instinctively my eyes sought the flock, but I could not see them, and that was why I was careless when I reached the ditch which bordered our land, and rolled to the bottom on to a bed of brushwood, from which I rose all bruised and bleeding and with my smock torn. For the second time that morning I showed myself a stoic and shed no tears.

Besides, I was too concerned about the sheep to feel sorry for myself. I ran across La Breure hoping to discover them gathered in some corner, but they were nowhere to be seen.

Then I made a tour of the quickset hedges. Down below on the valley side, between a pollarded oak and a vigorous cluster of nut trees, there was a breach in the hedge which led into a field of clover, of which the first cutting had been made, and which had been left to shoot again for seed. I dashed through the opening and soon saw sheep and lambs cramming themselves with the green clover, in spite of the heat.

My first act was to call Médor, who had left me in the forest to follow some trail. But Médor did not come. I tried to get the flock together by myself, and to drive them towards the hedge.

I succeeded after a lot of trouble, but instead of going through the gap, they went to either side, and scattered again among the clover; a second and a third attempt failed in the same way.

Desperate and weeping, I made for the house to seek help. There I found only my grandmother nursing my little sister Marinette, who was suffering from colic and moaning continuously.

The first words the old woman greeted me with were to tell me that I had brought the sheep back too late. When I confessed, sobbing, that they were in the clover, she threw up her arms, with a pitiable lamentation:

"*Ah! Là, là, là!* Is it possible? My God! Holy Mother of God!

Oh, they will all swell up. Oh! they will all be lost! What shall I do? My God! What will become of us?'

With Marinette in her arms, she crossed the yard, mounted the ridge which overlooked the big pool surrounded by willows, and started to call in a piercing voice:

"Ah! Bérot! Aaah! Bérot!"

At the fourth call my father answered with a prolonged "Aaah!"

My grandmother implored him to come quickly; then, having ordered me to remain there to tell my father, she ran along the sunken lane in the direction of La Breure, still carrying Marinette in her arms.

My father soon appeared; he stopped an instant quite out of breath, questioning me with a look, and when I told him what had happened, uttered an oath, and ran off again.

I followed him at a distance, very worried and whimpering all the time. When I reached the pasture, the sheep had been got out of the clover, but their bellies had swelled up and they looked tired, their heads lowered and their ears drooping. Behind them came my grandmother and my father, lamenting together, saying that they were all swollen up, and that not one would survive.

My grandmother proposed that she should go to Saint-Aubin to seek Fanchi Dumoussier, who "knew the prayer". My father was troubled chiefly at the prospect of having to go to Bourbon to tell Monsieur Fauconnet, the landlord, and he spoke of going to ask Parnière of La Bourdrie, who was rather skilful in such matters, to come and lance those which were most ill.

While I was walking beside them silently, they bethought themselves of me for a moment. The blood from my scratches, diluted with tears, made my face very dirty, and my smock and trousers were torn. My grandmother and my father misunderstood the cause of my sorry appearance; they thought that I had broken through the hedge for fun and that I was entirely to blame for the flock's escapade.

To clear myself I told them truthfully how I had spent my morning.

Then they swore a great deal at "that pig of an Auvergnat," who had taken me away. But my grandmother none the less considered me much to blame, and urged my father to punish me as I deserved. My father, always easy-going, replied that that would not undo the mischief, and left me alone. However, I did not get off so easily. My mother, on her return from the fields, gave me several slaps and a good whipping, which made me run off to the bottom of the hemp field, and hide in a big ditch bordered by young elms.

There I sulked and wept my fill. When dinner-time came my godfather came to look for me. He only got me to return with him by promising that I would not be beaten or scolded. I asked him for news of the flock. He told me that Parnière of La Bourdrie had lanced the ten animals that were most ill, and that only two ewes had died. They reckoned they would save the others, but a third one died, plus a lamb.

My friend, the Auvergnat, paid for the damage. That evening, when he came with his keg, my grandmother and mother called him all sorts of names, accusing him of being the cause of this great disaster which would ruin us all, and they forbade him to take any more water from our well. The poor man was very upset and tried humbly to explain, throwing out his arms with great gestures, as though calling the heavens to witness his complete innocence. When he saw how furious the two women were, and that no reasonable explanation was possible, he went off. In future he got water from the spring at Fontibier, beyond Suippière, a good three-quarters of an hour from his sawpit. I never saw him again.

The storms also caused me serious trouble in the course of that summer. I was ordered to return if there was a lot of thunder, because it was bad for the sheep to get wet. One morning the sky darkened over Souvigny, lightning soon zigzagged through the black clouds, and loud rumblings followed, so I took the flock home; I had only been away an hour. When I reached the sunken lane I heard the thunder rather less and felt that I might be making a mistake; however I didn't have the courage to go back on my decision.

As soon as my mother saw me she asked in a hard voice what possessed me to return so soon; when I spoke of the storm, she laughed and shrugged her shoulders, saying that I was a donkey not to know yet that storms were never for us when they came from the east. To get this better into my head, she gave me a couple of slaps and sent me off again without more ado.

"Once bitten, twice shy." When another storm came on, I judged it prudent not to pack up, seeing that it gathered over Bourbon. Without flinching I remained through all the premonitory rumblings. But they increased, and great flashes of lightning lit up the sky with their luminous twistings and writhings: the storm was coming towards Saint-Aubin. Although I was very frightened, I only decided to go when isolated big drops began to fall. I had hardly reached the lane, when the rain suddenly became heavier, and fell in a terrific downpour, mixed with large hailstones.

The sheep refused to move; I was wet through and was beginning to fret a good deal when I saw my father with a sack over his shoulders, coming to my aid. He told me I was crazy not to come back sooner in such weather. At the house my mother punished me again, after she had made me put on dry clothing.

So, having been beaten for going back when it was not necessary, and for not going back when it was, you can understand how afterwards stormy skies seemed doubly threatening to me.

IV

When I think that I was not yet seven when all these things happened to me, when I compare my childhood with that of the little ones of today, who are petted and cared for tenderly, and are not obliged to do any manual labour before they are twelve or thirteen years old, I feel they are really lucky. How much time I used to spend in the open air, while they spend theirs in school! While I was a shepherd I escaped the worst weather, for sheep are not sent out in rain or snow. But when I was nine they gave me the pigs to look after, and I no longer had any special advantages. Come rain or wind, come burning sun or biting north wind, come snow or frost, I had to go out to the fields. Oh, those terrible sentry duties of winter, when my legs were plastered with mud, my feet soaked, and I got colder and colder, whatever I did! I couldn't sit down, the leafless hedges no longer gave any shelter, my numbed, chapped fingers hurt me, my whole body was shaken by a convulsive trembling. How wretched I was!

We always had two sows that we called "old swill-tubs", and litters of little ones, usually about fifteen of them, depending on circumstances or the success of the farrowing.

They all wandered about, grunting and rootling in the soil. When the little ones were very young and still kept in the cowshed, the sows were particularly difficult to manage, the maternal instinct driving them nearer to their young. They got through the hedges with astonishing ease, and some strategy was needed to prevent them getting away; besides, it was impossible to make them stay anywhere for very long, but when they escaped they would at least go straight towards the house. But that was no longer the case when the little piglets were strong enough to follow them. They were terrific scavengers, and sometimes managed to get into a field of corn, where it was not easy to find them. I got a good many cuffs whenever I failed to keep them out of the wheat or barley.

After the corn came the fruit. My pigs knew, within a radius of several kilometres, where to find all the wild pear trees which yielded well. It was almost impossible for me to prevent them making a great circular promenade each day, to eat the fallen fruit. The same thing happened when the chestnuts were ripe, and the beech-nuts, and the acorns. In this late autumn we also had to protect the new-sown fields and the potatoes that had not been dug. Sometimes the families would divide, each litter following its mother in a different direction. At other times the little ones, too inexperienced, would wait about, some here and some there. On certain unlucky days, I could not get them all back together. Often at nightfall I had to set out again on a long search for the missing ones.

In addition to all the trouble the pigs caused in the fields, there was the business of keeping their lodgings clean. They were always kept in three small crowded sties, abutting the gable end of the house, and difficult to clean because of the gaps in the paved floor. I did my best, but my gradmother, who had a mania for inspecting everywhere, never found the sties clean enough, and urged the others to tell me off. My mother slapped me one day because I had put some new-born piglets on straw which was too stiff, and, according to her, this could have made their tails drop off.

These little miseries make the memory of that time bad enough, but the worst episode in my career as a swineherd was at the Bourbon winter fair, to which I went with my father, taking a bunch of piglets.

V

My godfather was suffering from a sprain, so my brother Louis had to stay at home to help him with the animals, and my sister Catherine had a bad cold. This is why I was chosen to go to the fair, and I was not at all sorry, quite the opposite. Since we had been at Le Garibier, I hadn't left the farm more than four or five times a year, to go to Mass at Meillers on important saints' days. From the day of the removal, when we had passed through Bourbon, I had retained a confused and vague memory of a huge town with great houses, fine shops, and so many streets that one would easily get lost. I was very pleased to be going to see those wonderful things again.

However, I found it very unpleasant to get up at three o'clock in the morning, and my mother had to shake me awake. She dressed me up in my best clothes, which were far from luxurious garments, having belonged to my two brothers before being handed down to me. Then she tried to make me swallow some soup, but I was too sleepy to be hungry. My head drooped on my shoulders or fell on to the table. My eyes were gummed up with sleep. My mother, realizing that I would later on regret having been so sleepy, put a piece of bread and some apples in my pocket:

"For when you are hungry, dear," she said.

She put a thick woollen muffler round my neck, and covered my shoulders with an old grey fringed shawl.

"You will be awfully cold, Tiennon," she said. "I don't like to see you going out in such weather."

That morning my mother showed me an unusual tenderness; her eyes and her voice were full of gentle sadness. I felt at that moment the mother-love which she rarely allowed to appear through her tough exterior.

At four o'clock she helped us get the astonished piglets out of the yard, then she wished us a good sale and went back inside. In the keen frost of that early dawn, there began for my father and me a long journey down strange frozen roads, and it passed off on the whole with very little weariness or discomfort.

By half-past seven we were installed in the field where the fair was to be held. We had a good place in the shelter of a wall; my father had brought a little dark linen bag from which he took handfuls of rye, and threw it to the pigs to help keep them patient. However, the cold soon made them grunt, their bristles stood on end, and it was hard work to keep them in one place.

I was very cold too: after the exertion of walking and the consequent warmth, the inactivity was torture. I shivered, my teeth chattered, my feet became painfully numb. I was desperately hungry, but my wretched hands were so stiff that I had to warm them against my body inside my clothes before I could get the food out of my pocket. And the stinging, icy air forced me to stop eating and warm my hands again. My father had difficulty in keeping warm too. He constantly stamped his feet, rubbed his hands together violently and beat his arms across his chest.

However, the fair ran its course, though nothing much happened. It was a "dead fair," said the regulars. Around us were other young pigs, some very small, grunting with cold like ours. Further off a number of two-hundred-pound porkers, protected by their fat, flopped down on the hard ground after eating; they staggered up with an angry grunt when a buyer struck them with his whip to examine them. At the other extremity of the enclosure were sheep, looking ill and miserable in their frost-encrusted fleeces. The cattle were in another part of the field, separated from us by a wall; we could not see them, but from time to time we could hear their wearied and plaintive bellowing. The men in charge of the animals, peasants in wooden clogs, wearing blue trousers, big smocks and caps, with their thin faces sunk in their very high shirt collars, shivered as one and, like my father, tried various devices to overcome the cold. There were few other people at the fair, only some big farmers wearing goatskins, and dealers in long blue or grey cloaks. They were all constantly on the move, hurrying to get their business done, that they might go and dine in some well-warmed inn parlour. Idlers, who only frequent fairs to kill time, had prudently stayed at home.

From time to time our master, Monsieur Fauconnet, passed by us. He was a man of forty, broad-shouldered and with a clean-shaven, somewhat twisted face. When in good humour he wore a perpetual benign smile, but when anything happened that did not suit him, he frowned, and his face became hard. That day he was very angry, for the fair was not good for much, and we had to sell at a low price or not at all. He was annoyed, too, because three of the pigs were of poor quality. He said that we ought to have left them at home, that the whole lot was spoilt by them.

I was still cold, and began to find the day very long. My father proposed that I should go and take a turn in the town, but I refused, being afraid of losing my way, besides being rather frightened by all the unknown people I saw moving about.

Several attempts at a sale having failed, we were thinking of going back when towards ten o'clock Monsieur Fauconnet returned with a very loquacious dealer. After a long haggle he finally bought the pigs, with the exception of the three poor ones, which he would not take. The master hardly tried to sell them and was not much concerned about the trouble we would have in taking them back.

We had to wait two whole hours on the Moulins road, where we were to deliver the pigs to the man who had bought them. The wait was long and dreary, although at midday the cold was less bitter. When the purchaser appeared, some kind folk, who were waiting like us, helped us to sort out the newly-sold animals. After payment had been made – in gold pieces, which my father cautiously sounded one by one on the damp pavement – we set out across the town, taking a steep, roughly-paved street which ran alongside the river Burge and led to the Place de l'Eglise, in the upper part of the town, where the road to Meillers began.

In this Place de l'Eglise, where the Aury road also began, my father left me. He wanted, as was usual, to hand the money for the pigs over at once to Monsieur Fauconnet. I was rather uneasy when I saw him go away, but he had promised not to be long, and to bring back some white bread and chocolate for my supper; besides, he wanted to ask Monsieur Vernier, a farmer from Meillers whom he expected to meet along with Monsieur Fauconnet, to take me home on his horse. These promises helped me to wait with patient resignation.

I threw the rye that was left in the bottom of the bag to the three pigs, but in spite of that they soon began to give trouble: one made off down the road leading to Meillers, which he no doubt recognized, while another ran down into the town again. Fortunately a man returning from the fair helped me get them together; they were quiet for a little while, but not for long; they soon began to run about, grunting, and I had hard work to keep them from escaping. During the few moments that they were quiet, I anxiously watched the street down which my father had gone, with the hope, always disappointed, of seeing him reappear. More and more I was gripped by cold and hunger.

I had been there a long time when I heard three o'clock chime from the tower of the Sainte-Chapelle. This tower, and three others more distant, the last vestiges of the ancient château, darkened naturally by the passage of the centuries, appeared more sombre still under the grey sky, submerged and faint in the thick mist of the frosty evening. Below, the silent, almost invisible town might have been annihilated by some unseen catastrophe. The Place de l'Eglise, where I was standing, was well in harmony with the gloomy atmosphere: skeletal trees, white and glistening shrubs, the square of worn grass which crackled under my feet, the rectangular pond where the boys' sliding had bruised the dull ice. At the far end of the square the church, its massive doors closed, seemed hostile alike to prayer and hope. To the right, in a garden behind high walls, a newly-built little château, with two square towers, looked like a prison. At the side of the Meillers road, facing the church, stood a fine one-storeyed house, but it was dismal too, for up its walls snaked ugly black stems, which in summer no doubt were clustered with roses and wistaria. A row of low cottages with a uniform line of narrow gardens in front contrasted with these opulent houses, except for one in the middle, which was evidently occupied by a cobbler, to judge by the big boot hanging over the door. At the town end of the square the house forming the corner of the paved street was both an inn and a grocer's shop; cakes of soap could be seen behind the transom window and a branch of juniper swung on the wall.

Like the church, all these dwellings were closed. No doubt inside them there were blazing fires and warm stoves, over which the inhabitants could laugh at the hostility of the outer world. The hostility of the outer world – where I was all alone and miserable with my three pigs.

The gate leading to the garden of the mansion opened and two priests came out. They bowed low to a hooded lady, who accompanied them to the gate. They passed close beside me, giving me an indifferent glance, and went into the house with the black snaky climbers, in which I supposed they lived.

A moment later one of the cottage doors creaked on its hinges. A big, untidy woman appeared in the opening and threw some water out of a saucepan into the garden. An urchin about my own age took advantage of the opportunity to escape: he came to the pond and began to slide on the ice. After five or six turns he went and knocked at the cobbler's door and called "André" three times. Another boy, rather smaller, at length appeared. They slid for a long time together, sometimes upright and following each other, and sometimes crouching down and holding each other's hands. But the big, untidy woman, opening her door again, ordered them to go in, in such a stern voice that they decided to obey her without delay. Once more I was alone in the square.

At long intervals a few farm labourers passed; they walked quickly, in a hurry to get home; some farmers on horseback went by, wrapped up in cloaks and mufflers. One of these, who rode a big white horse, stopped on seeing me.

"Where do you come from, my little lad?"

"From Meillers, sir," I stammered, my teeth chattering.

"Aren't you little Bertin from le Garibier?"

"Yes, sir."

"Hasn't your father come back yet?"

"No, sir."

"What a shame! He must have gone on a binge! Well, my boy, I was going to take you back with me, but now it's impossible, you can't leave your pigs. Keep moving about whatever you do, don't let yourself get numb with cold."

With this sententious advice Monsieur Vernier spurred on his horse and soon disappeared in the fog. I was heart-broken by what he said about my father – "What a shame! He must have gone on a binge." I had not thought of that, but now it seemed to me very likely. When my father attended Mass at Meillers he usually returned at once. But on market days he was sometimes not so sensible and I was often in bed before he returned. The following day he used to look tired and ill, and my mother reserved her harshest look for him, although she pitied him for having such a weak head and not enough strength to resist chance temptations.

At four o'clock darkness fell: it came down from the great sky low and black; it rose from the ground with the floating mist which suddenly thickened; I trembled with cold, hunger and fear. Having eaten nothing all day except my hard crust and apples, I felt faint, my stomach rumbled, and my eyes kept blurring. I was also weak with fatigue, the slight weight of my body was too much for my feeble legs. I regretted that I had not dared to set out alone earlier, even though I hardly knew the way. But now that the countryside was cloaked in darkness, I preferred to freeze where I stood rather than start on the road. The pigs, worn out like myself, slept at the bottom of the ditch: I took advantage of that to sit down near them, and tried to forget my misery.

A servant came out of the big house carrying an empty basket. He strode past the line of trees in the square, along the paved street and disappeared towards the town. He returned shortly after, the basket heavy with provisions, and carrying under his arm a long loaf with a golden crust, at which I looked with envy.

Five o'clock. It was quite dark. I could scarcely see a gipsies' cart which came from the town and passed our way. Two men walked beside the horse, hitting it violently with their sticks. Behind, came three lads in tattered clothes, quarrelling loudly in a strange language. From the inside of the wagon came sounds of wailing, the cries of beaten children and the voice of scolding shrews. I had heard that these people of dubious reputation stole children, tortured them and made little beggars of them. My blood froze even more and my heart beat very fast. But the group passed by, apparently without seeing me.

And two pairs of lovers who came by later did not see me either. They had probably been at a dance in an inn. The girls had flung their cloaks on anyhow in great haste to set out when they had seen how late it was. The young men held them closely round the waist in an amorous embrace, the cold giving them every excuse.

The sexton had rung the evening Angelus. The presbytery and the cottages had closed their shutters, through which filtered thin streaks of light. It was freezing hard: the mist had thinned out and a kind of vague twilight made all the surrounding objects appear mysterious and strange. I felt less pain but my vision became blurred more often, and the sound of bells rang in my ears like an everlasting Angelus ...

The pigs woke up again and gave me a lot of trouble. But despite the energy I had to spend on keeping them together, the cold reached my bones.

A noisy group of young men came up from the town, shouting. One very tall man walked in front, twirling his stick. Three others followed, arm-in-arm, staggering a good deal and pushing each other about. A few yards behind danced the other two, who had stopped to light their pipes. The one in front sang in a loud, raucous voice the refrain of a drinking song:

> *A boire, à boire, à boire,*
> *Nous quitt'rons-nous sans boire?*

To which the three in the middle replied with a formidable "Non," then all joined in, each in a different key and with comic gestures:

> *Les gas d'Bourbon sont pas si fous*
> *De se quitter sans boire un coup!*

When they repeated it this last word was prolonged into a lengthy "ouou" and was at its loudest when they passed me, without suspecting my presence in the black shadow of the great wall, in the deepest part of the ditch.

A wonderful smell of cooking reached me from the château, a delicious odour of meat being fried in sizzling butter. This revived the craving of my empty stomach. I wanted to climb the wall, to shout and scream my misery and my hunger, to beg one small portion of these good things. To escape from this temptation I drew nearer to the presbytery, but there too I could hear the rattling of spoons and smell of soup, which may have had a less penetrating smell than that from the big house, but it was no less pleasant. I realized that everywhere, in warm houses, people were eating their evening meal. They were all dining, the bourgeois and the priests and the poor people in the cottages whose soup, even if it had no taste, must still be so welcome to the stomach! Alone, left on the road, in the rime and frost, a little peasant boy, wrapped up in a grey shawl, was looking after three rejected pigs; and that little peasant, worn out by five hours' sentry duty, had eaten only a scrap of bread and three apples the whole day: and that little peasant was me! They had all seen me, the people from the château and the presbytery, and the housewives from the cottages, and their children who were the same age as I was; they had all seen me, but not one had deigned to give me one word of sympathy or wondered if I could have been unhappy. And not one had thought of coming to see if I was still there in the darkness ...

The clock of the Sainte-Chapelle struck seven. Sadly I counted the blows of the hammer striking the brass, which in the silence of that deserted place, in the wintry night, seemed to me as mournful as a knell. As I crouched in the ditch I felt my eyes closing and a terrible somnolence came over me. Sensations and thoughts faded. Some memories still haunted my half-numb brain. I remembered my family, including the dog Médor, in the forest, at La Breure, the people and the places which had held a place in my childhood life, all of which I felt I had left so long before. This caused me neither regret nor emotion, it was like a dream. I was no longer very certain of having lived that past life: I was convinced I would not live it again. I was drifting towards death and had neither strength nor will to resist the final torpor ...

I was roused by the sound of a step that seemed familiar. My father was arriving, coughing, spitting, walking rather unsteadily, but it was really he! I at once forgot all the misery, the terrors, the suffering, the long martyrdom of the day, in the great happiness of finding him again. Exulting with joy, I was about to throw myself into his arms. He was in the usual besotted state which follows a drinking spree, and at first he seemed astonished to see me there. Then memory returned, and he embraced me in an overwhelming rush of paternal love, as happens with drunken people who always exaggerate their feelings. My poor father wept to think that he had left me alone all day. He found in his pocket a crust of bread left over from his dinner, and a lump of sugar, the remains of the coffee which had followed that meal. I devoured those crumbs which gave me some strength. He was anxious to go back to the inn to buy me some food, but I said no. Since he was there, my protector and my guide, I had no fears, I felt strong enough to walk all the way home without anything more to eat. The pigs staggered about the road as though they too were half-stupefied with cold; that must have been why they had not run away, for I had certainly not been guarding them, even unconsciously.

The return journey was long, silent and painful, my eyes kept closing in spite of myself, and my father, whose hand I did not let go, almost dragged me along. Moreover, he had to keep lashing the pigs who tended to loiter; once he was obliged to stop and lean against a stone wall, his forehead in his hands: he exhaled a sickening smell of wine, his hiccups increased and shook him more and more; he must have felt terrible pain; finally he vomited; that relieved him, and he was able to go on again.

It was past eleven when we reached home. I went at once into the house, leaving my father to feed the pigs and shut them up. In the chimney corner, where the last embers were dying, my mother sat knitting, waiting for us. The whole evening she had been straining her ears listening to the sounds outside, always expecting us to arrive, getting more and more anxious as the night wore on. She asked me why we were so late. When I described the events of the day she began to caress me, shooting furious looks at my father when he came in. Then she ignored him altogether. He did not say a word, but went to bed immediately. I ate some soup and an egg cooked in the ashes. This feast consoled me, but all the same I could scarcely sleep. It took me more than a week to recover from the fatigue and heavy cold which resulted from my long watch. But it took my father and mother a still longer time to recover their normal relationship.

VI

The time came for me to go to catechism, my first contact with society. Society in this case was represented by an old rosy-faced priest with white hair, and by five urchins, of whom four at least were as uncivilized as myself. One only, Jules Vassenat, son of the tobacconist and innkeeper, was less awkward, because he some-times went to the school at Noyant, the village closest to us. Schools at that time were very far apart, and only the fairly well-off could afford to send their children to them, for the fees were high.

The boys' catechism took place at eight o'clock in the morning. It was a good league from Le Garibier to the church, so in winter I had to leave our house before daylight In frosty weather I got along very well, although I often stumbled and sometimes fell down, for the roads were rough. But in wet weather the mud got inside my *sabots* and bespattered my woollen stockings, making me very uncomfortable during the class. The curé used to be annoyed when I arrived with very dirty *sabots*: though to be sure he was no better pleased with my companions, for whom the roads were no better than for me. He had a very hasty temper. When we answered his questions wrongly and whispered and laughed, he used to fly into a rage.

"You great blockhead! You stupid ass!" he would shout.

Then he would give us bangs on the head with his book. But his wrath was short-lived, very soon he would tell us funny stories and laugh with us. He also did us little kindnesses which largely made up for his passing severities. Once on the occasion of a wedding, he shared with us the blessed *brioche* which the young couple had offered him; he also divided some sugared almonds among us after a baptism; and on New Year's Eve he gave us each an orange, begging us not to begin the new year badly by any naughtiness the next day. Indeed he was a good man, friendly with everybody, jovial and free from malice; he was free of speech even with the rich; he was indifferent to the power of money; he was not a toady like so many I have met.

I could hardly get back from the catechism before ten o'clock, but I often returned even later, because of the games I played with one of my classmates, Jean Boulois of Le Parizet, who would come to the end of the lane with me.

We used to pass the edge of a large pond close to the mill and we always stopped to watch the big wheel turn, and to listen to the grinding of the millstones and the clicking of the machinery. We also liked to watch the lads ride off on the big horses which carried the customers' flour on their backs, and brought back the grain to be ground. The covered wagons of the present day were unknown then, because there were no cart-roads.

The ingenious Jean Boulois always had some new diversions to offer me. He took me along the edge of a stream, where we made necklaces from the coral-red berries we found on the bushes. He taught me how to make snares with elder twigs and treacle, to catch birds in snowy weather. We looked for bullaces, which were eatable when frozen. So our journeys home took a long time. In the end I arrived home at eleven instead of ten o'clock, and told my mother that the curé kept us later and later.

"Go along then, get your soup eaten quickly", she would say, "the pigs are getting restless in the cowshed, they ought to have been in the fields two hours ago!"

I would then go out again to La Breure or some other fallow land for a long day with my pigs; but the solitude weighed more heavily upon me than formerly.

On day I was rash enough not to return until midday; that aroused everyone's suspicions. The following Sunday my mother went to see the curé, who told her we were always free by nine o'clock. She scolded me so much that it became impossible to dawdle any more: if I was not back by a quarter past ten at the latest I was sure to be punished.

In May 1835, after my second year of catechism, the good old curé allowed me to receive the sacrament. As my friend Boulois was my classmate, I went after Mass with my father, mother, and godfather to dinner at Le Parizet. They were comfortably off, and there was plenty to eat: there was soup made with ham, rabbit, chicken, a very fresh wheaten loaf, *galette* and *brioche*; there was wine (I drank a whole glassful) and coffee, which I had never tasted before. Perhaps I over-indulged in all the good things somewhat, for I was not very well during the evening ceremony and felt uncomfortable during the night.

I have often found out since then that every pleasure must be paid for – often rather heavily.

VII

There was another celebration in November of the same year, when my two brothers were married.

My elder brother Baptiste, who was my godfather, was almost twenty-five. Louis was twenty-two. To save them from military service, my father had insured them, before the ballot, with a *marchand d'hommes*, a man who provided substitutes.

Military service, which lasted at that period for eight years, seemed to us a frightful calamity. Mother often said, speaking of my brothers, that she would rather see them dead than going off as soldiers. The few lads who did go – victims of fate and poverty – went off on foot to some distant garrison and were usually never seen again until eight years later, after many wanderings and adventures. Now in our remote country parts nobody had any notion of what the outer world was like. The world beyond our district, beyond known distances, seemed full of mystery and danger and peopled by savages. And the memory of those great wars of the Empire, where so many men had fallen, was still with us. For all these reasons, the very idea of conscription haunted parents for years beforehand. To insure oneself before the ballot cost about five hundred francs, but if one waited until after the ballot and one's lot was drawn, then the cost was at least a thousand or eleven hundred francs. By dint of skimping and saving on the salt, butter and everything else, patiently accumulating big and little coins, my mother had managed to put aside the five hundred francs necessary for the preliminary insurance of each of her two elder sons. This achievement made her happy and proud.

My brothers were marrying two sisters, Cognet's daughters from Le Rondet. Louis had decided only at the last moment to propose to Claudine Cognet, for he had a nice little girl nearer home whom he wanted to marry. But our mother had made him understand that as he would no doubt always have to live with his brother, it would be better if they had two sisters for wives, for this would be some guarantee of harmony in the household. As she had considerable influence over him she succeeded in persuading him.

I was too young to take part in the ceremony so they made me stay at home with my grandmother and Marinette on the wedding-day. I even went out as usual with the pigs, but I brought them back early, knowing that nobody would notice in the general confusion.

My mother returned as soon as the ceremony was over. The dinner was prepared under the direction of a cook from Bourbon who, with Mother Simon of Suippière and the servant from La Bourdrie, helped my mother. Everything was topsy-turvy. The beds had been taken up to the granary. A large table, made of planks placed on trestles, divided the room in two diagonally. The fowls killed the previous evening and joints of meat brought by the butcher from Bourbon were being stewed in pots or roasted in the oven, and the smells were tempting. I regaled myself with giblets and some appetising *brioche*, which tasted deliciously of fresh butter.

The wedding guests arrived at nightfall. They had danced all afternoon at Vassenat's inn, where there were two musicians, a thin old man who turned the handle of a *vielle* and a chubby-faced one with a broken nose, who played the bagpipes. Lunch had been eaten early and hastily at Le Rondet before the departure for Meillers. Everybody was very hungry when they arrived, and dinner began almost at once. The big table was not big enough, so a little one was placed in the chimney-corner for the children. There were Uncle Toinot's two young children, three or four little ones belonging to relations of my sisters-in-law and those of the neighbours, the two lads from Suippière, and Bastien and Thérèse from La Bourdrie. I was placed beside Thérèse and I admired her fresh cheeks and the little locks of fair hair escaping from her calico bonnet. I hardly spoke to her all the time, for I was never very bold, and this invasion of strangers intimidated me still more. My table companions were not much more loquacious, but silent though we were we did full justice to the good things. My mother sat beside us to keep an eye on us and serve us, which was very wise; but for her we should certainly have overeaten.

By contrast, the conversation at the large table was very animated; everyone spoke loudly, but loudest of all was Uncle Toinot, who told the war story which he reserved for great occasions: it was about a Russian whom he had killed.

"It was two days before Beresina, a bitterly cold day, confound it! Twenty of us were sent out on reconnaissance, we had to search a little wood to the left of the column. We could see nothing, we expected nothing, when suddenly some Cossacks rushed out from a kind of ravine, firing at us, yelling like savages and trying to surround us. Then we wielded our bayonets, and we meant business, I can tell you! The leader of the bastards had an ugly face, I'd like to have had his guts for garters! But as I eyed him I saw that a big devil with a huge beard was waiting to knock me out with the butt of his musket. I jumped sideways to avoid the blow, I gave him such a violent thrust in the belly with my head that he staggered and fell down in the snow. Then, seeing my bayonet aimed at his chest he looked at me, rolling his two great eyes in terror, I'll never forget it:

'*Francis bono! Francis bono! ...*' he begged.

That meant 'Good Frenchman,' and his look added: 'Don't kill me!'

But with the misery we had in the bloody cold and nothing to eat but bits of dead horses, all raw, when you could get it, we didn't care a damn about pity! I'd only got one thought, a ferocious one: 'You can cry as much as you like, you bastard! You wouldn't have spared me if I hadn't seen you in time.' And *zing*, my bayonet went through him like a knife through butter.''

A shiver of horror ran through those at table, and for a moment there was silence. Everybody gazed at this man who had killed a man. He enjoyed his triumph. He drank two glasses of wine, and in order to keep everyone's attention be began to sing ribald army songs, which made the girls blush, drew coarse laughter from the men and intrigued us children so much that my grandmother reproached him for not being respectable. But he was so pleased to attract attention that he took no notice of her.

The outside door was suddenly flung open. Ten or so fantastically dressed individuals filed in and began to leap about, shouting and twisting around and pulling funny faces. They wore huge false noses and their faces were powdered with flour. Some of them had moustaches made with soot and black streaks all over their faces. From fifty mouths came the cry:

"The mummers! The mummers!"

At that time it was the custom for the young men of the neighbourhood to turn up in this disguise at all wedding dinners, under the pretext of amusing the guests.

They continued to play the fool, kissing the girls, whom they whitened with flour and blackened with soot. They were offered wine and *brioche*. They ate and drank, and then began to dance in the small amount of free space left: they capered about, whisking up their skirts and they howled like savages.

But the guests began to get tired of being at the table. My father lit the lantern and crossed the muddy yard, we all followed him to the barn and began to dance. In one corner they had built a kind of platform with some bales of straw, upon which they set the thin old man with his *vielle* and the chubby-faced, broken-nosed one with his bagpipes. The lantern was hung in the middle, very high up, and gave out a dim light, so that in the half-darkness the dancers looked alarmingly like spectres. That mattered little to them; mummers and guests spun round in eager rivalry or swayed together in time through the many figures of the *bourrée*. Leaning against a heap of sheaves, the old folks looked on, chatting, sometimes even joining in. We urchins ran among the dancers, following them and bickering among ourselves. At one time, when we were behaving pretty well, my godfather and his wife teased us.

"The little ones ought to dance, it's a good chance for them to learn."

We looked down and turned very red, but my godfather went on:

"Go on Tiennon, catch Thérèse and make her take a turn with you."

They insisted, and in spite of our confusion we had to make a start. Our heads were going round by this time; we bumped against the grown-ups, who drove us off to right and left; but we went on to the end, and when the dance was finished, seeing the others kissing their partners, I gave Thérèse two big kisses on her rosy cheeks, and got well teased by my godfather. This first attempt had given me courage, and I took part in nearly all the dances that followed.

The oil in the lantern was used up, the light suddenly went out, and in the dark barn arose cries of fright and gaiety, jostling and laughter, mingled with teasing exclamations:

"Baptiste, watch out for your wife!"

"Louis, I've stolen your Claudine!"

"The poor young couples, what will they do?"

After the first moment of surprise, whispering and the sound of kissing grew louder; anonymous, bold kisses gave rise to startled cries, wild dashes, entreaties, sighs.

My brothers sent me to the house to get a light. There I found some of the old people, who had left the barn, sitting round the table again, drinking and singing and cramming themselves with great pieces of roast fowl. Uncle Toinot, quite drunk, was lying across the table, fast asleep.

When the barn was once more lighted, the dancing began again, and went on until two o'clock in the morning. Only the newly-married couples had slipped away earlier to Suippière, where they were to spend the night. Some of the guests were put up by the neighbours. Others slept at our house, the women and children in the granary on makeshift beds erected by my mother, the men in the hayloft, where they found old blankets and worn sacks for covering.

The young men wanted to stay up, out of sheer bravado. When

they had eaten and drunk their fill they went out into the yard and played stupid tricks. They hid the tools, took the plough to pieces, pushed the ox-cart into the horse-pond, took the leather straps off the yokes and used them to tie Médor to the wheelbarrow, which they hung to the top of a pear-tree. The poor dog uttered such heart-rending howls that my father had to rescue him, which was not easy. During this time the young bloods concluded their exploits by placing in the path of the newly-weds great forked sticks, the meaning of which I did not understand at the time. They came back to the house at daybreak and pestered my mother to give them 'fried soup'. All this was in the tradition of the time, and if the details have been slightly modified since, they remain in essence the same.

Towards nine o'clock a procession was formed to go and meet the young married folk, and there was a fine laugh at their expense when they passed the forked sticks. I saw nothing of all this, for I had to go out with my pigs as though nothing unusual was going on. When I returned, breakfast was in full swing, but the gaiety was a little forced. Everyone was tired out, with sleepy eyes and drawn faces. There was one more dance in the barn.

The guests left before midnight, taking the leftover *galette* and *brioche* given to them by my mother.

It took a good many days' work after that to get everything back in place again.

VIII

After this double wedding our household was very numerous, especially in women. My grandmother, my mother, Catherine and my two sisters-in-law made five, all capable of working. There was also my little sister Marinette, who was nearly ten years old, but the poor child was half-witted. This was attributed to a bad fever she had had in infancy, after which she had grown up sickly and puny and had been a long time developing physically and mentally. She lisped, which made her difficult to understand. There was no gleam of intelligence in her brain, she could scarcely grasp the simplest ideas. She replied only in monosyllables and scarcely talked to anyone except Médor and the cats, with whom she liked to play. Reproaches left her indifferent; the gravest events never stirred her; at times she would go off into fits of laughter without any motive. Her understanding was to remain always that of a small child.

From that time I began to get used to all kinds of work. In late winter and early spring, down to May, when we were ploughing the fallow land for sowing in October, I became a kind of ploughboy, in charge of the oxen. I would take the pigs, who were so busy looking for worms along the newly-open furrows that they behaved quite well.

After grooming the oxen in the morning my godfather and I would start out at nine o'clock and stay out until three or four in the afternoon. I used a long, metal-tipped goad to drive the oxen, whose names were Noiraud, Rougeaud, Blanchon and Mouton. The first two were of that Auvergne breed I have already mentioned; there was at least one pair on every farm, for it was thought that the local white oxen were not strong enough to do all the work. The Mauriac beasts worked well, being old and experienced. But the two white ones, who were still young, needed constant watching. Walking on the loose soil tired me very much, chiefly because of the pebbles which soon got into my *sabots*. When I was tired of driving I used to ask my godfather to let me take over the handle of the plough. But in spite of all my efforts, my lack of practice and strength, or perhaps a clumsy movement by the oxen, would cause me to let the plough swerve. Then my godfather was angry, for he was hasty-tempered, and very particular where work was concerned. He would take over again quickly, saying I was useless. However, the same thing sometimes happened when he held the plough; then he would make out that I was guiding the oxen badly, and would give me a slap ... It was then I learned that even with the best intentions in the world the weak are always in the wrong, and it's miserable working for other people.

I often used to count the furrows worked in the course of the ploughing, compare them with what we had done the previous days and make a rough calculation of when it would be time to go. When I reached the hedge where the gateway was, I would steal a glance at my brother's face – nearly always impassive – and I had to turn the oxen round and do another length, at the end of which would be another disappointment, all the keener because of my growing expectancy. My godfather did not go, as a rule, until they called him from the house: he had no watch, and when the sun was not shining he had no guide except the amount of work done, or the degree of hunger rumbling in his stomach. The villages were so far away that we rarely even heard the midday Angelus, which would at least have told us we had accomplished half our daily task.

When the weather was fine, time passed not unpleasantly, but on bad days it seemed endless. I remember one March, when we were ploughing the chestnut field, the most distant of our fields. A strong wind was blowing all the time from Souvigny – that is right from the northeast – with cold, rain, hail, and flurries of snow, which soaked through my clothes, and wrapped me in an icy shroud; my hands became purple. One day, the showers buffeting us more than usual, I shivered with more than cold. My forehead burned, my teeth chattered, and my stomach was heavy; I kept yawning, and although it was late I was not hungry. I told my godfather that I felt ill and wanted to go home but he would not let me. At last, however, a really violent shower having forced us to shelter in a hollow oak-tree, my godfather took the trouble to look at me. Seeing me alternately flushed and pale he said, "Go home at once, you're feverish!" My legs shook; they were so weak and tired, I could scarcely walk to the house. I was sent to bed immediately. The next day, after a good sweat, my body was found to be covered with red spots. I remember that my mother told me to stay well wrapped up, to avoid worse catastrophes.

A fortnight later, when I recovered from this attack of measles and was able to go out into the fields again, April was radiant with sunshine, greenness and birdsong. The hedges were covered with young leaves and the cherry-trees with delicate white blossom. Nature seemed to be celebrating my recovery. I found pleasure in just moving about, in being alive.

The following winter, after my fifteenth birthday, I no longer looked after the pigs, I had to do man's work. They made me thresh with the flail, and help to clean out the cowsheds.

In previous years when I went out to the fields in the snow, I used to envy the ones who stayed behind in the barn to do the threshing. But when I had to take my turn at it, I had to admit it was no bed of roses either; if we had dry feet we also had pretty tired arms, and swallowed too much dust. At that time threshing was all done with the flail and went on from All Saints' Day to Shrove Tuesday, even into mid-Lent, almost without interruption, except for some days each month when, if there was a good moon, the hedges were cut and the trees pruned. In the daytime they threshed only between the morning and evening grooming, but worked at it again in the evenings. The year I began was one of abundant harvests and we threshed every evening by the light of a lantern, until ten o'clock. I know of no work so exhausting.

Wielding the flail with the same unflagging regularity, keeping the necessary rhythm, not being able to stop one moment, not being able to use your hand to wipe your nose even, or to flick off the grain of dust tickling your neck – when you're still awkward and unused to sustained effort, it drives you mad. I enjoyed only the days when we winnowed, when I saw the great grey-brown heap diminish little by little and disappear entirely into the hopper of the winnowing-machine. Then I could plunge my hands with delight into the clean, golden grain.

Cleaning out the cowshed on Saturday mornings was also very hard work. I did this work with Louis. We had a big oak barrow, which was heavy enough when empty, a pitchfork which we thrust into the thick beds of warm manure, heaping it on to the barrow in great forkfuls. Louis, playing on my vanity, would say:

"Let's put on a bit more, eh? You're doing fine, now we'll see if you're a man."

Of course I had to show I was a man, so I let the barrow be loaded so high that it nearly broke my back. At first I managed somehow but very soon I was sweating and choking. My strained sinews gave way and I could no longer hold the barrow which ran down the length of the cowshed into the big heap of manure in the yard. After that they reduced the load, but in vain – it always escaped me. Then my father and my godfather had to replace me, not without a jeer; and I made myself scarce, feeling dissatisfied and furious.

I have noticed since that all beginners have these setbacks. When you first start to work you try to rival the grown-ups, but you lack strength, skill and experience. The others vaunt their superiority, due to their age, and you smart under their merciless teasing.

IX

Monsieur Fauconnet came to our house about once a fortnight, on horseback or in his carriage according to the state of the roads. The women would rush out to take his mount and call my father, who, however far off he might be, always came hurrying back to show him the crops and the stock, and to give him any information he wanted.

Monsieur Fauconnet called everybody *tu*: young and old, men and women. When he was in a good mood he would even take off my grandmother's cap. This cap was made in three parts, a cone and two scrolls reversed; it was known as the Bourbon cap, which the younger women of the district had already begun to disdain.

"Eh! Are you keeping fit, then, mother? Yes, you're still good-looking; you'll live till you're ninety at least. With those caps all our women used to live to a great age. It's a mistake to change them; the new ones are too flat, they don't keep the sun off."

To my mother he would say:

"Your poultry doing well this year, Jeanette? You've got plenty of chickens at any rate: I see the yard is full of them. Don't let them eat the pigs' meal or get into the corn!"

He would tap my sisters-in-law on the stomach and ask "what they had got tucked away in there?" and when they were pregnant he would say complacently, "Won't be long now."

He chucked Catherine under the chin, telling her she was a nice girl, and that he would like to take her on as a maid.

"And you, you Auvergnat brigand," he would say to me, "you're getting as long as a broom handle."

He called me "Auvergnat brigand" in memory of the day when I had let the sheep get into the clover, while I was in the forest with the long-sawyer from Auvergne.

In bad years my father made loud complaints, and asked him to reduce the rent, to which the master would reply: "You're always worrying, Bérot: you make yourself old, my man. Reduce the rent! But you don't think: when you make nothing, I make nothing either, you old humbug. And when things do go well, do I charge you more?"

At Martinmas, when they had to settle the accounts for the year, they had to try to remember at which fairs they had sold stock and at what price. Since nobody could do sums, it was difficult to carry all the figures in their heads, and more difficult still to tot them all up and decide exactly what profit was left.

Concentrated and serious, their eyes glittering, my father, my mother and my brother would reckon up together:

"At the Bourbon winter fair – seven pigs at twenty-three francs."

"That makes a hundred and sixty-one francs –" said Louis very cleverly.

At first my mother would not agree:

"You say a hundred and sixty-one – are you sure? Let's see: seven times twenty-three – take first seven twenty-franc pieces, which make – which make – the five make a hundred, the two forty, a hundred and forty francs: then there are seven three-franc pieces, which make twenty-one; a hundred and forty and twenty-one make a hundred and sixty-one. That's right! Well, what else?"

My father had had time to think, and now went on:

"We sold some more on Ash Wednesday at Le Montet. There were five. They were big ones: we sold them for thirty-eight francs ten sous, I'm quite sure of that."

Then they would start working that out:

"Five thirty-franc pieces, five eight-franc pieces, five ten-sou pieces."

This went on evening after evening. By the time they got to the end they had forgotten the previous totals and often had to begin all over again. It sometimes seemed they would never get it right. In the end they would agree on a sum without being very certain that it was the right one.

When Monsieur Fauconnet came to settle our accounts he wasted very little time on the matter. Paper in hand he would say:

"The purchases come to so much – sales to so much; that brings you so much, Bérot."

In bad years our share was tiny; we were even in debt on two or three occasions. It never came to more than two or three hundred francs. When my father had hoped for more, he would often venture to say:

"But, sir, I did think I should have had more than that."

Then the master's face would assume its worst frown:

"What do you mean, more than that? Do you take me for a thief, Bérot? If that's so, I'll ask you to find another master, who won't rob you."

Then my poor father would say very humbly,

"I'm sure I don't mean that, Monsieur Fauconnet."

"That's just as well, for you know labourers are not scarce; I could find plenty as good as you."

However, when the difference was too marked, Monsieur Fauconnet would condescend to explain that he had carried over the October sales to the next year's account – "in case we had a bad season." This allowed him to use the money for the whole year, instead of sharing it with us then and there. But of course we had to accept this bizarre and illegal arrangement with a good grace or be thrown out.

X

Money, as you can imagine, was not plentiful in our house, and until I was seventeen I had never had as much as a twenty-sou piece in my pocket. All the same, on days off I now wanted to go to the inn and see a bit of life. We used to go to Mass by turns, there being only two sets of decent clothes among the four of us. My brothers had their wedding clothes, but these were saved for high days and holidays. A man's wedding-suit used to last him all his life, and serve for his laying-out when he died. My father and my brother Louis used to go to the town together one Sunday, and the following Sunday it was my godfather's turn and mine.

I saw that my friends from the catechism class were beginning to go and drink at Vassenat's and I was upset that I couldn't afford to go with them. On the second Sunday before Mardi Gras it was the custom for young people to have some fun. Being in my eighteenth year, I ventured to ask for a little money. My father gave a start and said,

"What do you want it for? At your age, good heavens!" My mother added that they could not go on keeping us all, if I was going to start wasting money already. I still contrived to get forty sous from them.

Away I went, as happy as a king, holding my head higher than usual, and sticking my chest out under my smock. After Mass, instead of slipping away, I boldly accosted Boulois from Le Parizet and offered to stand him a drink. He had been going to Vassenat's for a long time and knew all the regulars. Soon five or six of us were seated round the table. Not being accustomed to the place, I was bashful at first, and dared not say anything, even to those of my own group. I was astonished to hear the others exchanging dubious stories and passing in review the girls of the district, about whom they made rude or ironical remarks.

Behind the inn parlour was a room for dancing, in which the thin old man with his *vielle*, and the chubby-faced, broken-nosed man with his bagpipes, were already beginning to play. I went in with my companions. A side door opened onto an alleyway, and through this the girls entered. Over their thick serge dresses they wore little grey or brown shawls, crossed over the breast, and falling in a point at the back. Over their white caps they wore round straw hats without brims, trimmed with long black velvet braids. Thérèse Parnière was there. She was a fine girl of sixteen, still fair, and very well-developed. As I knew her better than any other girl there, I asked her to dance and she didn't say no. I took my place and began to dance like an old hand. She was my partner for nearly the whole evening. Between the dances I rejoined Boulois and the others in the inn parlour; we returned to the table where our empty glasses stood in a row, and drank a bumper, chatting gaily, but went out again at the first sound of the music.

It was nearly five o'clock in the evening when the last of the girls slipped away, and as we were very hungry we ordered bread and cheese. By the time we had drunk two more bottles everything was eaten. We had coffee, and then a brandy. I had never drunk so much before. I saw, as in a dream, people moving in the room, groups round the tables raising their glasses and making a row. When we rose to go I was not very steady on my legs. Fortunately Boulois took my arm, and by the time we parted, near Le Parizet, I had recovered my balance, thanks to the fresh air, and was able to manage on my own.

On reaching home I entered the dark kitchen noisily – everyone had been in bed since eight o'clock. I stumbled against a bench which fell over with a loud crash and began to talk to myself:

"Everybody asleep already? That's no life ... I'm not sleepy ..."

My godfather's two babies and Louis' three were woken up by the noise and began to cry. My mother and Claudine got up. I put my arms around them affectionately.

"He's drunk!" they exclaimed together. My mother gave me something to eat, sighing over my folly in throwing away their hard-earned money. Claudine nursed her youngest, who was crying, then she put him back in the cradle and began rocking him back to sleep with a lullaby:

Dodo, le petit, dodo
Le petit mignon voudrait bien dormir:
Son petit sommeil ne peut pas venir;
Dodo, le petit, dodo.

But neither the reproaches of my mother, nor her sighs, nor the singing of my sister-in-law, nor the baby's crying could move me. I went on playing the fool and keeping the whole household awake by my antics and noise for a whole hour. After that I went to bed and slept heavily until morning.

At work the next day my brothers jeered at me over my pallid and wretched appearance and because my mouth was so dry that I had to drink water from the ditch.

I had no chance to repeat that experience for some time. At Easter I was only allowed twenty sous. I had to wait until the feast of the Patron Saint, in June, before I got another forty-sou piece.

Fortunately at that time we could amuse ourselves without spending money; in fine weather we had dances in the open air, which we called *vijons*, and in the winter we gathered indoors for the *veillées*.

For the outdoor dances, we found when possible an open space, shady and grassy, and on Sunday afternoons the young girls and lads of the neighbourhood assembled there. Even married couples, old folk and children would come: anyone, in fact, with nothing better to do. When it was possible to have any kind of music, we danced to our heart's content, and even the old folk danced the *bourrée*. If there were no musicians, the keenest among us sang or whistled the tunes, and we danced to that.

In addition to the dances we used to play games. We would form a big circle, in the middle of which stood a victim who was blindfolded and only set free when he had guessed who faced him, touched his hand or something of that kind. Then there were forfeits, which allowed the young men to kiss the girls. Finally, for the men who were too serious for these childish pleasures, there were long games of skittles.

Lovers, for instance, could hardly get away on their own, there were too many people about; it would soon have been noticed and maliciously pointed out. Everyone behaved well at these daylight parties.

The winter gatherings often gave more opportunities for courting. We would meet one Sunday at one house and the following Sunday at another. We danced, we played games, we laughed. Sometimes, when a host wanted to do things well, he would provide a panful of chestnuts at the end of the evening. And when it got towards midnight, there was sometimes the chance of escorting one's chosen sweetheart home in the dark, and that was altogether delightful.

It was in such circumstances that I began courting Thérèse Parnière, my neighbour from La Bourdrie. Since my first visit to Vassenat's, in fact since my brothers' wedding, I had been attracted to her. At the *vijons* and the evening gatherings I was her recognized partner, and by the pressing of hands and tender looks I had let her see something of my feelings. But when I met her under other circumstances, I had nothing to say except a few commonplace words about the weather and the bad state of the roads, although God knows how my heart was beating!

On that Sunday the *veillée* had taken place at Suippière, and I was the only one there from our house: Catherine was ill and did not want to go with me, and since their marriage my brothers rarely went out. From La Bourdrie there were only Thérèse and her brother Bastien. I knew quite well that Bastien would want to go with the youngest Lafont girl from L'Errain, who had been his sweetheart for a long time. I said to him in confidence that it would be a nuisance for him to have his sister's company on the way home.

"Well, go with her yourself then," said he.

I told him that was what I wanted; he laughed and said:

"You've only got to ask her, stupid, she'll be very glad."

While we were dancing the polka, I screwed up my courage and said to Thérèse:

"Will you let me take you home this evening?"

"Yes, if you like," she replied without any hesitation. "As well you as anyone else."

As usual, the *veillée* ended about midnight. All the guests went out together, and in the yard sorted themselves into families or groups of friends. I rejoined Thérèse, who had deliberately left her brother behind, and we went into a large field which we had to cross to get to La Bourdrie. It was very dark. The west wind was blowing violently in wild gusts, and the fine drizzling rain which had fallen all day had made the ground slippery. We went cautiously, arm in arm, steadying each other when our clogs tripped us up.

I kept silent, much moved by the novelty of the experience. Thérèse said:

"It's no use going on, it's as black as the bottom of the oven. I'm frightened, I am really!"

"Oh, but when there are two of us –" I said timidly; and then suddenly I put my lips to her cool cheek.

It seemed to me that my boldness had not greatly surprised her. But as I showed some wish to keep her there, she said:

"Stop it, then, you great stupid," but her tone was more condescending than annoyed.

I took her hand in mine and put my left arm round her waist.

"Thérèse, for a long time I've wanted to say I'd like to be your sweetheart."

"You're very forward. You don't want to get married yet, do you?"

"Perhaps before very long –"

I tightened my arms round her waist, gripped her hands in mine and with a sudden movement I made her stand still.

"Would you like to?"

"What?"

"To marry me?"

And, wild with desire, without giving her time to reply, I put my arms round her again, holding her for a long time. My lips sought hers.

She had bent her head back with an instinctive gesture: I felt her tremble.

"Oh! stop it," she said again, in a fainter, half-pleading voice.

But she was not able to escape my caress; our lips met in a delicious kiss. Quite close to us an owl screeched mournfully. We resumed our walk with quickened steps, both deeply disturbed by these first exchanges of love and by the cries of ill-omen uttered by the bird of night.

The drizzle had started again, falling thick and cold upon my companion's baize cape and my thick cotton smock, and chilling with its icy touch our hot, clasped hands.

After crossing the field, we had to climb a stile in the quickset hedge which separated it from the La Bourdrie meadow. It was so dark that we had some difficulty in finding the stile. I went first, and as the meadow was at a lower level, I received Thérèse in my arms at the foot of the crooked stake which served as a step to mount and descend the stile. I hoped to make the most of this opportunity to embrace her again, but she disengaged herself so quickly that I had not even time to kiss her. We walked the whole length of the damp meadow soberly, almost in silence. We had to cross a very bad bit of pathway where we had to go one behind the other along a row of stepping-stones, placed rather far apart. To impress her with my gallantry, although the way was unfamiliar to me, I went first. Although I stepped carefully, I missed one of the stones and plunged into a puddle up to my knees. I came out of it very sheepishly, my trousers dripping and covered with mud, while she, undeterred by the water which had splashed her, laughed at my mishap. In the yard, however, before leaving her, I took her in my arms, pressed her to me in a passionate embrace, and gave her a lover's long kiss. This time she did not resist.

In a fever I found my way back to Le Garibier. I felt full of life and rapture. On that dark winter night of wind and rain my heart was full of blue sky.

From that evening, Thérèse was recognized as my sweetheart. I had no fear of displaying my preference for her at the other *veillées* that winter, nor at the *vijons* the following summer, nor even at the dances at Vassenat's on fête days. I often went to meet her down the fields on Sundays when there was no social gathering, and we used to spend long hours together under the discreet and scented hawthorn hedges, those accomplices of lovers. But our relations never went beyond innocent hugs and long, long kisses – repetitions of that first evening. Young and shy as we were, timidity, modesty, fear of consequences – all these things hindered us from the consummation of our love. Besides, I had quite decided to make her my wife.

XI

At the age of nineteen I had to leave the farm of Le Garibier, where my youth had been passed.

Monsieur Fauconnet, after a violent scene with my parents gave them notice to quit. My father had suggested selling one of the sows with her litter because fodder was scarce that year. But the master wanted to keep the mother and fatten up the piglets.

"We'll buy some bran," he said.

That remark was fatal. My parents were convinced that the last Martinmas accounts had included much more bran than had ever actually been purchased. Furthermore, the sale of two fat oxen, which had taken place in the absence of my father, had fetched a ridiculously low price. My mother had often sworn that Fauconnet would pay for that piece of trickery. So at the mention of the word 'bran' she told him that he need not set that down to expenses for he had been paid for it last year. When Fauconnet asked her what she meant, she accused him squarely of overcharging them.

"So you think I'm cheating!" he cried as usual. My father emerged from his usual passivity:

"Well, yes, you're cheating!"

Then he brought up the fat oxen and other old grievances, trying to give proofs. My mother supported him.

"Yes, yes, you're a cheat! If you had acted honestly I should have had three or four thousand francs put by, but instead I haven't a sou. Yes, you're a cheat!"

Fauconnet, despite his bravado, went white. He scowled heavily and began to threaten us.

"You'll tell that story to the magistrates! I shall sue you for libel and slander. You don't know what's coming to you. In the meantime, Bérot, you find another farm!"

He went out rapidly, saddled his horse himself and rode off, shouting:

"I'll show you, just wait!"

In risking this stand, my parents were prepared for an immediate dismissal. They had foreseen this from the start and took it calmly. But the threat of prosecution dismayed them very much, and their fear was shared by everyone. In court, even with the strongest case, downtrodden people are always in the wrong. That was a well-known fact. What would happen? They could only repeat what they knew to be true, while the master would produce papers, present well-ordered accounts: and what would be the good of stammering out the simple truth? The master would be bound to win.

My grandmother never stopped lamenting:

"The lawyers will take our all. They will sell our furniture and our tools at auction. *Ah, mon Dieu!*"

These terrors were vain, however: Fauconnet did not bring his action. At bottom, in spite of his superiority, he too perhaps had some fear of the courts. Until Martinmas he contented himself by inflicting upon us every petty annoyance he could think of, exacting the conditions of the lease to the letter, preventing us from using the clover for pasture, so that we either had to buy in hay, or let the cattle go hungry.

He found so many ways of worrying us, that when we left my father could not pay what he owed. The master then seized the standing crops and kept them all. He was the only person who had any profit from our last year's work.

Later, when I saw him send his sons to the great schools, making the eldest a doctor, the second a lawyer, and the third an officer; when, later still, I saw him buy a manor-house at Agonges with four farms, grow old and die a great landed proprietor, worth at least half a million and respected in consequence, I understood then how right my parents had been to call him a cheat and a thief. It was only by taking advantage of the lower orders that he had built himself up thus. By origin, he too was a poor man. His father had been steward of an estate, and his grandfather a *métayer* like ourselves.

XII

After much canvassing my father managed to find another farm. It was called La Billette, and lay near the market town of Saint-Menoux, at the foot of a hill, close to the Bourbon road. It had been bought by a certain Monsieur Boutry, a chemist from Moulins, who, having invested his money satisfactorily, settled there at the same time as we did. His house, a big square house in a spacious garden, was separated from our yard by a wall.

In several ways we were better off then at Le Garibier. The buildings were only two hundred yards from the main road, which bounded several of our fields. We could see people going by, on horseback, on foot, and in carriages; that was a change from our wild valley, where we never saw any strangers. We could not complain about the house or the land. But the thing that worried us, and soon seemed unbearable, was the constant presence of the master.

Monsieur Boutry was not a bad sort of man, and I would swear that our accounts with him were always straightforward. But he was fussy and interfering. He knew nothing about farming, but mistakenly took his role of managing proprietor seriously. He read books on agriculture, and wanted us to swallow all the theories he found in them. There was, perhaps, some sense in them, but they contained many new ideas, so contrary to our usual ways that we often laughed in his face as he unfolded them to us. And his appearance and gestures made us laugh too. Short, lively, excitable, bald-headed and short-bearded, he would come hopping towards us in the cowsheds or down in the fields, and timidly and politely make his suggestions.

"Look here," he would say, "it would be better to plough at such a time and in such a manner:" or even, "You don't use enough seed," or, "You ought to give the oxen so-and-so to eat."

I remember one day he came to look for my godfather and me when we were ploughing some fallow land. It was May, about ten o'clock in the morning, and very hot; Monsieur Boutry said very fussily:

"Baptiste, Baptiste, when it's as warm as this, you ought not to keep the oxen at it too long – three hours at the outside. If you work them longer than that at a time, it may result in very serious trouble indeed. I read that yesterday in a very good treatise on agriculture."

He stroked the backs of the oxen with his small apothecary's hand, white and delicate.

"See, they're already in a sweat, their sides are heaving, they're frothing at the mouth. Their tongues will stick out. You must unharness them, Baptiste."

My godfather shrugged his shoulders:

"We shall never get through the work, sir, if we are only to yoke them for three hours. Of course their sides heave and they let their tongues stick out in hot weather, but that doesn't hurt them; we're hot as well!"

He said all this in the plain, rough way of us country people, it was a great contrast to the affability of the master, with his pure French.

"It's a mistake: it may result in very serious trouble, I tell you. Don't keep them in too long."

"All right, not later than midday, don't worry," said my godfather slyly.

"As usual," I added maliciously.

M. Boutry could not help being aware that we were making fun of him. He went away displeased.

"Go on, you old duffer, have done," my godfather muttered, as the master disappeared. "What a nuisance it is to have that old booby under our feet all the time."

As you see, we had little use for a courteous approach. At Le Garibier, before the rupture, we had been polite enough to Fauconnet. But Fauconnet only came twice a month; he knew rural life, he had an undoubted capacity for managing a farm, and he knew how to be master. Whilst Boutry, putting his bookish ideas in the form of polite requests, seemed ridiculous to us; and then – well, he was always around.

By the conditions of the lease, we were obliged to do a host of little jobs for the master, for he kept no male domestic servant. We had to look after his horse, clean his carriage, harness and unharness it whenever he used it; also we had to work in his garden and cut his wood. I think he would have liked us to anticipate his wishes, or at least do our various duties with a good grace; and indeed, considering his character, we might have profited by acting in that way, by asking each morning, for instance, if he was going out that day and at what time, if there was anything to do in the garden, and so on. But instead, my father, who usually undertook the grooming and such duties, never failed to tell the master how annoying it was to have to stay at home when there was so much to be done elsewhere. He was absolutely ignorant of the art of dissimulation, so necessary in life.

In the spring especially, when the garden needed digging, my father was always furious, for at that time we were very busy on the farm, and in harvest time it was even worse; he would make fussy replies to Monsieur Boutry when he came to ask for anything.

"Oh, sir, that will hold us up; I've got to do this, or that – finish bringing the hay in from the meadow – bind the wheat in that field – set up a millstone – I shall never get through what I have to do."

And my mother and brothers were even worse. Then the master would say:

"But it won't take long, my friends. It is only a little job after all – you will soon get it done, my good Bérot."

"Longer than you think, sir. This is going to throw us out, I tell you that," my father would say.

These complaints worried Monsieur Boutry. He was afraid to come and disturb us unless it was absolutely necessary, and then he would ask us very humbly, as if he were asking us a favour.

Among the women matters were still worse. Madame Boutry, a thin, rather sour woman, past middle age, was not nearly so easy-going as her husband. She would say to my mother in a dry, disdainful tone:

"Jeanette, send someone to me tomorrow for the washing," or, "I shall expect Catherine on Sunday to help the maid, I am having visitors."

That admitted of no reply. She was also excessively suspicious. Since fowls and fruit were shared, like the other things, she frequently counted the chickens and often came at meal-times to scrutinize the table with a suspicious look. On market days, when my mother was starting out, Madame Boutry was always there, as if by chance, afraid, no doubt that the baskets might contain stuff which by right belonged to them. In fact, she spent a great part of her time ferreting and spying, always anxious to know the why and wherefore of the smallest things. My mother and sisters-in-law soon began to grumble a good deal about this.

One day Madame Boutry remarked to Claudine that some plums

had been taken from the tree near the road. Claudine, who was not particularly tactful, answered tartly:

"Well, what do you expect me to do about it! I can't sit there watching the tree all day long, I'm busy!"

Another day two chickens disappeared, probably taken by a buzzard, and the lady snapped:

"I find this often happens; you ought to look after them better."

"We'll hire a servant," my sister-in-law answered ironically.

The lady was much offended.

Both she and her husband were forever giving us advice about our health, something which irritated us all beyond measure. If they saw us sweating after some spell of heavy work, they would call out:

"Don't stay like that, go and change your clothes at once. Give each other a rub down, it will stimulate the circulation. And don't stand about in a draught!"

Perfectly sound advice, I dare say, but we had something better to do in the summer months than go and change our clothes and give one another a rub down every time we broke out in a sweat. We should have been doing this too often!

If they caught sight of one of the children running out of doors bare-headed, which of course they did most of the time, they would make even more of a fuss:

"Do be careful! What are you thinking of – you must never let children go out in the sun without a hat on – they will catch sunstroke."

Neither did they like to see the children out at dusk, nor when it was raining – their little lungs could never stand it. In other words, good advice for rich men's children – who are no better off for it – but rules to which working people's children are not accustomed to be subjected.

And if any one of us, young or old, were found to be ailing in any way the master and mistress would insist on us swallowing some mixture or other, whilst the doctor was sent for.

"They think they're saving our lives with their medicines," my father would say. "What rubbish! The more of them you pour down your throat the worse you feel. As for doctors, if we had to go running to them every time we had a tickle in our throats, I don't know how we'd make out. They don't know nearly as much about illness, it seems to me, as about ways of squeezing money out of people – it's easy to see the master was a chemist. They're in it together, the doctors and the purge-sellers, to cheat poor people."

And my mother, after one of these lectures on health, would say:
"There, how they do worry! If we believed them we should have
to wrap ourselves up in cotton-wool. But you have to have money
to do that; they seem to think we have."

My sisters-in-law grumbled still more when they had to listen to
advice about their babies.

Our relations with our employers were not without friction, then.
The mistress and Louis' wife were at daggers drawn. However, as
far as general interests were concerned, everything went well.
Monsieur Boutry seldom went to market and allowed my father a
great deal of liberty with regard to sales and purchases. From the
very first settlement-day we made quite enough profit to live on,
in spite of the seizure of our part of the harvest at Le Garibier.

XIII

During the first months that we lived at La Billette I had remained
faithful to Thérèse Parnière, and in spite of the distance I went to
see her nearly every Sunday. Those journeys were up hill and down
dale, across fields and meadows, sometimes I had to go through a
near-impassable sunken lane and even go through part of the forest.

Twenty minutes' walk from La Bourdrie I had to cross a piece
of waste land, vast and boggy, and there was only one path I could
take. Nearly halfway across, the path skirted a pond of greenish
water surrounded by pollarded elms. Nearby towered two rows of
old oaks which had never been pruned, extending towards the forest
which was close by.

It was certainly not pleasant to go through this spot at night on
your own; it was called the "Witches' Trysting Place". The sound
of the wind in the leaves seemed more mysterious there, and the
screeching of the owls more mournful. Without being afraid I was
not free from a certain apprehension when I reached that particular
spot.

Returning from my sweetheart's house one moonless winter
night I suddenly saw a white form emerge from the trees and
begin to caper about. Another followed, then a third ... My teeth
chattered with fright. However I grasped my solid blackthorn
cudgel in my hand, resolved to use it against the phantoms if they
attempted to bar my way.

After skipping about in silence for a few moments they all three stood abreast in my path and began to yell and howl interminably. The white shrouds they wore revealed neither head nor limbs and they waved abnormally long arms, also clad in white. When I was about five paces from them:

"Hold on, lads!" I threatened, with a slightly forced energy.

Instead of turning away they surrounded me, howling more loudly and stretching towards me their great threatening arms. I swung my cudgel in fury and laid it across the back of one of the three creatures who sank down with a long piteous cry – very human this time. Without waiting for more the others made off at speed.

"You've killed me you bastard, you've killed me!" groaned the phantom.

I unwound the drapery from the unfortunate man and recognized young Barret from Fontivier, a lad two years younger than myself, with whom I had always got on well.

"It's my back," he moaned, "you've broken my back, I can't move!"

His companions were the two Simon brothers from Suippière, childhood friends, but I wasn't on very good terms with them just then. I called first one and then the other, but there was no answering call. Barrett had a spasm and spat blood; I thought that he was going to die. I had a strong desire to leave him there to die on his own, in the dark, not out of revenge but out of selfishness, because I couldn't see how I could help him. By the light of a match I saw his face twisted with pain, his beseeching eyes, the red blood which was trickling from his mouth. I was overcome with pity and sorrow. I went down to the edge of the pond and soaked one of the towels which had formed his ghost costume. I bathed his forehead, his temples and the palms of his hands, I wiped his mouth. He appeared to recover a little.

"Take me home, I beg you," he said, "don't leave me all alone ..."

"You've only got what you deserve, though!" I replied, self-righteously.

"Oh, Tiennon, you've had your revenge ... I swear I didn't mean to do you any harm. I only wanted to frighten you so that you wouldn't come again to see Thérèse. I've been crazy about her for a long time. But you can be easy now: you're the one who'll have her, I'm done for!"

I reassured him as best I could and with great care I set him on his feet. By leaning on me he could stand up and take a few steps, but when his foot hit a stone he cried out with pain.

"Let's sit down; I can't go any further," he said, sobbing. We had not gone ten yards. I hauled him up onto my back and, taking great care to walk steadily, I went slowly on. But the unavoidable jolting hurt him even more and he groaned aloud in the most frightful way. I went on all the same, trying not to show any emotion.

There was one moment when the pressure of his arms relaxed and his body weighed more heavily on me because it was inert. I was exhausted, I laid him down on the ground and he did not seem to move. I ran to a puddle in the ditch to soak the towel again, and bathed him once more; he groaned without uttering a word. I lifted him into the same position as before and went on.

Barret hiccoughed in a way that seemed to betoken his death-agony. I congratulated myself that the martyred ghost's winding-sheet had saved my clothes, preventing my smock from getting blood-stained. In my anxiety my nerves were stretched to breaking-point, but I walked quickly, despite my heavy burden, the darkness and the rough pathway, and I no longer allowed myself to be upset by the groans of the unfortunate young man.

After an hour or more I reached the Fontivier farm-yard and, while attempting to calm the dogs who were barking furiously, I set the dying man down a few yards from the doorstep, laying him on the phantom's shroud.

I gave the door two great kicks and then ran off along a narrow path which led behind the farm buildings to the fields. The dogs followed me some way with angry yelps, but I was soon out of their reach. Then, in the silence of the night, I heard the exclamations which followed the melancholy discovery, and I was no longer afraid of being caught.

Poor Barret had not been mistaken. My cudgel had broken some-thing in his spine. He lingered for several months, suffering fright-ful pain, then died. Not once, throughout his slow agony, did he consent to give any explanation of the tragedy. When he was asked who had struck him he would reply:

"It was someone who had good reason; it served me right." And he begged his parents not to lodge any complaint.

The victim's two accomplices said nothing to anyone. Nothing happened to bring about a confession of their sorry share in the affair. I myself had every reason to keep silence. Barret's parents, if they had any suspicions, abstained from divulging them. Therefore no proceedings were taken, and after a thousand conjectures in the beginning, no more was said about the event, which remained for ever thereafter an unfathomable mystery.

Having acted in self-defence, more or less, I could not blame myself. But all the same it is a grief to know that one has caused a man's death – in such circumstances, at least: for it seems that there are times when it is a meritorious act. My Uncle Toinot was very proud of having killed a Russian! Often the image of that poor boy and the details of that sad night have returned to haunt me. I do not say that this memory has poisoned my life; but it has caused me many secret torments.

Soon after this, I had to break with Thérèse. Her parents insisted that I should either marry her at once, or not go to see her any more. They had heard that my father was not able to insure me and that I would have to go for a soldier if I was unlucky in the draw. Their ultimatum was as good as a dismissal.

Six months later Thérèse married the elder of the two young brothers Simon, one of the cowards who had accompanied Barret to the Witches' Trysting Place. The wedding took place the same week that Barret was buried. Life has some cruel ironies.

XIV

During our first year at La Billette, two important events took place at our house: the death of my grandmother and the departure of my sister Catherine.

My grandmother was over eighty. One day in May, whilst she was taking care of the goslings, she had a stroke – 'an attack,' we used to say. My father was alarmed when she did not appear at dinnertime and went to look for her: he found that she had slipped down into a ditch, her left side was helpless and her speech was slurred. They carried her to bed, from which she never rose again. She remained there for six months, suffering a great deal, and giving no little trouble. She would utter incomprehensible sounds, struggling to utter sentences, and then be very angry because we were unable to understand her. To satisfy her, someone had to be with her nearly all the time, in order to give her something to eat and drink whenever she wanted it, and so on.

I often heard people say to my mother or to one of my sisters-in-law:

"Do you think she's likely to last long?"

To which they would reply:

"It's to be hoped not."

I had no particular affection for the old woman, who had been rather hard on me when I was small, and yet I was upset by this talk; they seemed to want her to die. At mealtimes, I used to lift my eyes mechanically to her bed, and it hurt me to see her so still, with her face under the old-fashioned cap, or the painful movements of her lips making meaningless sounds. I often cut my meals short and took a piece of bread to eat outside, because I found it impossible to eat in her presence.

I think one of the advantages of being well-off is to be able to afford a house with several rooms, so that no-one need sleep in the kitchen where all the family eat, and each family can have a room to itself where it can have some privacy. At least then one could be ill in peace. But in the single living-rooms of poor families, where every type of scene takes place, the misery of each is exposed to the eyes of all, there being no way to avoid it.

Thus, while my grandmother lay dying, my little nephews proclaimed their joy in being alive, tiring her with their noisy games and shouts. Life went its usual round, indifferent to the suffering of a paralysed old woman.

At the beginning of the winter she had a second attack, and, after lingering for a day in great pain, she died. As soon as she was dead they stopped the clock, threw away the water that was in the pail, because they believed that the dead woman's soul had bathed in it before ascending heavenwards. As I had not seen mourning at our house before, all this impressed me very deeply. Seeing the terror of death close at hand gave me a complex feeling in which curiosity, disgust and pity mingled. Several times I went and stood gazing at her as she lay there, so stiff and straight – the being whom I had always seen going about her work in the familiar circuit of my life.

This death made no difference in fact to our daily routine; meals took place at the usual hours close by that bed whose drawn curtains concealed a corpse; a single note of mystery was created by the lighted candle set on a little table near the bed, on which there also stood a bowl containing holy water with a sprig of box steeping in it. We abstained from our daily ploughing, however. My brother Louis went to Agonges to tell Uncle Toinot and his family. My godfather went to register the death at the *mairie*, and to arrange with the priest about the funeral. I was sent to the neighbours to ask for bearers.

When my godfather returned from the village he busied himself fixing up a new plough, and I had to help him. The task finished, he said to me with a satisfied air:

"I've been trying to get that done a long while! I really needed a day like this."

Such an expression of calm selfishness distressed me. You're easily moved when you're young; later, when I was as old as my godfather was at that time, I became quite as practical as he.

The next day, in the cold thick fog, thirty of us followed the ox-cart which carried the coffin. At the entrance to the village, the coffin was lifted down and placed on two chairs borrowed from a neighbouring house. We had to wait a good quarter of an hour, for the priest was not there. He appeared at last, accompanied by a choir boy carrying the cross, and recited some prayers. Then we went on to the church. Four men carried the coffin on poles which they passed through slings hung round their necks. After the service was over, they proceeded from the church to the cemetery in the same way. At the grave, at the moment of the final sprinkling with holy water, I was astonished to see my mother and sisters-in-law weeping loudly. This open parade of grief surprised me greatly, for I knew they had so often feared that she would last too long. I realized that sobs were only a matter of form, that it was the custom to do that at such a time. For myself, the flow of tears which clouded my eyes when the coffin was lowered into the grave, had at least the merit of being sincere.

When all was over, our kinsfolk from Agonges came home to eat with us. Some preparations had been made, wine had been bought, and a piece of meat for soup, and my mother added an omelette. The meal lasted two hours or more, and towards the end the conversation became animated; I believe that Uncle Toinot once more told the story of how he had killed his Russian. I reflected that all such gatherings ended in pretty much the same way. whether the occasion was a wedding, a baptism, a funeral, or any lesser family event. Provided they were given a meal with something special in the way of food, a meal that gave them the opportunity to sit a long time at table, the moment always came round when they would start telling their reminiscences – each one, in the telling, making himself out to be a hero and everyone else in the story a fool – and telling, too, dubious jokes or anecdotes: tittle-tattle, malicious gossip, lies and stupid remarks. Only songs were forbidden over the funeral meals.

A little while after the death of my grandmother, my sister Catherine left home to go into service in the house of a relative of Madame Boutry, at Moulins.

Catherine was then twenty-four years old. Her pleasant face had at once pleased the lady, who had often employed her in the house to help her own maid. My sister liked her work and the ways of the house; she soon adopted the quiet, respectful manner necessary in those who serve the rich; she even came to be on quite familiar, though respectful terms with the Boutrys, who were kind to her. She was in love with a young man at Meillers named André Gaussin, who was doing his military service, and to whom she had sworn to be faithful. For five years she had kept her promise, going out very little and allowing no other suitor. Gaussin wrote to her three times a year: on the first of January, during the spring, and at the end of the summer. Catherine awaited these letters with impatience, but they caused her problems, for she had no one she could ask to read them to her and to write the answers. But after some months she told her employers about her romance, and they took charge of everything. Then, seeing that she had an aptitude for service, they thought of finding a place for her in town. Gaussin, who was an officer's batman, was already trained. Once married they could find a place together and earn a good living.

Catherine gradually got used to this idea, which had at first frightened her, due to her fear of the unknown. She was the more reconciled to it because my sisters-in-law reproached her for having given up farm work in order to work for the owners. In this way she left for Moulins during November, ignoring our parents' opposition but earning the enthusiastic approval of her fiancé.

XV

At that time I too was suffering a good deal from restlessness. The market town of Saint Menoux was a place of some importance; it boasted at least five inns, one of which had a billiard table, and another a skittle alley; and on Sundays and holidays there was dancing at two places. Since I had broken off with Thérèse I had fallen into dissipated habits. I went out regularly, almost every other Sunday, and each time I demanded forty sous from my parents. When they did accede to my request, they never omitted a lecture, to which I listened with bent head feeling nervous and irritable. Sometimes, though, I would say right out that I ought to be paid for the work I did. Sometimes they gave me only twenty sous, or even occasionally nothing at all; then I was furious, and spoke of going elsewhere.

There were five or six of us lads, belonging to the next conscript class, and we all had developed a taste for outdoor games; we played long games of skittles and nine-pins. On the days when we managed to get hold of some money, we drank a good deal, got tipsy, and returned home late. At such times it would not have been at all advisable to provoke us; we were not very approachable, nor in a humour to take a joke. It happened on a certain Sunday that we picked a quarrel with some lads of the town, young workmen belonging to different trades: smiths, tailors, carpenters, masons, and so forth. Between them and us there was an old, chronic feud. They disdainfully called us clodhoppers. We called them upstarts, because they had an uppish, conceited air, spoke better French, and went about in cloth jackets instead of smocks. They had their recognized inn, as we had ours, and we hardly ever ventured into each others' territory without a row resulting. That day, three of the town lads, who had been drinking earlier, and were in good fighting trim, came over after Mass to play at nine-pins with us. One of our group said:

"We don't want to play with townees."

"Never mind that, we want to play with clodhoppers; we've got money to stake."

I had had nothing to drink as yet, and felt a little timid with these lads, who, even when sober, had more effrontery than we had. Nevertheless, I said:

"You needn't trouble yourselves; us *clodhoppers*, us *ploughmen*, have as much money as you have."

I had exactly thirty sous!

One of my chums, a tall, rather daring fellow called Gustave Aubert, flung at them some insult or other. They answered it with interest. Finally it got to noisy brawling on both sides, and as we were by far the most numerous, we chased them out of the court-yard. After their departure the game began again and our party was in luck: Aubert won; so did I, and so did another of us. Of course, we immediately went on the spree. Towards eight o'clock in the evening after a good supper, the devil tempted us to go to the inn where the townsmen were gathered round the billiard-table. Our entry caused a sensation. There was a moment of silence, during which we eyed each other. Then one of the lads whom we had driven away that morning, a little dark youth, a cobbler, called out in a very loud voice:

"No swineherds allowed here."

"Say that again, you upstart! Say it again! Say that we're swineherds!" said Aubert, furiously rolling his eyes.

"Yes, yes," replied the other, "you're swineherds, mucky peasants, a lot of cursed clodhoppers!"

One of his companions, holding his nose shouted:

"Ugh! they smell of cow-dung!"

And a third said:

"No wonder; they only wash their legs once a year; they like having a coating of dung in winter to keep themselves warm."

The billiard-cues were laid down; ten of them were round us now, jeering. We tried to put a good face on it and return their insults as far as we could. Aubert, proud of his strength, raged:

"Come outside and say that, you damned braggarts, you town scum!"

The landlord intervened, and implored us not to fight, then urged us farm boys to go outside as we were the last-comers. But that did not suit us.

"We have as much right here as they have, why should we go out?"

However, with some pushing and pulling, the landlord managed to get us over the door. The others came forward:

"Put them out!" they cried, "put them out!"

They did not strike us, but elbowed us.

"Very well, if that's the way you want it!" said Aubert. "Take that!"

And he dealt a violent blow with his fist at the head of the little dark cobbler, who was the noisiest of the opposing party.

That was the signal for a general scrimmage. Blows and kicks rained down, while both sides yelled insults at each other. With gentle persistence, the landlord pushed us all, friends and enemies, out of the door. When the last were on the step, he shut the door so quickly that two or three fell over. An icy wind, heralding snow, swept along the street. The struggle continued with fury unabated; there were cries of:

"Here, take that, you lout!"

"That's one for you, swank!"

"The swine! he's broken one of my teeth!"

"Leave me alone, my nose is bleeding," cried a mason, to whom I had just given a formidable whack.

Aubert nearly strangled a farrier, who bit helplessly at his arm and face; a wheelwright came to his rescue, and together they managed to throw my big comrade to the ground. In a paroxysm of rage he took out his knife, struck at the hand of the one, and dug it into the cheek of the other. This caused yells of rage:

"One of the clodhoppers has got a knife!"

"Yes," said Aubert, getting up again, grinding his teeth, his cap gone, his eyes starting out of their sockets, his uplifted hand brandishing the bloody knife: "If anybody wants some, let him come and get it!"

Here the village policeman arrived, and some onlookers with lanterns.

"Look at that one bleeding like an ox!"

"What a pack of savages! Isn't it disgusting!"

Some men succeeded in parting those of us who were still fighting, and held us off at some distance. We ... we were so furious that we went on yelling and tried to get at each other again. The policeman took our names. The wounded were looked after. Our antagonists were taken away by their parents or employers. The father of the farrier who had got the knife wound in his cheek shouted as he went:

"Leave the ploughboys to themselves; let them fight each other if they want to!"

"The ploughboys are as good as you are!" cried Aubert. He was still panting to carry on with the fight. Our landlord and some neighbours who had come with him begged us to calm down. I was neither so drunk nor so angry as to be incapable of understanding. I said:

"That's enough, Gustav, we'd better go."

And we went – not very far, to tell the truth, for we decided to go to our own inn to drink cold coffee and cool down. Some people who were drinking there were talking about the brawl.

"They'll suffer for this; they were using knives."

"That will mean prison, I dare say!"

"Quite likely."

Aubert, still excited, thumped the table hard, saying he didn't care a damn for the law-courts:

"If we have to go to prison we'll go, that is all; and that won't stop me fighting again if they insult me. What I won't stand is to be taken for a good for nothing. No, never! The town lads wanted to give us a licking. Well, it was they who got it! They won't be able to say ploughboys are cowards now!"

We all agreed that we regretted none of it; in fact, that all the right was on our side. At heart we were none the less very uneasy.

The next day the gendarmes from Souvigny came to La Billette to question me. My little nephews, who were playing in the yard, were the first to see them:

"The gendarmes!" they cried, in a fright. They ran for refuge to the barn, where my brothers and I were threshing with the flail. The children crouched down behind a heap of straw and stayed there, not moving a muscle.

My parents were not altogether surprised, for they had seen my soiled clothes, and my face black with bruises; and I had to admit that I had been mixed up in a scuffle.

The gendarmes interrogated me briefly and ordered me to go to the *mairie* at midday the next day.

At the appointed hour we found ourselves, artisans and farm-lads, all together again at the site of the battle. The farrier whom Aubert had knifed had his face bandaged; another had his arm in a sling; several limped; black and blue bruises showed as witnesses, if not as glorious scars, on every face. Soon two gendarmes arrived one of them with white stripes on his sleeve: he was the sergeant in charge of the Souvigny police. It was he who conducted the inquiry. His sharp features, his cold gaze, his long black moustache gave him a stern and hostile appearance, suited to his job. He interrogated us separately, beginning with the wounded. A gendarme wrote down our replies in a great notebook. Alas! our arrogance of Sunday had vanished. Friends and foes, we contemplated each other now with no sign of hatred; our lowered eyes, our dejected faces showed only how much we regretted our foolishness and its ugly consequences. Gustave Aubert was the only one who had used a knife; the sergeant-major questioned him at greater length; but the poor boy was quite limp and pale, and trembled so much that he could only answer in monosyllables. Those who make the most noise when they have had a glass too much are nearly always the most cowardly, the most craven when caught in a tight spot.

I must say that the town lads made a better impression than we did during the inquiry: they expressed themselves better. It was the same on the day of the hearing, the following week. Country folk, used to solitary work in the open air, always make a poor show in the presence of the law and all these "gentlemen".

You can imagine the miserable time I had of it at home. There were reproaches about the expense, the annoyance, and the disgrace that I was going to cause.

"It's no light matter, my gracious!" said my mother. "You may have to go to prison! You will be in their bad books now! It's a terrible thing to bring up children who cause you so much trouble!"

My father lamented nearly as much; the others, too, were anxious, and indeed I was not easy in my own mind.

When Monsieur Boutry got to know about the affair, he hardly let a day go by without giving me a lecture, saying that it was unworthy of a civilized country for young people of the same commune to fight each other for no reason. "You behaved like savages, like barbarians," he concluded.

Nevertheless, he intervened on my behalf both with the sergeant of police, and with the mayor; then, seeing that it was impossible to keep the affair out of court, he busied himself to find a good lawyer to act for all the belligerents.

"This trial," he said to me one day, "ought to be a lesson to you, but more than that, it ought to be the means of a general and lasting reconciliation."

Poor Monsieur Boutry! all this happened sixty years ago, and the feud is still going on, at Saint-Menoux and elsewhere, between the lads of the town and those of the farms.

On the day of the hearing, we proceeded on foot, in two groups to Moulins, the town lads starting half an hour before us.

I remember how astonished I was when I crossed the bridge over the Allier. I had only seen the narrow Burge at Bourbon, and the very small streams in our meadows: it did not seem possible that there could be such wide rivers. Those of my companions who were seeing the county town for the first time shared my astonishment.

In the town we soon found ourselves in difficulties. We walked along slowly, gaping at the shop-windows like so many village idiots. It had rained the previous day and the weather was still threatening; our clogs slipped on the damp pavements. I was conscious that to the people of the town we must have looked ridiculous. And indeed the clerks and shop-girls, who were going off for their dinners just then, looked at us with curiosity and a shade of mockery.

I saw a man loading mud into a cart; I ventured to ask him if he knew the way to the law-court.

"The law-court?" said he, a little astonished, "it's in the Rue de Paris, a big red-brick building with a courtyard in the middle. You are still a long way off; first you had better go to the Place d'Allier, and then ask again."

He showed us the way to the Place d'Allier, and we were not long in finding it. As we were looking round for someone to direct us, we saw another group of youths standing in front of a large shop: they were our bitter foes, the lads of the town. Well, well – away from their usual environment, they were no more at home than we were; they were no longer themselves: our mutual hatred had died down all of a sudden. They turned towards us, and we smiled at each other.

"Well, better get going!"

The little dark cobbler answered:

"We were waiting for you – only we had begun to think that you had eaten the summons."

We went together towards the big red-brick building. We were ushered into a square hall with whitewashed walls, and furnished with seats; there we had to wait a whole hour and a half in the company of six tramps and three poachers. Our turn came at last, after all the others, and we filed into the Hall of Justice. At the end, on a kind of high platform, sat the three magistrates in black robes. On the wall behind them, a great plaster figure of Christ towered above them. The man in the middle examined us; he was a big man, red-faced and clean-shaven, and his eyes twinkled behind his spectacles. We all behaved like a lot of animals caught in a trap; we answered in such a plaintively humble tone that they might well have asked if we were the same raging maniacs who had made such a to-do a fortnight before. After the examination was finished, another man in a robe got up. He was a young man with black whiskers; he sat on a small platform to the left of the magistrates and a little in front; he spoke witheringly of our abominable conduct, called Aubert a "young killer" – and advised the Court not to hesitate to punish us with all the rigour of the law, in order to deter other young hotheads. But after this, it was the turn of our advocate, a short bearded man with rather a mocking expression. He spoke of our epic battle as youthful foolishness of no importance, said we were all excellent young men and hard workers, whose only fault had been that they had drunk a glass too much that day, and he begged the three men on the platform not to put us in prison. After exchanging a few words in low tones they agreed with him. Aubert, because of the knife-wounds, was fined twenty-five francs; all the others, sixteen francs.

When we left the court-house, we had a meal all together in a tavern in the Place du Marché, and afterwards started on our return journey, which we got through very well, except that several of us had blistered feet, and everyone was very fatigued. The little cobbler tried once or twice to provoke us, but he got no encouragement from his friends, so the relations between the two reunited groups remained cordial.

At home they were very glad that I had not been sent to prison; nevertheless, the cost of the fine and expenses together seemed to them enormous.

* * *

The time for the drawing of lots for conscription now approached. One fine day, my parents took me aside to tell me that I could not count on a substitute. They detailed their reasons: our removal, my grandmother's death, these had caused considerable outlay; my brothers had several children, which increased the household expenses; the dirty deeds of Fauconnet had lost us money; for a long time I had been spending a good deal at the inn; and finally that wretched trial had been costly. As a result of all this, they had found it impossible to save up the five hundred francs necessary to insure me with a merchant of substitutes or at the *cagnotte mutuelle** of Saint-Menoux. I was dumbfounded for I had always, in spite of everything counted on being treated like my brothers. I exploded with fury, and said right out that if chance did favour me at the drawing, I should not stay at home for long. My parents were much troubled, but made no attempt to curb my discontent.

I drew number sixty-eight; I was saved, for they only took up to fifty-nine. I remained at La Billette for the rest of the winter, and nearly all the spring. But when midsummer came, I announced again that I was going to offer myself for hire.

"You don't really want to go, Tiennon?" said my mother very uneasily.

---

* In the bigger villages conscripts' parents made a preliminary deposit of a sum agreed upon, to buy substitutes for those who had been drawn in the ballot.

"Why are you going elsewhere, when there is plenty of work for you here?" added my father.

"It's plain that you expected to be able to do without me, since you meant to let me go for a soldier," I replied maliciously. "I've spent all my youth working for nothing: it's time that I started earning some money."

My mother answered:

"When you have to feed yourself out of your wages, I can tell you there won't be much left. You won't have as much to amuse yourself on as we give you here."

They all begged me to stay: my godfather, Louis, my sisters-in-law, and even poor Marinette, poor little innocent, who was fond of me. The little ones clung to me.

"Tonton, don't go! Say you won't go. Do!"

I almost wept as I freed myself from the clasp of their little hands, but I remained obdurate.

XVI

You have to make a change to appreciate fairly the good aspects of your former life; in the monotony of daily existence you enjoy the best things unconsciously; they seem so natural that you can't imagine they no longer exist; only the tiresome things strike you, and you think they must be less in evidence elsewhere. Changing your way of life brings out the advantages you didn't appreciate and proves that troubles, in one form or another, exist everywhere.

I quickly discovered this for myself during the first weeks of my stay at Fontbonnet and sometimes regretted leaving my family. But I got used to it in the end and even began to feel better than I had done at home, because of the total independence I enjoyed during my free time. But now that I could no longer ask my parents for money, I could not go out, and I lost touch with my mates. There's nothing like empty pockets to teach you discretion!

I spent my Sundays rambling about the country and in the forest, for the estate skirted the end of the Gros-Bois. In that direction there was a forester's cottage, in which lived an old keeper, old Giraud, with whom I soon made acquaintance. I lent him a hand in various ways, helping him to cut grass for his cows in the clearings and to reap the patch of wheat that he had at the bottom of his garden. I always found something to do there that would take up a couple of hours every Sunday. He generally gave me a glass of wine when the work was done, and I used to stay with him a good part of the day. Old Giraud had a son in Africa, a soldier, of whom he often spoke to me, a daughter married to a glass-blower in Souvigny, and a second, unmarried daughter who lived with him. Mlle Victoire was a brunette with black eyes, a swarthy complexion, and a cold manner like her mother. I was not at all familiar with the two women: the daughter of the keeper seemed to me to belong to a station so superior to mine that I dared not even look at her.

There was, however, somebody else I did dare to look at: the little servant-girl at Fontbonnet. She was a little slim girl with a childish face, small white teeth and an enchanting smile. Her name was Suzanne, she was a hard worker and good natured. I might have thought quite seriously about her if she had belonged to a respectable family; but she was illegitimate. Her mother was a maid-of-all-work to a widowed shopkeeper, and had had three children and no husband. Poor Suzanne turned red to the roots of her hair if ever her family was mentioned. As for me, as I was only a hired labourer by chance and of my own free will, it would have been beneath me to marry a maid-servant: only the daughters of *métayers* had the same status as I had. A stronger reason was that I could not marry a bastard: my mother would have made a fine fuss about that! If however, I was not set on marrying Suzanne I thought hard about making her my mistress. It must be said that I was in that particular state of mind experienced at one stage, I'm sure, by all lads of my age.

At Saint-Menoux, Aubert and most of those with whom I had associated the year before, used to assert that they had tasted of the forbidden fruit. They even put a name to the girls: most of whom would have been given the Host without confession, as we used to say, so modest was their demeanour. Every time the subject girls came up, I used to put on a knowing air, as if I had known all about that for a long time. To speak about a matter that one knows nothing about, you only have to be able to season and serve other people's phrases with a blasé air: it always works. The fact is, I was entirely innocent, but had of course a great desire to be otherwise.

I attempted therefore to wheedle Suzanne by doing friendly little services for her, saving her the hardest tasks in the fields and house, going in her place to fetch water and wood, and so on. It was not long before she looked at me with affection, because of these little attentions. Besides, I was not bad-looking. I was of middle-height, rather thick-set, strong and vigorous; my face was rather long, with a strong nose; my hair was thick and curly; and I was full of life and energy. It was quite natural that she should like me. Be that as it may, one evening at nightfall it so happened that we met in the cowshed; I told Suzanne that she was pretty, and that I loved her, and I kissed her with as much ardour as I had kissed Thérèse two and a half years before. She seemed to like it so much that I really thought she was going to swoon away in my arms. But the sound of the master's footsteps, prowling round outside, caused us to spring apart.

A few days later, one Sunday, as we happened to be alone in the house, I began wooing her again, and after some soft words and a few – perhaps too few – embraces, I tried to slip my hand inside her skirt. What a surprise I had! She flung away from me at once, and with flaming eyes slapped me twice across the face as hard as she could. Then, getting behind the nearest chair-back, she hissed:

"Get away, you beast! So that's why you were being so nice to me: you just wanted to amuse yourself.... But I'm not that sort of girl, no matter what you thought I was! and if ever you dare lay a finger on me again, I'll go straight to the mistress and tell her."

"Little vixen!" I muttered stupidly, rubbing my red, smarting cheek.

"If I've hurt you, it's your own fault," she said, a little less angrily, "It'll teach you to treat me properly!"

I went out very sheepishly, and made no more amorous advances to the fiercely virtuous Suzanne. My conscience was awakened now and I realized what a cruel thing it would be to ruin her life for the sake of my stupid vanity, or for a few moments of pleasure. I felt guilty and despicable and I did my best to win back her friendship by helping her in the same way as before, but never again speaking to her of love.

Soon afterwards a new amorous adventure also turned out to my disadvantage. On a neighbouring estate, at Giverny, there was another servant girl, much older, an indolent, tow-haired woman who was said to have had lots of affairs. Even at La Billette I had heard of this Hélène and her lax morals. At Fontbonnet it was quite different. At work, the men used to talk about her every day, and when they were tired, they used to cheer themselves up by swapping coarse stories about her.

"There are only two sorts she'll refuse," the boss would say, "the ones who won't and the ones who can't."

I very much wanted to know her better.

One day, while we were eating our dinner, she came over to Fontbonnet to take back three stray bullocks which had escaped from pasture. She sat down with us without ceremony, talked freely of this and that, and answered in kind the chaffing of the boss and the lads. It so happened that she went out at the same time as I did. Once outside I was able to speak to her alone. I made a few suggestive remarks, which did not appear to bother her in the least; on the contrary I think it was I who blushed at her replies.

I felt we were now well enough acquainted, and the following Sunday, the devil driving me, I went over to Giverny. I loitered about in the maize-field by the farm until I caught sight of Hélène coming back from milking the cows. She carried her pitcher of milk into the house and came out again a few moments later wearing a white cap, a clean blouse and freshly blackened sabots. She untethered the cows and drove them out of the yard. Five minutes later, out of sight of the farmhouse, I met her as if by chance in the lane.

"Hullo, is that you?" she said, looking surprised.

"Yes, I'm going for a walk for the good of my health."

"Well, do you want to come and help me look after the cows?"

"That's just what I was going to suggest."

Side by side, we went down a shady, lonely lane, until we reached a marshy meadow, bordered by a little copse. I was rather excited to find myself alone with this dispenser of love and I painfully pondered over some suitable phrases, all rather silly. She played with her stick, she was gay and relaxed, making all the conversation. I was annoyed to see, at the other end of the meadow, a labourer's cottage, round which some children were playing. But my companion, as though she had read my thoughts, made a suggestion:

"Shall we go into the wood and pick nuts?"

I accepted eagerly, but when we were there, my heart beat fast. I plucked up my courage: putting my arm round Hélène's waist, I said how pleasant it would be to lie down on the soft grass under the green trees. She answered ironically:

"Are you tired? I didn't come here to lie down, I can tell you that."

Then, having by a quick half-turn escaped from my embrace, she began to bend down the branches and gather the clusters of nuts, which she slipped into the pocket of her apron.

It puzzled me that she appeared to be putting obstacles in the way of what must have been a commonplace to her. In my bewilderment I hesitated to take action. I pointed out that the nut-trees were not so numerous now.

"Let's go a bit further, we'll find more there," she said.

She glided in and out of the branches with surprising agility, considering her weight; I had some trouble following her. We had been walking for a few minutes along the track which ran through the copse, when we suddenly found ourselves face to face with a black-bearded man, stocky, strong and still young. She showed no surprise; I had an idea that I was being made a fool of. The man said, half-laughing:

"Hullo? Have you brought an assistant to help you pick nuts, Hélène!"

I blushed as deeply as Suzanne would have done, but I tried to extricate myself with a show of cheek:

"Two's company," I said.

"Yes, but three's none, puppy."

He thereupon set on me, punching me and jeering:

"There, take that, and that, and that too! That'll teach you to come prowling round where you have no business, my lad!"

In any other circumstances I should certainly not have allowed myself to be thrashed without a protest. But I was so taken by surprise that I had no chance to defend myself. Without waiting for more, I ran off like a hare, followed to the end of the wood by the jeers of both of them. After which, rather late in the day, I swore never to go near "Big Hélène" again.

*   *   *

My youthful amorous escapades did not amount to much, as you see, and I have no reason to be proud of them. But that did not keep me later, like all the other lads, from boasting of my exploits, and speaking with an experienced air of my great feats when I was a youth, or saying even:

"Oh, there were plenty of women around, good Lord yes! I was spoilt for choice."

To tell the truth, it was my lawful wife who took my virginity.

XVII

The following spring I went to the Fête at Meillers to see my communion class-mate, Boulois of Le Parizet. His young brother having died, he was the only son, and he was proud of his position, for his parents were well-off. In our conversation I happened to speak of old Giraud the keeper, and Boulois asked with a sly smile if he had not a daughter. I replied that he had two, one married and the other still free. Then Boulois said that a relative had pointed out Victoire to him at a fair at Souvigny, telling him that she would do nicely for him. He then questioned me about the character and habits of this girl; and when I departed he charged me to approach her in order to find out if she would consent to marry a young gentleman.

"If she seems likely to say 'yes,' you might speak to her about me," he concluded.

The thought of this delicate mission worried me the whole week. However, in order to comply with my promise, I went the following Sunday to the forester's house. Chance favoured me: Victoire and her mother had returned early from Mass, and old Giraud was getting ready to go at ten o'clock. I went away with him, making a pretence of going back to Fontbonnet, and trying to appear quite natural. But an hour later I turned up again at the Girauds', knowing this to be a propitious moment, for Victoire was alone in the house, her mother having taken the cows to the pasture in the clearing some way off. I came straight to the point, and said that I wanted to catch her alone for a moment to ask if she would ever consider marrying a peasant. For a moment she fixed her large dark eyes on me; her questioning gaze seemed to search my mind, but she made no answer.

"It is one of my friends who wanted me to ask you this question," I added.

"Oh! – one of your friends?"

I thought I could discern in these words a note of disappointment. After another moment's thought, she said:

"Well! I should have to see the friend; I couldn't say, without seeing him, could I?"

"Oh, you will see him! But you wouldn't mind him being only a farmer?"

"Why should I mind? Don't I work on a farm myself?"

There was a moment of embarrassed silence. Victoire, seated in the chimney corner, poked the fire and did not take her eyes from the rosy flame. I was standing with my back to an old oak cupboard near the outside door, my head down, agitated and thoughtful. The crackling of the logs on the fire, the tick-tock of the clock, the singing of a cricket in the wall, the clucking of a hen in the yard, all these familiar sounds assumed a strange significance. And I had the audacity to blurt out, all in a rush, the idea that had suddenly sprung up in my mind:

"No! I don't want to go on lying to you! It's not for another, it's for myself that I've come, Victoire, would you have me for your husband?"

She lowered her eyes towards the large black flags which paved the room. I saw a slight colour rise in her brown cheeks.

"I don't dislike you; but I cannot give you a definite answer without speaking to my parents. Go to the dance at Autry next Sunday; I shall arrange to be there, and I'll tell you if you may make an offer or not."

I stammered a "thank you," and went away at once without even trying to come closer to her, so confused did I feel, and so much did her cold and serious air continue to impress me.

During the days that followed I thought I must have been dreaming. It did not seem to me possible that I had betrayed Boulois' confidence, that I had sought for myself this girl Victoire, who did not even particularly attract me, – it was just that she was well-off. How great events hang on a mere trifle: a chance circumstance, a fleeting inclination, a moment of boldness or a moment of thoughtlessness.

Victoire, who did like me, must have managed it all very well, for she told me at the dance on Sunday that I had a chance, although her parents had made many objections. When I asked for her hand, her father and mother admitted straight out their displeasure that I was without a single sou. They had promised to give her a bed, a cupboard, a little linen, and three hundred francs, which was a good deal for that time.

"Get your father to give you a sum at least equal to Victoire's, he owes you that, as he didn't buy you out of conscription. On that condition we will consent to the marriage, for we know you are a hard worker and a good lad."

The parents' acceptance of me astonished me nearly as much as the daughter's had. I found out the reason later. Their son, the soldier in Africa, had been wild in his youth; he had cost them a good deal of money, and given them a great deal of trouble when he was a clerk in a cotton warehouse at Moulins. Their son-in-law, the glass-blower, was no credit to them either: he drank and was a bad husband. I profited by their bad examples, for in Giraud's eyes they had lowered the prestige of urban professions.

My father had received from Monsieur Boutry eight hundred francs on account of the second year, and I had not much trouble in obtaining the necessary three hundred francs. I was then definitely accepted, and the wedding took place at Martinmas, 1845, two months before my twenty-third birthday.

My wife stayed with her parents, and I continued my work at Fontbonnet, where I was hired for a second year.

Each evening, after the day's work was done, I returned to the forester's house, and each morning, as the sun rose, I went back to my post. On Sundays I continued to do some of the harder tasks for my father-in-law, and this made me welcome at the house. Victoire was amiable; I had no responsibilities and no worries; that time was one of the happiest in my life.

XVIII

However, we could not go on like that for ever. In the course of the year, I learned that a holding was vacant at Bourbon, very near the town, on the borders of Les Craux, a large stretch of thin, stony land, the lower slopes of a fertile granite upland, its rough pastures falling to damp meadows, watered by an alder-fringed brook. I went to look at this holding. I thought it would suit us all right and rented it for three years. We settled there the following Martinmas, exactly a year after our marriage.

But alas! our poor six hundred francs, how soon they were exhausted! The purchase of two cows, which were absolutely necessary, used the greater part of it. We had to borrow from old Giraud in order to buy a cart, a barrow, some indispensable household utensils, a quantity of fuel, and some measures of rye. Victoire, who at home had been used to a certain amount of comfort, suffered more than I did from our early hardships. Moreover, with her cold and reserved character, she was not in the habit of showing much satisfaction, though she knew how to give weight to her complaints.

I often had to tell her in this respect that she was exaggerating. She would say in a complaining tone:

"I must have another stewpan," or, "I need some more dishes," or, "I can't do my washing without a tub."

These would be bought, but there was always something else needed. Then she turned her mind to baby-clothes and a cradle, for she was now expecting a child. I did my best to cheer her up.

But above all, our lonely evenings in the winter months were often monotonous. I found it hard to get accustomed to this, I had been so used to the liveliness of large families. However, thanks to continuous activity, I was preserved from boredom. I made a lot of useful things, my plough first, then a ladder, then a barrow, and last of all, two or three hay-rakes. That carried me through to March.

In the early mornings, and in the evenings towards four o'clock, Victoire went to the town to sell fresh milk. I used to carry her pitcher to the Place de l'Eglise, that very place where I had suffered so much on the day of the fair when I was a little lad. From there, she went the rounds from door to door, selling to regular customers and casual ones. To begin with, she made twenty-five or thirty sous a day. But when the weather grew cold and the cows gave less milk, she did not even make as much as twenty sous, though she sold it to the last drop, not even keeping a little to whiten our soup. And the task of taking it round was no joke. Her hands, holding the pitcher, turned blue with cold, her numb fingers could scarcely be made to do their work. And things got worse. One frosty morning, Victoire came home weeping, her pocket half-empty; she had slipped coming down the steep paved street, and the remaining milk – two-thirds, at least – had run out of the overturned pitcher. This accident worried me, for she was in her seventh month of pregnancy, and I was afraid it might cause trouble. So I resolved to take the milk round myself. I had to endure a lot of jeering and chaffing from the people in town, for it was unusual for a man to be seen selling milk. In the evening the small boys would follow me in a gang, shouting:

"Look at the milk-seller! Look at the milk-seller! Give us some milk, Tiennon. This way, Tiennon, this way!"

I realized that it was better not to take the little rascals' impudence too seriously, nor that of the grown-ups either. By the end of the week they all left me in peace. And on the other hand, my customers praised me for being a model husband.

There were some things about the job that I found rather enjoyable: for instance, the awakening of the town each morning interested me greatly. When I arrived, the only visible activity was in the blacksmiths' shops. There one could see the forge already glowing and the fiery sparks rushing up from the white-hot iron which was being shaped on the anvil by mighty strokes of the hammer. Work was going on also in the back of the butchers' shops, in the bakehouses, and the workshops of the sabot-makers. But the shops were still shut. Like the clerks and the bank-managers, the shopkeepers were asleep behind their closed shutters. I, who had been rushing about for two hours or more, wide-awake and alert in the sharp morning air, used to hammer on doors and on shop-fronts with malicious pleasure. The house-keepers would soon appear, some fat, some thin, wrinkled, untidy, toothless, with uncorsetted bosoms, and rings round their sleep-encrusted eyes, a sorry sight! The slovenliness of their dress betrayed their ugliness, their deformities. Many came to the door in their bare feet or in down-at-heel slippers, with petticoats half done-up showing their chemises, or in shabby and often ragged night-gowns, or in dirty or greasy night-caps.

They would say with a yawn:

"It's very cold this morning, isn't it, Tiennon?"

"It is indeed, missus, it's freezing hard."

"Brr! It was so nice in bed!"

I chuckled inwardly to see them in their natural state, these fine ladies of the town, who in the daytime were always so well corsetted, combed and curled.

"My word," I thought, "I won't let myself be taken in by appearances after this! Oh, no!"

However, it was not long before I was taken in terribly.

As soon as I got back from my morning round, I used to take off my clean smock and trousers, and put on my working-clothes. I would toss some more straw into the cowshed and fill up the manger with hay; then, after eating a bowl of onion soup and three potatoes baked in the ashes, I would go round to old Viradon, an elderly neighbour, where for eight sous a day, I helped him thresh from nine o'clock till three. After that spell of work, I ate some more soup and perhaps a stew of pumpkin or beans; then there was the grooming to do; then the milking, then the milk round in the town and many other little jobs, which kept me busy till seven o'clock; then I would settle myself by the fireside and work with my tools, while

I tried to prove to my wife that we were getting on quite well, and that we should have no difficulty in pulling through.

* * *

But in April, when Victoire's confinement took place, it was indeed a different matter; I had to take care of her and undertake all the household tasks besides. The previous month I had visited my parents, and had asked my mother to come and stay with us for a few days when the baby arrived; but the illness of one of my little nephews had prevented her from keeping her promise. Mother Giraud was ill and found it difficult to leave home because of her cows. So in addition to the midwife there was only our old neighbour's wife, Madame Viradon, to help us and give us advice.

At the same time the work on the land had to be done, the garden dug, and the barley, oats and potatoes sown, so you may well believe that I didn't have time to turn round; I nearly lost the habit of sleeping, and the summer was not the season either for catching up on lost sleep.

During the summer I went out to work as a day-labourer. Although I had enough to do on my own holding, I was afraid that the income from that would not be sufficient if I earned nothing outside. When I came home from work, about ten in the evening, I often set to work again in the vegetable garden, by moonlight. This was on the advice of my neighbour, Viradon, who informed me that vegetables sold well in the season when the town was full of strangers. I often worked till nearly one o'clock in the morning, hoeing, weeding and watering. At three o'clock I went out to work again; Victoire had for some time given up the milk-round – the cows being near to calving gave no more – but she was able to sell a few lettuces and a few baskets of beans, and this brought in enough for our household needs.

When Martinmas came, we had the satisfaction of paying the landlord punctually, and being able to repay old Giraud half the sum he had lent us.

XIX

There were certain kinds of work of which I had very little experience: for instance, before I had started on my own account, I had never done any sowing. The sowing was always done on the farms by the master or his eldest son: with us my godfather had taken over from my father. I believe that the custom of keeping to one's own job still exists to some degree. There is always the cowman, the gardener, the sower. The cowman never works in the garden, the gardener knows nothing of field-work, nor how to care for the oxen. When they come to separate, each finds himself at a loss. Consequently, the first time I sowed, I did it unevenly and too thickly, and my harvest was affected by it.

However, that year even the best sowers did not obtain very wonderful results. After a winter of night frosts and warm sunshine, we had had a wet spring, and the harvest of 1847 was bad everywhere. Wheat sold at eight francs the double, and rye at six francs. In country places poor people were going hungry, and in the towns, especially in Paris, it appeared that it was still worse.

I got this information from Monsieur Perrier, an old schoolmaster, who had become a insurance agent: he lived in the Place de l'Eglise, and was a customer of ours for milk. Monsieur Perrier read the newspapers, and when anything important happened, he never failed to tell my wife, charging her to repeat it to me.

It was in this way that I heard the news of the Revolution of February 1848, the poverty of the working people in the capital having caused a revolt there. Then I remembered that when I was shepherd at Le Garibier, I had heard the long-sawyers talking of something of the kind: revolution in Paris, a king turned out and replaced by another king who called himself Louis-Philippe, the tricolour flag instead of the white flag, and so on.

The next day, when I went on my milk-round, I told Monsieur Perrier about these recollections. He told me that they had just got rid of that same Louis-Philippe, and that instead of a king we now had a republic; and he went to some trouble to explain the difference it made.

In the country we don't worry our heads about that sort of thing. Whether Peter or Paul is at the head of things, the same jobs still have to be tackled, the same woes still have to be faced. All the same, the change of régime did send a ripple through our backwater.

The Republic did at least one good thing, for which I was grateful: it lifted the salt-tax. Before that, we had to pay five or six sous a pound, and we were nearly as sparing with it as with butter: afterwards, it cost only two sous. It was in my view a mean trick on the part of the old government to allow such an enormous tax on one of the chief necessities of life, which neither the poor nor the rich could do without.

Another innovation, no doubt a good one, was the establishment of universal suffrage. I knew that the workmen in the towns made a great fuss about that, and later I understood their reasons. But just then I did not think the right to vote as important as the suppression of the tax on salt.

As might be imagined, such reforms found no favour with the rich. Cereals kept rising in price: it was said that out of hatred for the new government, the rich were storing up quantities of corn, which they were going to throw into the sea so as to cause a famine.

Soon after, there were elections to appoint deputies. I received several papers on this occasion, and I used to go to Monsieur Perrier and beg him to read them to me. The Republican candidates spoke of liberty, justice, the welfare of the people, and promised numerous reforms: the establishment of schools and the making of roads, the shortening of the terms of military service, assistance to the infirm and aged poor. The Conservatives spoke chiefly of the France which they wished to see united, great and strong; they desired peace, order, prosperity; they counselled us to distrust the revolutionary Utopians who wanted to overthrow everything to make a clean sweep of our age-old traditions, and consequently lead us to destruction. I was far from understanding the exact meaning of all those fine phrases, but it seemed to me that the Conservatives were trying to dazzle the electors with big words which meant nothing, while the Republicans had a few good, practical ideas. I told Monsieur Perrier what I thought, and he quite agreed with me.

"Be sure and tell your friends and neighbours," he urged me, "that the Republicans are the only ones who wish to see your condition improved. The others are rich *bourgeois*, who approve the old order of things; they have reason to be contented with their lot, and naturally the lot of others is of no importance to them."

This strengthened me in my early beliefs. But the evening before the vote, whilst I was at work, the local priest came to our house and told my wife that all Republicans were blackguards. He told her about several persons of bad repute, idlers and drunkards, who shouted, "Long live the Republic" very loudly in the streets of the town when they were drunk.

"If people of that sort came to power," concluded the priest, "nobody would be safe; they would take the earnings of honest folk, and they would live like lords themselves. You ought to vote for the

ones who represent order and good principle – that is, the Conservatives."

Victoire recounted this to me the same evening:

"There," she said, "that is what Monsieur le Curé told me to tell
you. Now you can do what you like."

I knew in fact that all the riff-raff of the town boasted of their
Republicanism at every turn. But I reflected that the candidates
would not be like the brawlers and drunkards that we saw around
us. Besides, Monsieur Perrier, that excellent man, educated and
intelligent, was a Republican. Many other good people whom I
knew were also Republicans. And when I heard that the illustrious
Fauconnet was campaigning in favour of the Conservatives, I said
to my wife:

"Listen, as for property, all we possess is our two cows; I don't
think they will come to carry them off – and the people who are
supporting the priest's candidates are not such fine people, after all:
Fauconnet, who is probably the biggest thief in Bourbon, supports
them also."

"You surely don't compare Fauconnet to the drunks and
brawlers who shout in the street?"

"Oh, no! I don't want to insult *them*," I said, laughing; "they are
not his kind!"

In my heart I realized, nevertheless, that those same riff-rafff
were doing the "reds" a lot of harm. I have noticed since that the
worst enemies of progress are the people of doubtful repute who
draw attention to themselves under pretence of supporting it. The
best programmes, the best candidates, are lowered by such support;
discredited somewhat in the minds of those, who (like nine-tenths
of the peasants including myself) base their opinion upon a sort of
instinctive sympathy which they feel for the apostles of the various
ideas in the country.

All day Saturday I was torn by contrary feelings; but on Sunday
I returned to my first resolution: I put my voting paper in the
ballot-box for the Republican. That was my way of thanking the
new government for having reduced salt to two sous a pound.

Six months later, there was another vote, to elect the President
of the Republic. All the influential people, the landowners, the
great farmers, the priests, were charged to say and repeat everywhere that the one idea of the "reds" was to favour the town-
workers; we no longer knew what to think. Among all the groups
of farm labourers who collected on Sundays after Mass, on the

Place de l'Eglise, or at the Town Hall, the election was the topic of conversation.

"My master says that if a Republican was made President, wheat would sell for only twenty sous the measure –"

"Mine has said the same thing," took up another. "The Republicans want those in the towns to get their bread for nothing." "They will lower the price of meat, too, you may be sure." "We shall not be able any longer to live by working on the land."

These rumours spread widely and influenced us: like my neighbours, I voted for Napoleon.

XX

After having lived at La Billette for six years, my parents were obliged to leave, the relations between them and Monsieur and Madame Boutry having become impossible. They went to the other extremity of the Commune of Saint-Menoux, on the Montilly side.

My father did not live long at the new farm. In the month of January 1849, two months after he had gone there, one of my nephews came to tell me he was seriously ill. I went to see him the next day, and found him very weak and emaciated with a high fever, which flushed the sunken cheeks above his long beard.

"My poor lad, I'm done for," he said. "Never mind, I'm very glad to see you again before I die –"

For a long time he looked at me with his wet eyes; I could scarcely keep from weeping.

He was not mistaken: he died three days later, on a sad, snowy dawn.

I mourned him sincerely, for, since I had grown old enough to judge him impartially, I had realized that he was a good man to whom life had not been kind: his brother had lived at his expense, his masters had exploited him, his wife had bullied him. His rare moments of pleasure had been at the inn, where he stayed longer than he should.

My sister Catherine, who was married to Gaussin, was unable to attend the funeral; she and her husband had had jobs in Paris for the last year.

* * *

After his death there was a further revolution in the household.

For some time my mother had been at daggers-drawn with Louis and his wife, and tried to set my godfather against them, with the object of separating the two families. But in spite of occasional disagreements, my two elder brothers got on fairly well; they reckoned it was better to stay together until their children were grown up. So my mother, bad-tempered and obstinate, left the house herself. She rented a wretched cottage on the road to Autry, at the entrance to the market town of Saint-Menoux, and to this she retired, to live the life which women live who are alone and without resources: gleaning, taking in washing, doing all the disagreeable and difficult tasks which come their way. As long as she was able to work, she kept the few hundred francs which were her entire savings untouched in her cupboard.

Marinette remained at the farm with my brothers; they kept her, partly out of charity, but also because she was useful to them. The poor child had, in fact, a great love for animals and made a very good shepherdess, except that she was unable to count the sheep when she brought them home. She could spin, and do certain kinds of field work. In short, she earned her keep. Since she never went beyond the boundaries of the farm it cost very little to maintain her.

XXI

Victoire, pregnant a second time, presented me with a little daughter. Fortunately our affairs were not in a bad way. Old Giraud was entirely repaid, I paid my rent regularly and had a few hundred-sou pieces saved. Success gave me satisfaction and therefore encouragement. When it was possible, I continued to work outside my holding. I had found a steady job to work at during bad weather. This was at the quarry of Pied de Fourche, not far from the church, at the east end of the town; there I broke stones for a contractor who made roads. I went to this task, to which I could go at my own convenience, when I had finished my morning's grooming, and I returned in time for that of the evening. In the spring I took my food with me and stayed later.

At times we were as many as twenty stone-breakers in a row, each working kneeling on a rag mat, in the shelter of a straw windbreak. Our yard, on the same level as the old château on the hill opposite, overlooked the entire central part of the town which stood in the middle of a narrow valley. We looked over the roofs of the main street where chimneys of all shapes stood like an outcrop of mushrooms, the smoke rising from them either peacefully or else blown about in the wind – all more noticeable about midday. The main street especially seemed to us like a precipice, and we were tempted to pity the inhabitants of the town for their lack of air. To tell the truth, even if we were able to breathe and felt ourselves caressed by healthy breezes from the countryside and the forest, we might well have been objects of pity too, for there is not much recreation about stone-breaking. Being always in one position and bent, our legs stiffened at the joints, and our hands were torn by contact with the holly-wood handles of our hammers. We were often overwhelmed by monotony and weariness.

My right-hand neighbour took snuff, and he would often throw me his snuff-box, from which I would take very small pinches, in order to do as the others did, clear my head by sneezing. But little by little I acquired a taste for tobacco, and I got a snuff-box for myself made of cherry bark, and had it filled; Victoire was annoyed, and said that we were not so rich that I need put money up my nose, and also that it was disgusting. But her remarks were in vain: my new addiction was already too strong.

And tobacco was not all. This work near to the town led to other expenses which I carefully concealed from my wife. To get to the stone-yard, I had to pass the house of the contractor, who kept an inn near by. When he chanced to see me arrive in the morning, he never failed to call out:

"Hullo, Tiennon! Come along and 'kill the worm,'" which meant drink a glass of spirits. He offered to stand treat, and I could do no less in my turn; it meant that two glasses were drunk and four sous spent.

When we had our meal, there would be a new attack: there would always be one of my companions who would say:

"How dry this wretched bread is! If we only had the price of a quart!" By contributing three sous each, we got a quart between four. That glass of wine certainly did us good, but three sous counts in a daily wage of fifteen or twenty!

On pay-days one had to drink again. I didn't have the courage to refuse, for fear of being conspicuous or being considered a spoilsport, but these abnormal expenses worried me; and besides, in spite of my precautions Victoire had realized what was happening, and often reproached me for it.

I realized then what a real calamity it is for workers in towns and cities to have too many temptations. Although they earn more than we do, they are not better off, for gradually they find it natural to spend something every day at the inn, and it adds up to quite a lot at the end of the day. They are more to be pitied than blamed. I know that in their shoes I should not have acted differently. But I resolved to remove myself from these temptations and seek work elsewhere.

*   *   *

That was how in the winter of 1850, I took to clearing, in the neighbourhood of César,* a field of brushwood that was being brought under cultivation. There it was real country; I earned rather less than at the quarry, but I gained in the end, because my only debauch was my snuff-box.

One March day when the sun was shining – it was very warm even then – among some roots of broom I found a viper just awaking from its winter sleep. Since my boyhood experiences I have not been afraid of reptiles; I watched it moving about for a minute, then I called to Monsieur Raynaud, a baker of the town, who was bundling up some branches of thorn and juniper which he had bought for his stove.

"Come here and see this beautiful viper, Monsieur Raynaud. It's already half awake."

The baker came near, examined it and said:

"The devil! It's more than *half* awake; it's wriggling about like anything." After he had looked at it for a while, he said in a half-serious, half-teasing tone:

"You ought to take it alive to the druggist: he would give you at least a hundred sous for it."

"Are you pulling my leg, Monsieur Raynaud?"

"Certainly not! I assure you that druggists use them to make their drugs and they buy all the vipers they can get."

I looked questioningly at the group of woodmen who had come to see what was going on.

"Monsieur Raynaud's right," said one, "I'm sure they buy them, sure."

"It's the first time I've heard that," said another.

"And I," said I.

"Well, you try," said the baker. "Take it to him alive and you'll see that he'll pay you a hundred sous and maybe more."

* Hamlet near Bourbon, where Julius Caesar had had a camp.

"It isn't easy to carry it alive –"

"Put it in your food tin."

"That's an idea: if I could be certain of selling it for a hundred sous, I'd take it in the food tin and then buy a new one."

Monsieur Raynaud said for the third time, "It's absolutely true, what I'm telling you!"

Although it was not dinner time yet I ate my soup quickly, without even taking time to warm it; then with the aid of a split hazelwood stick, I seized the reptile and pushed it with a good deal of trouble into my empty can, on which I put the lid quickly. The baker and the woodmen watched me and laughed.

"You'll have to stand us a drink, old chap," said the baker as he disappeared. "I've helped you earn a day's pay. Be sure you tell the druggist that you come from me."

Rejoicing at this piece of good luck, I left work earlier than usual and called at the house to put on my clean clothes. When I told my wife about the business, she cried out:

"Take it out of the house at once! The nasty creature – suppose it should lift the lid and slip out under the furniture!" She added: "They can make you believe any silly things, you fool! You'll have to buy a new can for your trouble – another twenty-five or thirty sous. I don't want to see that thing any more, do you hear? Throw it in the ditch, do what you like with it, but don't bring it back here."

My face lengthened; I began to think that my wife was right, but I pretended to be absolutely certain of returning with my hundred-sou piece. So I went boldly to the druggist.

"Good evening, Monsieur Bardet."

"Good evening, my friend, good evening. What can I do for you?"

"Monsieur Bardet, I have been told that you buy living vipers – it was Monsieur Raynaud who told me. I found one in the clearing and I've brought it."

"Oh, yes! I buy them. Monsieur Raynaud is quite right."

He lifted down a big blue bottle.

"Look, there are three of them in here; the one you've brought makes four. If you find any more, bring them to me; I'll take them all at five sous each."

I felt myself going pale.

"How much, Monsieur Bardet?"

"Five sous."

Monsieur Raynaud told me a hundred sous –"

The druggist smiled in his grey beard.

"Raynaud is a bit of a joker; you obviously don't know him. A hundred sous for twenty, he meant to say."

"I've been made a fool of then, I shall have to buy a new food tin; this'll cost me money.... Damn! I wish I hadn't brought it."

Monsieur Bardet seemed sorry to see me so vexed.

"Well! This should teach you not to believe everybody. But you're wrong about your can. You need not throw it away. Look, I'll give you something to disinfect it. Dissolve a little of this white powder in a quart of boiling water. After you've cleaned it with this liquid, you may use it quite safely; it'll be as clean as ever."

The powder cost three sous; I had twenty centimes left over. But I had reckoned without Victoire, who swore that the can was of no more use, and threatened to break it herself instead of cleaning it. So I had to return to the town in the evening, where I bought a cheaper one from the ironmonger's at twenty-five sous. It was not nearly so good as the old one.

I have often made people laugh at my expense when I have told them about that adventure, and I amused myself by imagining some comic episodes intended to make it still more funny. But I bore the baker a grudge, especially as he made fun of me again the next time he saw me.

"Well, Bertin, how about that viper?"

"Well, Monsieur Raynaud, I shall never believe you again; you are a thorough liar."

"What! didn't the druggist want it?"

"Yes, but instead of a hundred sous, he paid me five."

"Five sous? Well, that was what I told you; you misunderstood me."

And he went away laughing.

XXII

From time to time I used to see Fauconnet, whose hair had whitened and whose shaven face, with its wrinkles and perpetual grimace, had a rather diabolical appearance. When he crossed Le Craux, going to Meillers, he would stop and speak to me, and forced myself to appear amiable, in spite of the contempt I felt for him.

One time it happened that his servant was ill and he came to me to take his place. It was after the August harvest and there was not much to do on the holding: so I agreed. When one is poor it is necessary to take work where one can get it, even with employers whom one considers to be rogues.

In this daily intimacy I got a close view of that upstart farmer, who was on the point of becoming a big landed proprietor. At home he was coarse, sullen and grumbling. He used to wander about aimlessly from kitchen to cowshed, from cowshed to garden, untidy in dress, smoking his pipe, yawning, never troubling to do any work. I realized during my stay in that house that idleness is not really enviable. Work is often painful, hard, oppressive, but still it is interesting, and the best antidote to tedium. Fauconnet was terribly bored. He was always bickering with his wife and the servant, to whom he made contemptuous remarks or unreasonable reproaches. At times he would pour into himself great bumpers of brandy, seeking in alcoholic excitement a remedy for his bad humour and idleness. He was pleasant enough to me; he would call me into the kitchen to have a glass in the morning, but at meal times he never gave me any wine, on the excuse that working men ought not to get used to it.

He rarely spent the whole day at home. He was proud of his fast horses and very particular that they should be carefully groomed and the harness bright. Astride his horse or in his carriage, he became once more the public man, Fauconnet, the rich farmer, conscious of his power. He went to the fairs, where he knew he was looked at, envied, respected by the merchants, bowed low to by the workers. In addition to his trips to the fairs or to the provincial capital he went round his estate to give orders, to arrange the coming sales or to flirt with some young *métayère* who was not too virtuous and dared not refuse anything to the master.

The only time I saw him really cheerful at home was the Sunday when the hunting season opened. He had invited to dinner five or six of his friends, with whom he had been hunting in the morning, also his eldest son, a doctor, who had just set up in practice at Bourbon. That was a feast with a vengeance, a real debauch. I had to wait at table, which I did very clumsily, because I had never done it before; but even my clumsiness was of use, since it gave the guests occasion to laugh. And that was all they wanted, occasions to laugh. After they had eaten and drunk hard, they told each other ribald stories; accounts of orgies, and illicit love affairs. They talked also about their *métayers*, whom they mocked for their stupidity and submissiveness, and about the landowners whose lands they managed, whom they made to swallow improbable lies. I realized that they considered themselves to be very superior people, dominating the rest of humanity with all the weight of their big bellies, with all the breadth of their red faces. Only the young doctor was apparently not amused. He had settled down in a house of his own next to the hot spring,* and he visited his father's house very seldom. His two brothers also made brief and rare appearances.

"They haven't got their father's habits; they're not his sort," the servant said to me.

I concluded that they, too, most likely considered themselves to be superior men, superior to this farmer who was their father, and to his friends, whom they no doubt despised. That is the way of the world. Everyone sees and thinks in his own way. However superior a man thinks he is, he will always have some neighbour who despises him. There is some consolation in that for those who are not superior at all.

* * *

When the servant was well enough to return to his duties, as I had some time at my disposal, Fauconnet kept me to work with the threshing machine on his Bourbon estate. The threshing machine had just been introduced in that district; after hesitating a long time, the farmers had finally decided to use it. In those days they still provided a third of the hands as they had done when threshing was done with the flail. They have since freed themselves from that obligation, which they found too costly, and now they leave all the labour costs to the *métayers*.

The threshing was begun at La Chapelle, the estate on the road to Saint-Plaisir. We were all very surprised and a little afraid to find ourselves in the service of this monster, whose wheels turned so quickly. But the work was not so hard as it is now, because we worked at a very moderate pace and we soon adapted to it.

The women were the most at a loss because they had never had so many people to feed. Now they have got used to it: they buy great quantities of meat and cook *pot-au-feu*, *boeuf en daube*, various ratatouilles, they kill rabbits and even chickens. But at that time the housewives had been too poor for fifty years to think of such things, and yet the ordinary cooking did not seem good enough for

---

* Bourbon is a winter spa.

strangers. The *métayères* of Fauconnet's farms must have put their heads together and this is what happened:

At La Chapelle, for the morning meal they served *galette* (a flaked pastry cake) and *tourtons* (pasties). I have always had a great liking for our country pastry and these were fresher and with more butter than usual; I can tell you I stuffed myself. But at the midday meal they again served *galette* and *tourtons* only, and the same in the evening. At each meal I found them less and less good; my appetite diminished, and it was the same with my companions. I expected that there would be something new the next day, soup, haricots, something, anything. But disenchantment came. When I arrived in the morning, I noticed that the fire flamed in the oven, and I saw a new pile of *galettes* and *tourtons* that they had prepared for cooking. At the three meals of that day, they gave us nothing else. The warmth and the dust always made us thirsty, and this heavy pastry did not go down at all well. Our tired stomachs rebelled. That evening I left without sitting down to the table, and many of the others did the same. As we were going to another farm the next day, we hoped that the obsession would cease: nothing of the kind! The pastry abounded more than ever; *tourton* in the morning and *galette* at midday. It was too much; everybody demanded milk, even old milk, or skimmed milk, milk of whatever kind.

The housekeeper consented to go round with her milkpan, but she made it plain that she did not like to serve us with such common food as milk. However, it was such a success that she had to go round three times with her pan to satisfy us all. But the *métayère* did not take the hint; at the next meal the table was spread as usual with the inevitable *galettes* and *tourtons*. I ate nothing at all, and feeling that I was about to fall ill, I told Fauconnet that I could not work any longer at the machine. The food at home, the onion soup, the rye bread and cheese, seemed better after that experience.

XXIII

One December evening when there was snow and a hard frost, the capons began to crow. It was at the end of the evening, towards nine o'clock. We were getting ready to "use the sheets" as one says.

"What are they trying to say, damned creatures?" said Victoire, immediately on the alert.

"Nothing, you may be sure," I answered, feeling as worried as she did.

We were both convinced that the crowing of cocks between sunset and midnight was an evil omen: it is the time for sleep, they should be silent.

On reflection, this infringement of the rule on the part of capons ought not to seem surprising, for as they never go out of the dark shed, they gradually lose the sense of time. But we did not think of that and were worried because as children we had seen our own kinsfolk worried by this occurrence. Besides, in the deep silence of the winter evening, the shrill crowings had a melancholy sound, especially when there was a chorus of them: the Viradons' cock replied to ours, then some from the neighbouring cottages joined in, and for half an hour there was a concert of piercing cock-crows, as though it had been the hour before dawn.

When the noise was at an end, Victoire suckled our little Charles (we had a third child, two months old), but she was not reassured and still trembled after she had gone to bed. That night we slept badly and decided that the unlucky fowls should be sold as soon as possible.

*　　*　　*

It chanced during the months that followed, that we suffered all kinds of misfortunes. As I have grown older I have lost a good many of the superstitions of my youth; but because of that incident I have always retained my fear of cocks crowing after sunset.

In the corner of my cowshed I had a reserve store of potatoes. The better of my two cows got loose one night, greedily swallowed a big potato and choked herself. In the morning I discovered her lying on her back, in the throes of death; her stomach was swollen, her tongue protruded and her legs twitched. The potato had got stuck in the oesophagus and was obstructing her breathing; my attempts to push it down were as useless as the desperate struggles of the poor beast, who had no wish to die. Nothing was left for us to do but to call in the butcher, who gave me thirty francs for her: I had relied on selling her for three hundred francs at the end of the winter.

I remember that my wife had wanted to buy some clothes for our little Jean and some drugget trousers, a cap and a smock for me. But we had to postpone such abnormal expenses till times were better. A little later, a pig, which weighed at least a hundred and fifty pounds, also died. Then we had a lot of trouble with the cow we had bought to replace the one that had choked to death.

On account of the children, Victoire had given up carrying the milk to town and had begun to make butter. But it was impossible to make butter from the cream which we got from that cow. We spent hours and hours working the churn; our arms ached with moving the beater up and down: nothing happened. One evening I got angry: without interruption, from six o'clock till eleven, I worked the beater in the watery liquid; I succeeded in exhausting myself, in making my shirt wet, in staving in the churn, but not in making butter. The next day I told old Viradon about it and he said it was a spell. A similar mishap had happened to him in his youth; he had consulted a *défaiseux de sorts* (a person who removes spells) who had given him the following advice:

"Go, a little before midnight, to the crossroads at the Place de l'Eglise and put there a new six-sou pot full of this worthless cream; walk twelve times round the pot while twelve o'clock is striking, dragging at the end of a cord six feet long the chains which are used to fasten the cows; at the twelfth turn, stop sharply, make the sign of the cross four times in four different directions and then leave as quickly as possible, leaving the pot and bringing back the chains.

"Cut from each beast a bunch of hair, from the ears, from the mane and from the tail; soak them in the drinking trough every day during Holy Week before sunrise; carry them to Mass on Easter Day and burn them in the fire without being seen."

"I did that and it worked," concluded Viradon, "but the *défaiseux* had to do his part, too."

In spite of my worries, I laughed heartily as I listened to the good man telling me, with utter conviction, the details of the bizarre ceremonies which he had been made to perform. I fancied I could see him traipsing round his pot, and clanking his chains.

The *défaiseux* was dead; but he had left the secret of his power to his son, and my old neighbour urged me strongly to go to him. I refused, however, not having faith in such nonsense.

Victoire went to the priest to tell him our troubles. He came the next day, sprinkled the cowshed with holy water, and told us not to have any fear of sorcerers.

"It is simply that your cow has milk of a bad quality," he concluded; "probably because she is in an advanced state of gestation; improve her food, give her each day a little salt in her ration of meal and you'll find that her milk will improve."

We followed the priest's advice and found that we could make some bad butter, which improved quite naturally when, in the good weather, our cows went out to pasture on Les Craux, and when they had new milk. If we reasoned sensibly, I don't think we should have much occasion to believe in spells.

*　　*　　*

Towards the end of the winter, we had a more serious alarm and on that occasion we decided, as a last resort, to go to a healer.

Our little Charles was suddenly attacked by a serious illness of the throat; he refused the breast; his breathing became hoarse, then rattling. Victoire took him first to the midwife, then to the doctor, but he showed no sign of getting better, rather the reverse. But, on the road to Agonges, there lived a man who treated children for diseases of the throat; people went to him from all the communes of the canton and even from other places: he had cured babies despaired of by the doctors. One evening the little one seemed so much worse that we decided to take him to the healer there and then.

It was a sad journey. I carried the little invalid in my arms on a pillow covered with an old shawl; Victoire followed weeping; in the silence of the night our footsteps made a mournful sound on the dry, frosty ground. At about ten o'clock we were relieved to be knocking at the door of the healer. He was a little old man with grey hair and a vacuous face, attired in cotton drawers and a nightcap. He muttered some prayers, made signs over the child's body, anointed his neck with a kind of grey ointment, and breathed into his mouth three times. This strange scene took place by the light of a dim smokey lamp. I was deeply moved. Victoire wept silently all the time. After he had finished the man said:

"He will be better tomorrow; you did not bring him any too soon, though. As soon as he is well you must go and burn a candle before the altar of the Virgin."

When we asked him what his fee was, he said:

"I never charge poor people anything: however, I have a box here in which each may put what he wishes."

He took from the mantelpiece a small square box of fumed wood with a slit in the lid: I slipped twenty sous into it and we went away in haste, being uneasy about the two elder children, whom we had left asleep in the shut-up house.

The healer had not deceived us. Towards morning the baby

vomited some watery matter which was like hard phlegm, and at once took the breast. Two days later he was entirely recovered.

I have often wondered, without being able to find any answer, if that cure was natural, or if the grimaces of that old man really did have any effect. I know a number of people, very sceptical, very level-headed, who resort to these country healers to improve their teeth, or to get them to say special prayers when they have sprained a foot or wrist. And many claim to have been cured. With such examples, a poor simple man may well be perplexed, unable to choose between those who affirm and those who mock. That's the way I still feel.

XXIV

One day at the Bourbon fair, during the Carnival of 1853, my father-in-law drew me aside in the Place de la Mairie, where I was talking to some men, to tell me that he was in a position to get me engaged as *métayer* on an estate in Franchesse, his original commune; he knew the steward very well as they had been friends when they were children.

I had been considering for some time whether I should take a farm, for I realized that if I stayed where I was, I should have to let my children be hired out as soon as they were old enough to take charge of animals, and I disliked the idea of that. I should have preferred to have waited a few years; however, on reflection, I thought it better not to miss this opportunity. The following Sunday old Giraud and I went to see the farm in question. It was situated between Bourbon and Franchesse, two hundred yards from the road which joined the two communes. It was called La Creuserie. It was part of the property of Monsieur Gorlier, who was known as "de la Buffère," the name of a small neighbouring château where he lived during the summer. The estate comprised five other farms: Balutière, Praulière, Le Plat-Mizot, La Jarry d'en haut and La Jarry d'en bas, a holding called Les Fouinats, and the steward's house, which was close to the Hall.

The name of the steward was Monsieur Parent. He was a man of middle height, with a very large head and a fringe of grey beard; his protruding eyes gave him an air of being constantly astonished; his thick lower lip hung down, uncovering his broken teeth, and allowing a continual jet of saliva to dribble. He said at once, that out of consideration for my father-in-law, he would engage me as a *métayer*, although the fact that I would be working alone would be a disadvantage. He showed us the farm buildings, which were old and not very comfortable, and he took us to see all the plots of land and the meadows. When we returned to the house he stated the conditions.

Two thousand francs would be needed to pay for the lease of the cattle, but they would be satisfied with half that amount; they would add the interest on the remainder at five per cent, to the fixed annual tax* of four hundred francs, and there would be a retention from the profits for amortisation. I should have to do all the carting for the château and the property; my wife would be obliged to pay as rent out of her produce, six fowls, six capons, twenty pounds of butter: the turkeys and the geese should be divided equally. The master would reserve the right to alter the terms each year or to dismiss us, giving at least nine months' notice.

Afterwards Monsieur Parent began to speak about the proprietor, whom he called Monsieur de la Buffère, or more often Monsieur Frédéric and for whom he seemed to have a great respect.

"Monsieur Frédéric does not wish the *métayers* to approach him directly. You must always speak to me or ask me for what you consider necessary. Monsieur Frédéric insists that you shall always be respectful, not only to himself but also to his staff: he made me give the present tenants of La Creuserie notice because they spoke rudely to Mademoiselle Julie, the cook. Monsieur Frédéric will not allow the game to be touched: if he found that anyone had set a trap or had been shooting, that would mean instant dismissal. When he hunts you must keep out of his way, even if it means stopping work. Also you must see that the butter for your rent is of good quality, and the fowls nice and fat, to satisfy Mademoiselle Julie."

In reply to a sly question from my father-in-law he answered in a low tone that Mademoiselle Julie was not only the cook, but also the mistress of Monsieur Frédéric, who was a bachelor. That was why one had to humour her, for her influence over him was considerable.

I did not know quite what to think of Monsieur Frédéric. According to the steward, who, however, spoke of him as a very

---

* the *impôt colonique* owed by the sharecropper to the proprietor was paid in cash and was somewhere between 5 and 20 fr per hectare (approx. $2\frac{1}{2}$ acres) according to the farm.

good man, he appeared to be a potentate whose slightest wish must be obeyed. That alarmed me somewhat.

I asked Monsieur Parent to let me have eight days to think it over, especially in order to discuss the matter with Victoire.

She irritated me, for she did her best not to give any opinion. "Oh! do as you like," she said, in her coldest, most indifferent manner, "it's all the same to me."

She was in a bad mood because she was pregnant again, and that made her unapproachable. One day when I insisted more than usual, she made a semblance of assent.

"For goodness sake! If you like that farm, take it, that's all."

"But will you be happy if I take it?"

"Me! Oh, I might as well be there as anywhere."

I could have hit her. I decided, nevertheless, to take the farm, and at Martinmas, 1853, we settled down at La Creuserie. Victoire had given birth prematurely to a little boy, who was still-born. She was very tired and weak and totally unfit for coping with the heavy work of a move. Fortunately her mother was able to help us this time.

XXV

Our house had two rooms of equal size connected by an inside door: these were the kitchen and the bedroom. The floor was lower than the yard, into which both rooms opened through great ogival doors darkened by the weather and strongly bound with iron. In the kitchen, a kind of concrete had been laid at some former time: but the surface had been worn away by continual sweeping, and there was little left but a quantity of sharp stones sticking up from one end of the room to the other. In the bedroom the floor was of ordinary earth, sunken in the middle, uneven under the furniture, with little humps and holes everywhere. The ceiling matched the room: it was of boards, low and dilapidated, and supported by great joists very near each other and covered with patches of white mould; and in each room was an enormous rough-cut beam supported by a vertical post.

Grains of wheat and oats escaped from the loft, falling through the open joints of the boards, and the rats laid up their stores on the beams. The light entered only through narrow windows with four small panes; in winter, when it was dark and the cold prevented us from keeping the outside door open, it was difficult to see, even in full daylight. The kitchen was the communal room, where all the main tasks were carried out. By the entrance, on the left, was the kneading-trough, and above, a rack with wooden arches to separate the big loaves of a batch when they were placed there side by side; on the right, there was a round-topped chest for the linen, and a chest of drawers. In the middle of the room stood the massive oak table that we had bought second-hand; it had benches on either side where we sat at meal-times. At the back of the room, a clock stood between two beds: our bed was in the corner, nearest to the fire, as is the custom, and on the other side was the bed shared by the servant and our little Clémentine. To the left, in the wall at the gable-end, the stone fireplace projected wide and high; above the fireplace was the black hole of the oven. The bedroom was cleaner and less smoky: my wife had placed there her wardrobe and the new beds we had had to buy for our staff.

The house faced the sun at nine o'clock, but it was much later before it shone on the threshold, because of the proximity of the barn and cowsheds, which were built in front and parallel to it fifteen yards distant at most. In the space between the two blocks of buildings, were the drains, and these formed a kind of dark, stagnant pool on which floated husks of wheat from threshing-time until the middle of winter. Near to that we also stored the sheep-manure, which we used for manuring in the spring-time. Also in that space, was a wooden trough, long and shallow, from which the pigs fed, and an old wheel placed horizontally on three posts which served as a night perch for the turkeys. The tip-cart and other wagons were often there, and along the walls were the smaller tools, sticks, and goads; some waste straw and wood, stones and broken tiles were scattered here and there.

The farm was situated high up on the side of the valley, which gave us a magnificent view, from the top of the granary staircase at the gable end of the house. The valley extended over a good part of the communes of Bourbon, Saint-Aubin and Ygrande, and was like a gigantic amphitheatre. On the upper parts of these slight undulations could be seen distinctly green, russet, or greyish fields encircled by thorn hedges; there were other fields of which one could see just enough to make out whether they were fallow land, stubble or pasture; and in the low-lying areas one could only see the tops of trees growing here and there in the quick-set hedges. At the far end of a long meadow could be seen the mysterious lozenge-shape of a coppice, which was already vast. Lines of giant poplars could be seen in some places, and at wide intervals among the hedges and trees, the ruined buildings of a cottage or a farm were visible; those were the domains of Baluftière, Praulière, and Le Plat-Mizot, arranged in a triangle quite near; La Jarry d'en haut and La Jarry d'en bas were a little further off, then some others whose names I knew, and further off still, domains of which I knew nothing, and finally, at the other extremity of the valley, was a thin line of buildings forming the village of Saint-Aubin. Beyond that one could see, like a great sombre ribbon, the forest of Gros-Bois; and on clear days, still further off, many other valleys, many other villages; and beyond known distances, one could see black masses silhouetted against the blue of the heavens, a line of peaks which were said to be the mountains of Auvergne.

Behind our house was a narrow valley of fertile meadows, and beyond them a little hill upon which was perched the village of Franchesse, with its small square belfry.

On the first days after our arrival, this landscape was everywhere shrouded in mist; later I saw it in its winter dress, with the bare fields washed by rain or spangled with frost, and the hedges like mourning-borders embellished by the skeleton trees. Later, a mantle of snow lay over everything, disguising the landscape as if for a masquerade. I saw the landscape come to life again, quivering in the warm April breezes, displaying gradually all its magnificence, with its white flowers and fresh shades of green; I saw it in the full glare of summer, when the harvest lay golden amongst the darker green of the trees and hedges, and the whole panorama seemed asleep. I saw it when the leaves took on their russet tints, which is their time of white hair, preceding briefly their contact with the earth from which all comes and to which all returns. I saw it grow light as a gentle dawn revealed its gay elegance, and I saw it decline slowly into the purple shadows of a fine evening. And I saw it when it appeared a setting for dreams, bathed in the mysterious light of the moon.

How often when contemplating all this have I said to myself:

"There are people who travel, who go far, out of ambition, necessity, or pleasure, to satisfy their taste, or because they have to: they have the opportunity to go into ecstasy over a variety of landscapes. But how many others see always the same thing! For how many is life bounded by such a valley as this, or even by one of its undulations, by one of its minor recesses! How many people, down the ages, have grown up, loved and suffered, in each of the dwellings I can see from here, or in those which preceded them upon this expanse of fertile country, without ever going as far as the horizon!"

This thought consoled me for not knowing anything outside the two cantons of Souvigny and Bourbon. I came to find some charm in the varied aspects of my familiar landscape; I found even a certain pride in the possession of that vast horizon, and I pitied the inhabitants of the low-lying places.

XXVI

Monsieur Parent, the steward, often came to see us and was very liberal with his advice. But his advice about cultivation, besides being of only mediocre interest, took second place to his lectures on the subject of Monsieur Frédéric's habits and how we ought to behave to him when he came back.

It was June when the master arrived for his annual stay at La Buffère. By a chance which was no doubt calculated, he paid his first visit to us in the evening, when we were all together at supper in the kitchen. Monsieur Parent accompanied him. I rose and made a sign to the others to do the same, and leaving the bench I went towards the visitors. Monsieur Gorlier eyed me from head to foot.

"Is this the *métayer?*" he asked the steward.

"Yes, Monsieur Frédéric, it is."

"He's very young ... The wife?"

"That's me, monsieur," said Victoire, approaching.

"Ah! You don't look very strong."

"She has three very young children," said Monsieur Parent, in a timid voice.

Monsieur Frédéric asked us our ages, and questioned us about our upbringing. We were both very nervous in the presence of this powerful and formidable man, about whom so much had been dinned into us. He saw this and took the trouble to speak in a friendly tone:

"Don't be afraid! Good Heavens! I don't eat people! Parent has told me that you work well and have your hearts in the right place. Keep on like that and we shall get on all right. To obey and to work, that's your job; I don't ask anything else. For instance, don't ever bother me about repairs. It's a principle of mine not to do any. And now, good night. You can go to bed now, good people!"

He spoke slowly, rolling his r's a little; his small grey eyes blinked constantly; his complexion was a deep red; his beard and hair were jet-black although he was over sixty. (I found out later that the black was artificial; he used a dye.) His expression, in spite of an appearance of good health, was disagreeable and bored. Those who have tasted every pleasure rarely look happy.

Monsieur Gorlier often came to see us, sometimes at our house, sometimes in the fields. He would chat for a moment about the weather and the work, while playing with his stick, then leave abruptly. He was never polite as he had been that first evening. Like Fauconnet, he "thee'd and thou'd" everybody, and as he had no memory for names or perhaps as a matter of policy, he invariably addressed the person he was speaking to as "What's-your-name."

"Well, What's-your-name, d'you like this weather?"

"Mother What's-your-name, we'll soon be taking two of your chickens for rent."

Mlle. Julie, the cook-mistress, a fresh-coloured woman, already mature, with a white skin and voluptuous figure, came one evening to ask for the two chickens which Victoire had been specially fattening for several weeks. She weighed them, felt them, and deigned to say that she was satisfied.

"You must always have them like that, Victoire; they seem perfect. That's a magnificent cock."

"Yes, Mademoiselle," said I. "Indeed, I wish it was my stomach that was going to be his cemetery."

The big woman noticed the remark.

"What did you say?" she asked.

I turned pale, fearing that I had displeased her.

"Go on, say it again!"

"Mademoiselle, I said that I wished my stomach was going to serve as a cemetery for that fellow there. It is a country saying, which I used as a joke; you need not be vexed: I know well enough that fowls are not for me."

Mlle. Julie laughed uninhibitedly.

"I shall remember that saying, Tiennon, and I'll serve it up to others whom it will amuse, you may be sure. I've never heard it before."

She repeated it without delay to Monsieur Frédéric, and the next time he saw me, he said:

"What's-your-name, you've got some capital sayings; my friends Granval and Decaumont are coming on a visit shortly: I'll bring them to see you, and you must try to think of some amusing things like the one you told Mlle. Julie the other day about the cock."

He kept his word. Several times during August, he came in the evening with the two gentlemen. They arrived smoking their pipes, while we were at supper, and sat down near the table.

"Carry on talking, my good people, don't take any notice of us," they said each time.

But we could do nothing of the kind, you may be sure. We spoke only to answer them when they addressed us directly. The farm servants, who slept in the next room, were able to escape as soon as they had finished eating, but I had to provide them with amusement until ten or eleven o'clock. My wife and the maid had to stay there too. It mattered little to them how late they went to bed; they were able to get up late too! It mattered little to them that I lost my sleep, though I had to be up at four o'clock as usual. And it was simply, as I say, to make me provide them with sport that they came and hung around my house. They only made me talk, so that they could laugh at my incorrect speech, at my simple and awkward replies. If I said anything which seemed especially comic to them, Monsieur Decaumont would bring out his notebook.

"I must make a note of that," he would say. "I will use it for the rural scenes in my next novel."

Mademoiselle Julie came one day and I ventured to ask her why Monsieur Decaumont wrote down the uncouth things which I said in spite of myself. She said that he was a great man, whose business was writing books, and that he was famous. A great man! A famous man! That fat little man with a face like a priest's, and ridiculously long hair, falling upon his shoulders!

"Ah! A famous man is like that, is he?" said I.

Mademoiselle Julie began to laugh.

"Good heavens! Yes, Tiennon, he is much like anybody else, in spite of his cleverness. With his long hair and his funny ways one would take him for a fool instead of a learned man; and he is amused by everything, like a child."

Well, I did not find the actions of this maker of books quite fair. I was irritated with him for writing down my answers to publish them, so that other bourgeois like himself could also laugh at them. Was it my fault that I spoke incorrectly? I spoke as I had been taught. He, who had no doubt remained at school till he was twenty, had learned to turn fine phrases. But I had had other things to do during that time. And currently I was employing my faculties quite as usefully as he was. Producing bread is, I suppose, as necessary as writing books! Ah! if I could have seen him working with me, that famous man, ploughing, scything, or threshing, I believe that in my turn I should have had occasion to laugh! I have often wished that I could put to work in the fields for a few hours all those clever people who sneer at peasants.

XXVII

I was not the only one who served as a butt for the mockery of the master and his friends: my neighbour, Primaud of Balutière, also suffered. I must say that good old Primaud's face at first sight invited ridicule: he had a flat nose, a big, toothless mouth, which opened wide at every opportunity in a foolish, noisy laugh, and he had a comic way of looking at the sky with one eye when anyone spoke to him. He was as simple as could be, and anyone who took the trouble could make a fool of him. Finally, he had the peculiarity of being passionately fond of bacon. Now, Monsieur Frédéric knew of that peculiarity. Nearly every Sunday morning, under one pretext or another, he sent for his *métayer* to come to the château, and he would give him an enormous slice of bacon. He was left alone in the kitchen, and he regaled himself, as one can imagine. After a quarter of an hour, the master would join him.

"Have you had enough to eat, Primaud?"

"Oh, yes, Monsieur Frédéric!"

"But there's still a big piece of bacon on the dish; you mustn't leave that. I know you can manage to get that down." And he would put it on Primaud's plate.

"It is too much, Monsieur Frédéric, my stomach's full! I can't take any more."

"Go on, Whatsit, you're joking; no doubt you're thirsty. Julie, give him a glass of wine."

On his way home, Primaud used to pass through our yard. He would often call at the house or come to see me in the cowsheds.

"Tiennon," he would say to me, "I have had another good meal!"

"Ah, so much the better," I would reply. "That's always a good thing; I bet you've been eating as much bacon as you wanted."

"More than I wanted, old man! Just imagine, Monsieur Frédéric came in and served me himself with a huge piece, with his own hand, y'know. I couldn't refuse, especially as he made them give me some wine."

He felt himself much honoured by this flattering attention. It never occurred to him that in it there was something hurtful to a man's dignity. Perhaps he even considered that the greasy tricklings from the bacon on each side of his mouth were marks of glory. He went home delighted.

But the other *métayers* and I were less pleased. Unknown to himself, no doubt, Primaud played the sorry part of informer. Through him Monsieur Gorlier obtained all the information he wanted about the people on his estate, and the inhabitants of the commune. Three years before, when Napoleon III – whom they then called Badinguet – had brought about a kind of counter-revolution in order to get himself styled Emperor, two men of Franchesse had been sent to Cayenne, through, it was said, some careless gossip of the bacon-eater.

The master had made him understand that it would be a very good thing for the country to be rid of those who proclaimed their preference for the Republic; and the poor man had eagerly mentioned all the 'reds' he knew.

One might excuse Primaud's part in this because he was stupid and not spiteful, but I can find no excuse for Monsieur Frédéric for using such means to obtain information, any more than for using his influence afterwards to injure the people of his country.

When I realized what was going on, I only told my neighbour things that there was no need to hide.

At that time Primaud already went by the name of the "bacon-eater." He has been dead a long time, but the nickname has survived, and there is a kind of legend attached to his name in Franchesse; they still say of anyone who has a great fancy for bacon, "he's a real Primaud."

XXVIII

My life was laborious and fatiguing, but it had its pleasures. Being head of a farm, I felt that I was a kind of minor king. My responsibilities often weighed upon me, but I was proud of sitting at the head of the table beside the loaf, from which I cut big slices at the beginning of each meal. Above all, I was proud of having the corner seat, the place of honour in the fireside circle.

I was head cowman, and I helped with the grooming of all the animals. In summer I never missed getting up before daylight for the ploughing or mowing; and before starting on that, I always gave a little bran to the sheep, prepared the pigs, and went to see the oxen in the pasture. I was often up an hour before the servants, but that did not prevent me exerting myself and getting about as quickly as possible at work during the day. I led the team and the others, in their places behind me, were obliged to regulate their pace according to mine, and I can say without boasting that they had a hard job keeping up with me.

I had had the luck to find a good foreman, a lad of just over twenty, named Auguste; we called him Guste. He was strong and plucky, and worked as hard as I did. My second servant was a boy of fifteen, half-shepherd, half-labourer. I also hired a day labourer for the summer; during the first years this was a certain Forichon, an old, experienced man and a good worker, but a great gossip and rather slow. He always had some story to tell and I believed that, by trying to interest us in what he was saying, he hoped to get us to slacken the pace of the work, and take it a bit more easily. One day, by prearrangement with Guste, I resolved to work more quickly than usual, so that he would not have time to talk. When we had mown three swathes at that speed, old Forichon tried to call a halt.

"If we carry on like this till midday, we shall have cut a lot!" said he.

"If the boss wants it, we'll try," said Guste.

Old Forichon went on: "Once at Buchepot, at the Nicolases', we mowed like that three days running. It was big Pierre who was at the head: he kept a good edge on his scythe, that brute, and he worked damn fast; his brother-in-law could only just keep up with him. The big chap teased him, and they started to quarrel. I thought they would come to blows. The fact was they had a grudge against each other already; I knew all about it. This is what happened –"

He believed that I was going to lean on the handle of my scythe, as usual, to listen to what had passed between big Pierre and his brother-in-law; but, instead, I went on mowing at the same fast rate; and when Guste and I got to the end of the row, he was a bit behind.

"Curse it!" he said, "I have caught an ants' nest and spoilt my edge. I once mowed in a meadow where there were so many anthills that we had to hammer our blades out at the early meal break."

He turned round and seemed astonished that we were not listening, but were already a long way off. From one swathe to another, he got more and more behind. There was one place where, the grass being very tough, we had to sharpen often, which slowed us down. Then Forichon thought he could catch us up; but he got to where we were just as we found soft grass again, and we went on quickly, while he pegged away, unable to keep up.

When the servant brought the soup, old Forichon did not want to eat until he had caught up. When he arrived panting, his face streaming, his shirt soaked in sweat, we were just getting up to start work again. He was furious and seemed to want to cut out lunch so that he could come and cut his swathe alongside us. To make him consent to take his meal, I was obliged to tell him that we would wait for him, which we did, though Guste was very anxious not to. Poor old Forichon sulked for a week at least, but he was not cured of his passion for reminiscing; and he referred to the incident at least twenty times, saying:

"My scythe isn't very good; if I still had the one I broke two years ago, you wouldn't have left me behind, I can tell you."

*　　*　　*

But I did not always have the servants on my side. There were times when I felt that they were all allied against me: Guste, old Forichon, the boy, and the servant-girl. Their hard faces showed discontent and hostility; I was the boss, their enemy. On very hot days, especially, after the midday meal, they would be overcome by fatigue and idleness; they wanted to have a siesta. I, too, would have liked a rest; I was as exhausted as they were. But I pulled myself together and tried to find words to encourage them.

"Come along, lads! Let's get a move on and load up; it looks stormy; the hay could get wet."

Sometimes I tried to get at them through their pride:

"We're going to be the last to finish: at Baluftière and Praulière they're further ahead than we are; if we want to get the harvest in at the same time as Le Plat-Mizot, we'll have to stir our stumps."

They would get up, relieving their feelings by great oaths:

"*Bon Dieu de bon Dieu!* no one can work in such heat; not even animals could stand it."

Forichon said:

"I'd like to commit a crime and go to gaol, to see if it's any worse there than here!"

As we worked, I strove to cheer them up by telling them jokes and dirty stories, which made the servant-girl blush. They would laugh and tell even dirtier ones; so the time passed, and work got done. To be cheerful, friendly, and not to spare yourself, that's the way to get the best out of others.

Sometimes in the course of those hard days of haymaking and harvest, on those scorching afternoons, we would see Monsieur Frédéric and his friends sitting in the shade of a group of trees, round a little table covered with cold drinks.

"Look at those lucky bastards," said Guste, who, at a distance, showed no respect for class differences.

The others also made disrespectful remarks, but I kept silent, or even tried to stop them if they went too far. A poor labourer, caught between the hammer and the anvil, has to know how to be diplomatic.

Working without respite from dawn to dusk, hurrying with one job and immediately beginning another which is behindhand, having only five or six hours of light, uneasy sleep – it's a régime which isn't fattening, but it prevents monotony. For six months of the year I followed that régime. After the harvest came the manuring, the ploughing, the sowing, which are busy times as well, and until about Martinmas I continued to get up at four o'clock in the morning.

The ploughing was particularly hard, owing to the situation of the farm on the side of a valley. Our fields were on the slope, and consisted mostly of red clay mixed with stones. All that made the work hard both for the ploughman and the oxen. The poor oxen got up reluctantly when we went before dawn to fetch them from the meadow, which was their pasture in September. They were nearly always asleep under the same oak tree, white masses in the mist of the early dawn, and we had to give them hard prods with the goad to make them move.

"Get up, you good-for-nothings!"

They hated having to go to work and, really, I felt sorry for them: there was a good spring of clear water in the meadow; the shade from the hedges was dense and cool; the grass was wonderfully tender. I hated taking them out of that paradise to put them under the yoke and force them to drag the plough for hours up and down our steeply sloping fields. Sometimes I felt that I had to apologize to them:

"It's a nuisance, of course, but it's got to be done ... I would rather be resting too, my friends, but I have to work. So let's get on with it cheerfully."

They had some good times during the winter months, and my work was not quite so hard either: I did not get up until five o'clock and went to bed at eight. But the head of a farm has his worries at all seasons. At that time it was the question of fodder which occupied me most. One had to be very careful with it, and at the same time contrive to fatten the animals, to give a sufficient ration to the newly-calved cows, to the heifers to be sold in the spring, and also the working oxen, which I liked to keep in good condition. I used to measure my hay-loft, taking some points as landmarks, marking off such and such a portion to last up to such and such a time, and in that way I managed never to be taken unawares. In bad years I had to mix a good portion of straw with the daily ration, and even then I had great trouble to make it last out; as I saw it shrinking fast, I used to tremble all winter with the fear of being without at the end of the season. If you have to buy fodder even for one month, you can lose most of your profit for the year! I used to distribute all the cattle-fodder myself, and on days when they went out I was rarely absent at grooming times. For this reason I went very little to the inn, well knowing how the time passes there, and that there was great risk of being late when one got talking to others. The memory of my father's weakness, and the fight at Saint-Menoux which cost me a court case, often haunted me and gave me a salutary fear of debauchery.

My one passion was snuff, and I was taking more of it than I used to. I had already been taking, since our move to La Creuserie, five sous' worth of tobacco each week, and this increased gradually to ten sous' worth. When ploughing, when I came to the end of a furrow, and stopped an instant to examine the next one, with a view to straightening out any curves, then mechanically I drew out my snuff-box; when mowing, at the end of each swathe, Pop! – a pinch; when hoeing, if I stopped a moment to straighten my back and take a breather, my hand slid automatically into my pocket to take out the snuff-box. The worst days were those when I ran out. I dared not, chiefly because of Victoire, send anyone specially to Franchesse to buy snuff for me, but how long the time seemed, and how irritable I was! I wanted to quarrel with everybody.

It was indeed an excusable weakness; but the inward satisfaction that I felt in my work was certainly the greatest of my pleasures, and the most healthy. To contemplate the returning green of my meadows; to follow passionately in all their phases the growth of my crops and potatoes; to see my pigs improve, my sheep grow fat, my cows have good calves; to see my heifers develop normally into fine specimens; to keep my oxen in good condition in spite of their fatigue, to keep them clean, well-groomed, their tails combed so that I could be proud of them, when, in company with the other *métayers* I went to do the cartage for the château; to fatten properly those I wished to sell – all that made my happiness. You must not think that I thought only of the practical result, the legitimate profit which would come to me from my share of the harvest or the sale of the animals; no! Much of my effort was due to the desire to be able to say: "My wheat, my oats, will be talked about. When I take my animals to the fair they will be admired. The *métayers* of Balutière, Praulière and Le Plat-Mizot, will be jealous when they see that my oxen are fatter than theirs, and my heifers better."

When I met my neighbours going to or returning from the fields, or in winter when we cut the boundary hedges, we always talked about our animals, and I was usually modest about mine.

"Oh! my calves are nothing much this year. My sheep are not fattening as I expected. My oxen have worked too hard, I shan't get anything out of them."

Sometimes the same neighbours would come in to spend the evenings with us and I would invite them, as is usual, to go round the cowsheds. Then I enjoyed their surprise, and their compliments were very gratifying. When, some days before the fairs, we brought the oxen from the six farms to weigh them, if strangers singled mine out for praise, I enjoyed it even more. The greatest joy was if the same thing happened on the day of the fair, and in order to gain still more admiration, I would reply:

"They haven't had too much rest, poor fellows: they worked up to the end of the sowing! I can't reduce expenses any more. They've only eaten two sacks of barley meal and three hundred pounds of oil cake."

"Go on! You haven't got them like that with nothing!" the others would say incredulously.

The fact is, I often lied a bit.

In that way I gained a reputation in the district for being a good cowherd. Some words which Monsieur Parent had used at an inn at Franchesse in the presence of a few big-wigs, were repeated to me. He had said:

"The best worker I have is Tiennon of La Creuserie; he gets the best out of things, and he's got a wonderful way with animals."

I was extremely proud of that tribute, and the memory of it, especially when I was grooming, made my heart beat faster under my greasy smock. A general praised after a successful war must have much the same feeling; and was not my satisfaction as legitimate as his? And less likely to arouse future remorse, as it derived entirely from my own efforts and not from the sacrifice of human lives.

Sometimes, while working in the fields, especially in spring or autumn, when the weather was fine, and the breeze, caressing like a loving woman, brought odours from afar, gentle breaths of life and health, I had the same feeling of proud contentment bordering on complete happiness. It was for me a joy to live in contact with the soil, with the air and with the wind; I pitied the shopkeepers and artisans, who passed their lives between the four walls of a room, the industrial workers imprisoned in unhealthy workshops, and the miners working so far underground. I forgot Monsieur Gorlier and Monsieur Parent; I felt myself the true king of my realm, and I found life beautiful.

XXIX

Victoire was often ill, and she had aged a good deal. She suffered frequently from stomach trouble. Migraine attacks forced her to wear a handkerchief tied round her head for several days at a time, and this made her tense face look even thinner, her cheeks were hollow and she had circles round her eyes. This did not improve her taciturn and difficult character. She lived in a state of perpetual irritation, brooding on the dark side of life and exaggerating the worst aspect of things. She would complain constantly of the troubles she saw ahead:

"We shall have to make the bread on Friday, and the same day we have to churn the butter and pluck the geese. We'll never manage!"

Or, else:

"We simply must do the washing: we haven't any more clean clothes. And the bad weather keeps on. What a nuisance it all is!"

She lamented in the same strain if one of the children was ill, if the harvest promised badly, if the eggs were not a success, if the garden was short of vegetables, if the cows gave less milk. Everything was a subject for complaint. At meals she never sat at table, but busied herself preparing the food and serving it, or looking after the children.

"But look here, wife, do take time to eat!" I would say sometimes.

"Oh! I've had as much as I want," she would answer.

The fact is, she took nothing but a little clear soup, which she swallowed as she moved about; I was ashamed of my healthy appetite, of my two dishes of thick soup. On the days when "it took her in the stomach", she withdrew into herself, saying that nothing tempted her. I urged her to make some better soup for herself, or to boil an egg, but she said she did not want anything, and stuck to the soup from the communal dish.

Although the servant did all the rough work, Victoire still had a great deal to do; the children, the poultry, the cooking and a good part of the housework, without reckoning, when there was enough milk, the butter and cheesemaking; all this was enough to keep a more robust person busy. She was very economical and knew how to make the most of the produce which she carried to the Bourbon market every Saturday. She often scolded the servant when she was wasteful with soap, lights or firewood. Indeed, the poor girl had no easy time.

Our house became somewhat discredited; people complained that I hurried the work too much, that my wife was ill-natured and selfish. For these reasons servants thought twice before engaging with us. We were forced to pay them more than the standard wage.

Fortunately Victoire was an excellent mother and the children seldom suffered from her bad temper. She complained about them, declared that they were unbearable, but she never beat them.

For my part, it was only very rarely that I had the leisure to occupy myself with the children: even on Sundays I hardly found a few minutes to dandle them on my knees; but I can truly say that I was not a churlish father. If, because of our laborious life, they were not cuddled and petted, at least they were not cuffed, and my wife and I had the satisfaction of feeling that they loved us.

When any of our relatives came to see us, Victoire made an effort to be amiable. Except on the Patron Saint's Day, we rarely had visitors and we never considered old Giraud a visitor. He had retired to Franchesse, and came to see us frequently. One day the poor old man came with sad news; he had just been informed, by telegram, of the death of his son, the soldier in Africa; he had succumbed to a bad attack of fever some months before the expiration of his second term of leave, when he had reckoned on returning to France with a job.

My brothers' children came one after the other to invite us to their weddings. On each occasion we made some preparations to receive them, as was the custom. On the wedding day I would go to Saint-Menoux, almost always on my own. I would drink hard on these occasions and held my place well at table. Sometimes, caught up in the general excitement I would forget my cares for a few hours, I would let myself go and dance and sing like the young folk, all the more as Victoire, who had little taste for going out, was not with me.

One unexpected visit was that made by Gaussin and his wife, who were making a tour in the district, after an absence of ten years. One evening they arrived unexpectedly with their little boy, and they laughed a great deal at our extreme surprise. I hardly recognized Catherine in the lady wearing a hat, and who spoke so well; and her husband, with his clean-shaven face and his fine cloth garments, was not much like the Gaussin of former days. Their little Georges was polite, lively, and as gentle as could be; he wanted to play with Jean, Charles and Clementine; but they, too little used to seeing strangers, were sullen, and remained aloof in spite of all our efforts. I spent a happy evening chatting with my sister and my brother-in-law. They went off the next day, for they had only a fortnight's leave, and as they wanted to see all the members of the two families, they could not make a longer stay in each house.

Two or three times the glass-blower from Souvigny, who had married Victoire's elder sister, came with his family. He was a middle-aged man, stout and tall, with a fat, pale face, and a thick red moustache. He coughed; his chest was doubly exhausted by his work as a blower and by drinking. He thought of little else than revolt and death. The idea of death haunted him

"In our work," he would say, "we're worn out by forty; not many live to be fifty. As for me, it won't be long before I'm pushing up the daisies."

That prospect made him anxious to enjoy what remained of his life; he demanded good cooking, meat and wine every day, and that did not keep him from spending a good deal of money out of the house; two or three glasses in the morning, an apéritif in the evening, and great binges on paydays and holidays. As a result, although some months he made as much as ninety francs, money was never plentiful with them. There were times when the butcher, baker and

grocer refused to give any more credit; on those days he had frightful fits of rage, and scolded his wife and children furiously. His wife,
who looked much older even than Victoire, had prematurely white
hair and a fearful, resigned expression. The children were thin little
creatures, cunning and sly, and precociously depraved.

My wife, in whom her sister had often confided, knew how bad
it was in that household. To please her testy brother-in-law, she
spared neither money nor trouble, though she did not do it
willingly. The glass-blower's visits worried me also. I understood
as little of the political questions about which he talked, as I did of
the matters concerning his work, and his sarcastic humbug did not
amuse me. He affected to despise farming. That created constraint
between us: I felt real relief when he went. On days following these
visits, Victoire showed herself more peevish than usual, as though
to make up for her efforts at amiability. It was a good thing for all
of us that the visits were rare.

XXX

The temptations of the devil are for the rich, who, not knowing how
to kill time, run off in all directions as the fancy takes them, in the
hope of finding something new.

But a life so well filled as mine should have preserved me from
this. However, during the fifth year of my residence at La Creuserie
it happened that I was unfaithful to my wife.

The thing happened entirely by chance, and I can't help thinking
that there were extenuating circumstances. Victoire, due to her
poor state of health, was very much detached from the pleasures of
love. Since I was strong and in good health, despite fatigue, it was
natural that I sometimes felt the desire for more proximity. But I
did not dare show my feelings, for I knew I would not be well
received, a fact that made our relations cooler. However, I did not
seek opportunities elsewhere.

I could have found these in the house even, among the servants,
some of whom would not, I think, have been so severe as little
Suzanne of Fontbonnet. But I know that in these conditions the
thing always ends in discovery and in quarrels difficult to make up,
and it is a deplorable example for the children.

So, about the middle of July, after the ground had been watered by thunder rain, I took advantage of the lull between haymaking and harvest to harrow one of my fallow fields. The field was a good way from our house, to the right of the road between Bourbon and Franchesse, and near to the smallholding of Les Fouinats.

I started the harrowing very early in the morning, and as I wanted to make a long day of it, Victoire had sent my meal out by the servant. I stopped my oxen under the shade of an old pear-tree, not far from the cottage; I could see the mud walls and thatched roof, on which grew some green plants. The labourer who lived there, a little red-haired man who stammered, always worked on farms a long way off; his wife, a blonde, attractive woman, also did a day's work occasionally: they had no children. Now that July morning was warm and the soup was too salt; after I had finished eating I was very thirsty and naturally I thought of going to ask Marianne for a drink; I knew she was at home, for I had heard her call the fowls. My oxen were resting, puffing and ruminating at their ease. By way of precaution, I unhooked the chain which attached them to the harrow, and hastened to the cottage.

Marianne was dressing, and was wearing only a short petticoat and a chemise. She had drawn her loosened hair forward in order to comb it. A ray of sunlight playing over this hair made it look silky and attractive, and it seemed surrounded by a halo like that which adorns the figures of saints in pictures and stained glass windows. Her face, although tanned by the sun, had rosy tints in it; her bare shoulders were rounded and full; the nape of her neck showed white and velvety, and her breasts, rounded and tempting, showed above the opening of her chemise.

As soon as I saw her, I felt a little fever run through my body.

"Good morning, Marianne, am I disturbing you?" I said as I entered.

She half-turned her head:

"Oh, it's you, Tiennon! Look what a state I'm in!"

"You're in your own home; surely you've got a right to do as you like ... I've come to ask for a drink."

"That's easy enough."

Without even taking the time to tie up her hair she went to the dresser and took down a big yellow earthenware pitcher, which she filled from the bucket behind the door, and offered it to me. I told her it wasn't necessary to get out a glass and drank almost all the water straight from the pitcher.

"You really were thirsty", said Marianne, smiling through her loosened hair, "unless you find it tastes better here than in your own house."

"Perhaps it's both," I replied. "You know that change . . ."

I even added a few words whose meaning was perhaps more obvious.

She had no difficulty in understanding: her cheeks flushed, her eyes became brighter, her smile became mocking.

"That depends . . . Some things always taste the same," she said.

"Do you know that from experience?" I asked mischievously.

And since she did not move away I plunged one hand into the golden waves of her flowing hair, and the other into her gaping chemise, between her tempting breasts.

Marianne did not repulse me, she seemed rather to provoke my caresses, and we went on to complete the sin.

I was deeply troubled when I left the house, half-expecting an ironic glance from the entire outside world. But my tranquil oxen were still ruminating quietly in the same place. The sun still shone as before. The green lines of the hedges, the fields of corn, the potato patches still looked the same. My fallow field had the same reddish tint of washed clay. The quails still called in the yellowing wheat. Swallows, warblers and wagtails flew round me as though nothing abnormal had taken place. And when I returned to the house, after my day's work, I found no change in the attitudes of my wife, children and servants, nor in that of Monsieur Parent, the steward, who came during the afternoon. That made me think of my unremediable act as something less grave.

My relations with this woman continued for eighteen months, more or less regularly, according to circumstances. We were both careful not to get ourselves noticed, in order to save appearances. So I had to have good reasons for going alone to the neighbourhood of Les Fouinats, either to do some urgent work or to go and see my animals in the pasture. At certain times good excuses were hard to find, and then I did not see her for several weeks. But in the country everything is noticed, prudence is no use, the slightest hint leads to trouble. Marianne never asked me for money, and I did not offer her any, naturally. But I allowed her to put her goats into the neighbouring fields, and also to take grass from them for her rabbits, and I willingly shut my eyes when her fowls did some damage to the land sown with corn. The servants and the neighbours were puzzled by this tolerance; they watched; they saw that I stopped at her house, and that caused gossip. The matter having been reported to Monsieur Parent, he dismissed Marianne and her husband. They went to live a long way from Franchesse, on the road to Limoise. Thus ended our love affair, of which I imagine Victoire never knew anything ... her father, however, had heard rumours, and scolded me severely one day when we were alone -- and I listened to his reproaches with all humility ...

XXXI

In various ways the progress of the century was reaching our valley, despite the fact that each in his own sphere of action -- Monsieur Gorlier, the proprietor, Monsieur Parent, the steward, and my wife -- did all they could to thwart it.

The schools were beginning to fill. The shopkeepers of the town and the best-off of the country people sent their children: there were a few free places for the poor, and these chiefly benefited the children of the mayor's *métayers*.

I should have liked to have had my Jean learn how to read and write, so that he could keep the accounts. Monsieur Frédéric was a municipal councillor, and a friend of the Mayor, so I thought that I might speak to him about it. One day when he came to our house and complimented little Jean on his good looks, I ventured to say timidly:

"Monsieur Frédéric, what he needs now is a few years at school."

He took three great puffs on his meerschaum pipe and finally answered:

"School, school! Good heavens! *You* didn't go to school: that doesn't stop you from working and earning your bread. Put your little lad to work early, it'll be better for him and for you too."

"But there are times, Monsieur Frédéric, when to be able to read and write and count is very useful. I will try to do without him a few years longer at least during the winter, so he can be less stupid than I am."

"Just tell me what more you could have if you were able to read and write and reckon? Education is all right for those who have time to waste. But you manage to spend your days well enough without reading, don't you? Well, your children can do the same, that's all. Besides, you ought to know that a year at school costs twenty-five francs. If you send the eldest to class you can hardly help sending the others. You'll need a lot of money!"

"Monsieur Frédéric, I had thought that you might perhaps obtain a free place for me."

"A free place! The number of free places is very limited: there are always ten requests for each one. Don't count on that, Whatsit, don't count on that. I tell you again, send your boy to take care of the pigs, that will be better than sending him to school."

Monsieur Frédéric rammed his pipe angrily; his voice, his gestures, betrayed impatience. I understood that he objected to schooling. I feared to make him angry by insisting, and I didn't try again. And my children did not go to school.

As to farming matters, I was certainly not one of those who like to throw themselves into novelties and expenses without knowing what the result might be; but when I was convinced of the superiority of a tool I adopted it without delay. Since my arrival at La Creuserie, I had supplied myself with two good ploughs which went more quickly than the very best of the old kind. I should have liked the steward to do for the land what I did for the tools; I tried especially to persuade him to use lime, knowing that everyone who had any experience was delighted with it. But Monsieur Parent became more and more frightened and pulled a long face, saying that it would entail considerable expense. There was only one end to attain: to give the proprietor a sum equal at least to that he had been given the previous year. In fact, if for one reason or another the revenues happened to be lower, Monsieur Frédéric also made a wry face and grumbled:

"The income from my property will no longer be enough to pay the taxes!"

However, we the *métayers* of the six farms, agreed to return frequently to that question of lime; we insisted so strongly that Monsieur Parent ended by speaking to the master, who answered with his most morose air:

"If I wished to occupy myself with the management of my property, I wouldn't employ a steward! You must manage the farms so that they give the most profit. That's your business and not mine."

Monsieur Parent remained in a state of perplexity, hesitating between the fear of laying out money immediately and the desire to increase the future profits. But fear won and he did nothing.

But one day the master came to see us in the harvest field, and being in a good mood, he asked me if the harvest was likely to be good.

"Neither good not bad, Monsieur Frédéric," I replied; "it certainly would have been better if we had used lime."

"It gives good results then, this lime?" he asked, with an indifferent air, twirling his cane round the head of a big thistle.

"Oh yes, Monsieur Frédéric, one often pays the expenses the first harvest; after that the harvests of hay and clover which follow the wheat are worth much more, and that's clear profit; what is more, they say the land feels the benefit for quite a long time."

The master went away without saying a word; he visited Primaud of Balutière, Moulin of Le Plat-Mizot, and all the farms in succession; he asked each the same question, and being convinced of the unanimity of the opinion, he immediately gave the steward orders to satisfy us.

Three days later Monsieur Parent told us that he had arranged with the Bourbon carters to bring some lime to our fallow lands.

It was also for reasons of economy that Victoire opposed all reforms in her department. As a result of the improvement of the small mills in the country, it had become possible to separate bran from flour. A good many people began to take advantage of this improvement, there were even some who were using wheat instead of rye and eating the same kind of bread as the bourgeois. However, we spoke of those people with a little irony; we said that they were going too far, that ... they were on the road to ruin.

Without going so far as that at one stroke, although I still continued to put two measures of wheat and three of rye in each sack, I was quite determined to be done with the bran. Each time I sent the grain to the mill I made the same suggestion, but Victoire disapproved.

"We have to pay the servants enough already, without feeding them on white bread."

In order to overcome this stubborn resistance I devised a stratagem along with the miller. When he brought the flour back he apologized for having taken out the bran, as he now did for everybody. I scolded him, pretending I was angry. But we had enough flour for three months. After that even Victoire did not dare suggest a backward step. From that time we always had good bread, especially as I lowered the proportion of rye until it was left out altogether; that was when the quantity of wheat had increased at our harvests, owing to the use of lime.

It was a great day for me when I saw the round loaf, which in my childhood had been set aside, put in the most prominent place on the table, and when I cut a share for each person from that round, appetizing loaf. The young people of today consider our good wheat bread not good enough if it is just a little hard. Ah! if they were deprived of it, and had it replaced by the black and gravelly bread of former days, they would soon learn to appreciate it!

I quote these three examples of opposition to new ideas, but there were many others on Monsieur Gorlier's part with regard to general improvements, on Monsieur Parent's part with regard to farming, and on my wife's part in the concerns of the kitchen.

XXXII

There are years of great disaster which form sad landmarks in a farmer's monotonous existence. For those of my generation 1861 was such a year. That year was twice cursed for me, for in addition to my share of the collective calamity, I suffered from an individual catastrophe.

In the spring, on one of the last days of April, while putting a couple of young bulls to the yoke I was knocked over and trampled on, in an unlucky, clumsy moment. Result: a broken leg, two ribs battered in, to say nothing of lesions and bruises.

After I had suffered intensely for two hours Dr Fauconnet came to repair me; he bound up my leg with strips of wood and linen bandages and ordered me to stay in bed for forty days.

It was a nightmare; my broken leg tingled, my body was crushed and bruised, the fever was so troublesome the first two weeks that everyone was afraid of serious complications, the result of internal injuries.

The neighbouring women, who took the opportunity to visit me, wore me out with their endless chatter round my bed. All the noises of the household irritated me also: the tapping of metal-tipped *sabots* on the concrete pebbles, the clatter of the cooking-pots, the sound of plates and spoons, even the talking. On bad days Victoire would become irritable too, and would cry. The doctor, whom she sent for several times again, only came when it suited him – late in the afternoon or the next day.

In the country you've got time to die ten times over, as they say, before getting any help. And this is not the least inconvenience of peasant life, especially in our district of isolated farms.

Doctor Fauconnet was even less reliable because he was absorbed in politics and spent several hours at the café every day. He was a Republican, and fiercely opposed to the great bourgeois of the country and to the government of "Badinguet" – Napoleon III. All the "advanced" people of Bourbon swore by him. Some of them, after spending the evening drinking, would go to his house and shout "Long live the doctor! Long live the Republic!" outside his door.

That delighted him but dismayed his old father, who had retired to his château at Agonges.

As soon as I was calmer and capable of conversation Dr Fauconnet used to talk to me about the subjects dear to him. He wanted to tax capital, to suppress regular armies, dues and tolls, and he wanted free education. He told me about Victor Hugo, the great exile, and pitied the victims of the 1852 coup d'état. Then he began to attack the *maire* of Bourbon and his colleagues. No doubt all municipalities make silly mistakes, all *maires* are guilty of favouritism and it is not difficult for a well-read man to criticize them. But although the doctor appeared to talk sensibly I was not too sure if he ought to be taken seriously; for this great overthrower of the bourgeoisie lived a bourgeois life himself. I am sure he would have done more for ordinary people if he had gone to see his patients regularly and charged less for his examinations instead of haranguing at the café every day while he drank cool glasses of beer or fine liqueurs.

Besides, I had other things to think about than the doctor's discourses. Imagine me tied to my bed at the very moment when all the important work was beginning, forced to leave all initiative to the servants! Our son Jean was only fourteen years old and not able to act as master; I was constantly wondering how the animals were being looked after, if the men were getting on with the work, or if they were wasting time. As my illness subsided my anxieties increased, but anger and irritation were pointless; I just had to wait.

I felt an almost childish joy on the day when my dressing was removed and I was able to get up and move about. My leg was still weak, but I was not at all lame. As each day passed, walking with the aid of a big oak stick, I managed to go further from the house. I visited my fields and was happy to see that the harvest promised well.

"My accident has cost us dear," I thought, "but, thank God, it's going to be a good year, we'll be able to make a decent recovery from this set-back."

Alas, I had reckoned without the hail, which came on June 21st and did terrible damage. Right in the midst of a summer's day it grew suddenly as dark as night, the sky had turned so black. At every moment jagged flashes of lightning pierced the darkness, and after every zig-zag of fire the thunder rumbled more loudly. And then the hailstones came down, first as big as partridges' eggs, then like hens' eggs, battering roofs and breaking windows. This was followed by a downpour of rain and the house was flooded. Since the floor was on a lower level than the yard the water came in under the door whenever it rained heavily; but this time water came down from the granary through all the joints in the boards. It fell onto the beds, onto the table and the cupboard; it streamed between the sharp stones in the kitchen, and in the bedroom all the holes in the floor became pools of water. The women interrupted their moans and lamentations to put sheets over the furniture, but too late.

It was a sad business walking round outside, once we could venture out. Old broken mossy tiles were piled up along the walls of the buildings. On the west side especially there were big holes in the roof, through which we could see the grey laths, many of them broken. The countryside looked bruised beneath the premature defoliation of the hedges and trees. The sweetbriar petals and sprays of acacia lay mingled on the ground with twigs and small branches. Among this pitiful wreckage we found the dead bodies of many little birds with ruffled feathers. There were no longer any ears on the corn, the broken stalks leant over in a horrible tangle.

The hay, covered with mud and as though flattened with a mallet, lay over the meadows like a dirty, greasy lump of plaster. The clover showed the underside of its riddled leaves. The tops of the potatoes were broken off. Garden vegetables no longer existed.

The whole valley had suffered in the same way: at Bourbon, Saint-Aubin and Ygrande the destruction was total everywhere. Building workers were more or less the only ones to benefit from this catastrophe. Calls for masons and tilers came from everywhere at the same time, so that for several months they did not know where to start. On the day after the storm the tileworks ran out of supplies, their reserve stocks were exhausted at one stroke. The ordinary output was not enough to meet the abnormal demands, and more than one proprietor was obliged to use slates to recover his damaged buildings; that is why here and there you can still see roofs with tiles on one side and slates on the other. All the old people like myself know that these are souvenirs of the great hail of '61.

We had to begin earlier than usual to gather in the unrecognizable rubbish which was all we had for crops, and it was almost worthless. The hay, soiled and dusty, made the animals ill. The small amount of grain which we were able to get from the cereals was unusable, except to make bad meal for the pigs; even the straw was too battered for use. We had to reduce the litters. We had to buy grain for sowing and for food. The few sous I had saved disappeared that year; I was even compelled to borrow from the steward to pay the servants.

XXXIII

As a result of his reduced income and the expenses incurred for indispensable repairs after the hail, Monsieur Gorlier spent all the autumn and a great part of the winter at Franchesse.

He was in an impossibly bad humour, swore continually and did not take the trouble even to dye his beard: the scattered greyish white hairs showed up against the dark red skin of his face.

All the same he went away during January to the south, where he died suddenly from an attack of apoplexy, less than a fortnight after his arrival there. It was rumoured that Madesmoiselle Julie had appropriated the dead man's savings. In any case, afraid no doubt of meeting his heirs, she never returned.

The property passed to a nephew, a certain Monsieur Lavallée, an infantry officer in a northern town. As a result of this windfall he resigned his commission and came during the summer to settle at La Buffère with his family.

The Sunday after his arrival he summoned the steward and all the *métayers* to the château, of which I knew only the kitchen. But this time we were taken into a fine room with such a well-waxed floor we could scarcely stand up. Old Moulin, from Le Plat-Mizot, nearly fell down flat, and that amused us, but we dared not laugh for fear of being impolite. We kept near the door, standing in silence, gazing at all the astonishing things that we saw before us. There were armchairs and sofas covered in fabric patterned with blue flowers and trimmed with fringes, and they looked surprisingly soft. A little table in front of the fireplace was covered with a cloth that matched the armchairs, and presently I saw that the wallpaper also had the same blue flowers. On the mantelpiece of pink marble veined with red stood a beautiful gilt clock under a globe, and there were also six-branched candlesticks, each carrying a pink candle. These objects were reflected in a great looking-glass which rested on the chimney-piece, its frame veiled with gauze. On each side, in flower-painted *jardinières* standing on delicate round tables, were plants with broad green leaves, very similar to those which grew near the spring in my big meadow. One of the corners was occupied by a whatnot of attractive carved wood, covered with knick-knacks of all kinds – statuettes, little vases and photographs. The only large piece of furniture in addition to the table was a kind of large box in dark red wood, of which I could not guess the use. In a low voice I asked Monsieur Parent what it was, and he said it was a piano. That beautiful room contained in fact only beautiful, useless things. I thought of our dark kitchen with its dilapidated concrete, our bedroom with its little humps and holes, wondering if it was fair that some people should be so well set up and others so badly!

We had been there ten minutes or so when Monsieur Lavallée appeared. He was a man of about forty, rather small, fair, thin and very fidgety. He made us sit down in the fine armchairs with the blue flowers, which he took the trouble to place in a row himself, facing the French windows opening on to the grounds. Monsieur Parent and Primaud, the bacon-eater, shared a sofa. The master sat down in front of us, and after observing us briefly he asked us about our families, our land and our way of working it. He told us that he was determined to carry out good farming, adding that he was counting on us to adopt his ideas.

"In a few years from now we must shine in the competitions!" he concluded.

Monsieur Parent, much moved, applauded, stammering, shaking his big head, and rolling his big eyes; his lower lip hung down more than usual, and allowed a still bigger jet of saliva to drip. That interview gave the master a chance of judging that Parent was not a man to revolutionize agriculture: and shortly afterwards he dismissed him.

Parent was replaced by a rather rough young man with an expressionless face, Monsieur Sébert, who had studied in a big agricultural school. He began his duties at Martinmas, at the same time that the master left La Buffère to spend the winter in Paris. When Sébert came to examine my cattle he declared at the outset that they would all have to be changed.

"Take care of your oxen, we'll sell them; we'll sell the cows too, as soon as they've calved; we'll sell the heifers, the sheep and the pigs; and we'll buy other oxen, cows, sheep and pigs, select animals of good breeds."

At each of the six farms he said the same thing. We would have understood if he had sacrificed the inferior animals, but we found it strange that he wanted to sell all of them, the good and the bad. Every week that winter we had to travel about at night and freeze for hours at some fair or other. We went as far as Cérilly, Cosnes and Le Montet – twenty or thirty kilometres away. It was very fatiguing, very tiresome and expensive, for we could not come back without food, and the innkeepers made us pay a big price for bad stews. And the work in the fields did not get done while we were travelling about this way.

However, when Monsieur Sébert was buying he didn't worry too much:

"Here's a suitable animal", he would say, "I want to have it. Good animals are never dear."

"It's easy to satisfy your whims when you're spending other people's money," was what we *métayers* said among ourselves.

We were all furious with this queer fellow who was ruining us.

At his first visit, in April, Monsieur Lavallée asked me:

"Well, Bertin, how do you like your new steward?"

"Monsieur, he is too fond of trading, he only buys and sells; that can't help us."

"Oh yes, it will. He's renewing your stock with choice animals. In two or three years from now, you will be going to the shows and taking prizes."

All the time that the master was at La Buffère, Monsieur Sébert restricted himself to making us sell those of the new beasts which showed any defects. But after Monsieur Lavallée had departed, the business of the preceding year repeated itself. He made us change everything again, for no reason that we could see, out of pure whim.

The following spring the unanimity of our complaints made the master understand that his steward had cheated him. In the private deed which they had drawn up it was stipulated that, in addition to his fixed salary, the steward would be paid five per cent on both sales and purchases. That clause explained all: the improvement of the cattle had been Sébert's last concern: it was solely to fill his pocket that he had bought and sold without intermission. Monsieur Lavallée wanted to discharge him at once; but the private deed held him to an engagement for six years. Before he would consent to go,

Sébert demanded an indemnity of thirty thousand francs, then he compromised and deigned to accept the twenty thousand francs which the proprietor offered him. The knave had actual saved, in the course of his two years of management, as much as that, if not more. He went to Algeria and settled there, where he became a great vine grower, and where he was no doubt much respected.

That costly experience had one good result: the master was no longer interested in projects for scientific farming. He no longer wanted to be the gentleman who took prizes at shows! Besides, we all assured him that the rewards did not always go to the most deserving and that even the prizewinners suffered worry and loss.... Moreover, he began to find less enjoyment at La Buffère, and his wife was thoroughly bored by it. After that, Monsieur Lavallée's only ambition was to draw as much money from his property as he possibly could. He kept the management in his own hands and merely engaged as an assistant a young man from Franchesse named Roubaud, who could read and write. He was foreman and looked after the accounts. We *métayers* had more freedom and things went better.

XXXIV

The master's two children, Ludovic and Mathilde, often came to our house with their father, or with one of the servants. Ludovic was the same age as our Charles and the little girl was three years younger. I was astonished one day to hear the cook, and another time the coachman, address these children as "Monsieur" and "Mademoiselle," I asked the coachman if he was obliged to address them like this. He assured me that he could not do otherwise, adding moreover that it was the custom to do so with all the children of bourgeois families, even if they were still in the cradle. I told them this at home, adding that they should remember it if necessary. Everybody began to laugh.

"To say 'monsieur' and 'mademoiselle' to those two brats!" said the maid servant. "That's too much!"

They were in fact unbearable, the "monsieur" and the "demoiselle". In their father's presence they were more or less quiet, but with the servants they played all kinds of tricks, and it was another thing altogether when they got into the habit of coming on their own. In the house they ferreted everywhere, upset everything, knocked down with sticks the baskets which hung from the beams, climbed onto the benches and even the polished table with their muddy boots on. Outside they frightened the fowls, separated the little chicks from their mother and chased the ducks until they were exhausted: in fact one evening two of them died. Once the children opened the rabbit hutches, a dozen of them escaped and several were lost. Another time they scattered the sheep and we had endless trouble in getting them together again. In the garden they ran across the beds, over the new seed and the vegetables which had been hoed up; they shook down the unripe plums and pulled off the pears before they were ready. In fact, since no one dared to say anything to them, they became real little tyrants. The little girl in particular seemed to be much happier when she saw we were dismayed by her tricks. Sometimes I would venture to remonstrate timidly:

"Now look, Mademoiselle Mathilde, you're causing a lot of harm; it isn't nice to do that."

She would smile maliciously and go on to do something even worse.

"It amuses me, so there!"

To such reasoning any reply was useless.

But it was little Charles who suffered most from the master's children. They wanted him for a playmate, but as he was unwilling, his mother and I forced him to agree.

"Now, Charles, go and play with Monsieur Ludovic and Mademoiselle Mathilde, since they're so kind as to want to play with you."

But the poor child did not think much of this honour. To play with companions to whom he had to say "Mademoiselle" and "Monsieur" seemed more a duty than a pleasure.

Besides, experience soon proved that they did not want him in order to treat him as a companion, but as a slave, and to torment him.

One day they took him into the park where Monsieur Lavallée had just put up a swing for them. He was obliged to push them one after the other, more or less fast, as they ordered him, and for as long as they chose. Then the two tyrants made him take a turn on the seat, and they pushed him backwards and forwards violently, laughing very loudly because he was afraid. It frightened him to see that it needed very little more to make him strike his head against the post; his head swam and he expected to see the ground open below him. But the more he begged them to stop, the more they swung him fast and roughly. When he did manage to get down he was pale and unsteady and had to sit down on the grass to save himself from falling.

"Oh! what a coward he is!" said the two little bourgeois, delighted.

They were crunching sweets; Ludovic, who was good-natured at times, offered Charles some.

"Have some, they'll make you feel better."

But his sister interfered.

"Mamma has forbidden us to give him any, for it will give him a taste for them. You know quite well he is not like you; he and his father are only tools to serve us."

I had a strong feeling of unease, anger and revolt when my poor boy repeated those words. I was certainly not angry with the vicious little girl, but with her mother, who had taught her to despise the workers.

I took a great dislike to that fat, flabby woman, with her languid, haughty look, who spent her days – so said the servants – half lying on a sofa, varied by short spells at the piano.

"The 'tools' are quite as good as you, you doll," I thought; "without them you would die of hunger, with all your wealth, for what useful work are you capable of?"

Another time the children were playing at horses and carriages, Charles of course being the horse. Long strings called reins were tied to his upper arms. Ludovic held the ends behind, and Mathilde cracked sharply a little whip which was more than a toy.

"Get up then!"

The horse made the round as in a riding school, and the master hardly moved. Then came a moment when Charles was tired and wanted to go at a walking pace. But that did not please Mathilde.

"Gee up then! Run, will you?"

As he showed no willingness to obey, she struck him full in the face with the whip, making a red furrow. Charles began to weep; he wept silently, not wishing to make a noise so near to the big house. Ludovic went up to him, touched to see him weeping.

"Has she hurt you?"

"Yes, monsieur."

"It's nothing. You just bathe it with fresh water."

Ludovic dragged him into the château kitchen and the servant washed with a wet towel the red weal which burned on Charles' face.

Mathilde looked on pitilessly:

"It serves him right: the horse wouldn't run."

Just then Madame Lavallée happened to come into the kitchen to give orders for dinner; she found out what had occurred and said:

"Mathilde, you are very naughty. Ludovic, you shouldn't let your sister behave like that."

She then spoke to Charles.

"You see, my boy, Mathilde is short-tempered; when you play with her you shouldn't cross her."

She made the cook give him a biscuit and a little wine, and sent all three away to play together again.

"Go along, go back to your games, and try not to quarrel."

As a result of that experience Charles avoided the two little tyrants as much as possible. He came into the fields with me; he hid to escape from them. One day they wanted to start playing with him again. He was in a low, damp, meadow taking care of some cows. Before their arrival he was amusing himself making a *grelottière*, (a kind of small oval basket woven with rushes, in which two or three pebbles are placed: when the object is shaken the pebbles make a faint noise like little bells). Mathilde wanted very much to possess this rustic toy, but Charles refused to give it to her, for he bore her a grudge after that cut of the whip. As she insisted trying to take it from him, he pushed her, saying:

"You're always plaguing me; you shan't have it. And I won't call you 'mademoiselle' any more. You're just a mean little cat."

Then she began to whine.

"I will tell *maman*, yes, yes, yes—I'll tell her that you struck me, that you were rude to me, horrid little peasant! And you'll be sent away from the farm, you and your parents."

She went away, furious with rage.

Ludovic was at the edge of the pond nearby, throwing stones at the frogs which he could see near the water. After his sister disappeared he went to Charles and said:

"You know she's quite capable of saying that to *maman*: you were stupid to do that."

"I don't care what she says. I can't bear her teasing any longer; I don't want either of you to come looking for me; you treat me as if I was your dog!"

And he called his cows together and led them out, leaving Ludovic to his frogs.

Monsieur Lavallée came the same evening to speak about the

incident, for Mathilde had fulfilled her threat. The master spoke without bitterness.

"Decidedly our children don't agree," he said. "I have forbidden mine to come seeking Charles, and I will see that they obey my orders."

A week may have passed during which we did not see them; then they came as before. Fortunately, not long after, they departed for Paris.

I heard afterwards from the gardener, who had it from the cook, that Madame Lavallée had been very angry at the affront to her daughter. For a time she had insisted that we should be sent away, as the child had demanded with screams, but her husband had refused to make a tragedy out of the children's quarrel.

The following year Charles, who was almost in his thirteenth year, began to be regularly employed: that gave me a pretext for saying to the little bourgeois that he had no time now to play with them, and he was able to avoid the tyrannical companionship with which no doubt they would have continued to honour him.

XXXV

My mother was now very old and unhappy. She still lived at Saint-Menoux, in the same cottage, and although much bent by age, she continued to go out to do a day's work when her rheumatism allowed her. But for several years it had been difficult for her to leave her fireside in winter.

I went to see her every year at Christmas, when we killed the pig, and took her a basket of fresh bacon and some black pudding. In 1865, when I paid my usual visit, I found her in bed, ill and changed. Her rheumatism had kept her in bed for weeks, and there was no one to help her except another old day worker, her neighbour, who brought her food and helped her to make her bed.

"I shall die here alone. One fine morning they'll find me dead!"

Then she began to rail against my brothers and their wives, then against me. All the rancour accumulated in that bitter old heart poured out in bitter words. Nothing was left of the small savings she had taken with her when she left the family home, and she declared that my brothers had fleeced her. This suspicion, caused no doubt by spiteful gossip, had grown during her long solitary reflections and had become a certainty. She called my brothers rogues and my sister-in-law Claudine a slut. She repeated these revengeful words endlessly:

"The rogues! The slut!"

Stretching her long wizened hands out from under the bed-clothes she made threatening gestures, and sometimes she sat up straight in furious excitement: her face was darker and harder than ever and the grey locks of hair which escaped from under her black headband made her look like a witch pronouncing a curse.

I tried to make her see things more fairly, then I busied myself with lighting the fire for it was cold.

"Don't burn so much wood; can't you see there's hardly any left?" said my mother.

Her store was indeed low, there were only a few scattered bits in the corner of the hearth, and two or three barrow-loads of big, uncut logs between the cupboard and the bed.

"I've been so careful with it that I've let my potatoes freeze. The house is like ice; the wind comes through the trap-door to the loft."

The potatoes were under the kneading trough, and some had rolled across the floor. Those on top were as hard as stone, but the others were not frozen, and I told my mother so, to console her.

When the fire was burning I helped her to get up and to get the soup ready; then I chopped up the rest of the big logs, and went to a neighbouring farm for two trusses of straw, which I put in the loft to prevent the cold wind from coming through the door.

As she ate, my mother became slightly better-tempered; she talked about Catherine, her favourite, who, each year, at Martinmas, sent the money for her rent; and when she came to visit, she brought with her a whole store of good things: sugar, coffee, chocolate and even a bottle of spirits.

"If I could let her know how I am," she moaned, "she'd be sure to send me a parcel of tit-bits."

In order to satisfy her wish I asked the schoolmaster to write a letter to Catherine, and then I ordered and paid for a cartload of wood. Finally I called on the old neighbour, gave her some money and promised to pay her regularly if she would keep an eye on my mother.

On reflection this did not seem to be enough, and I decided to see my two brothers. They had not been living together for a long time. My godfather, who was a *métayer* at Autry, had had bad luck with his animals, and two of his children had been ill for a long time.

Louis was at Montilly and was doing very well – which made Claudine proud and rather arrogant.

The next day I went to see first one and then the other. I pointed out what I believed to be our joint duty towards our mother and said what I had done for her. Louis promised to pay for her bread. My godfather undertook to supply her with vegetables and to send his youngest daughter to take care of her when her rheumatism kept her in bed.

I returned to La Creuserie the next day, fairly pleased with what I had done. Thanks to my initiative my good mother did not lack any necessities during the three years of life which remained to her. My conscience was more satisfied as a result.

XXXVI

Our children were growing up. I was much pleased with our eldest boy, who enjoyed his work and did it with enthusiasm. He ploughed well and began to help me out with the grooming. He was fairly extravagant, though – every Sunday he would go either to Bourbon or to Franchesse and not return until late at night, after a good meal at the inn. Ah, those rare forty-sou pieces, which my father gave me when I was young, would not have gone far with him! And I think he would have been very upset if he had had to be satisfied with so little. Times had changed and business was better; servants' wages had doubled or trebled, and money circulated more. As a result we dressed less roughly, which was reasonable. But perhaps it was a mistake to give up the simple amusements of the past: *vijons*, *veillées*, games with forfeits. The inn was now beginning to be the background for all diversions.

Jean, our second son, was passionately fond of billiards, did not dance much and remained shy with the girls. We had at that time an old-looking, plain servant named Amélie, whom we called Mélie; she had a mannish face, a large mouth and rotten teeth. It was partly because of her age and her ugliness that we kept her, despite her rough manners. If there are comely servants in a house with young lads there is always a tendency for them to have close relationships, with disastrous results, or else there are quarrels, which are also a nuisance.

I believed I could see this unattractive Mélie making eyes at Jean, looking at him lovingly. He was tall and dark, with regular features and a moustache that was already well grown. He was a good-looking boy and I did not think he was stupid enough to respond to these advances.

One winter evening they went together to crush the potatoes and prepare the pigs' food in the cowshed built against the barn wall. I decided to find out if the couple were taking advantage of this tête-à-tête to do something foolish. Leaving the house without allowing the door to creak I crossed the yard and walked quietly the length of the barn as far as the wall of branches which closed off the shed. The lantern gave out a faint light in the interior, which was full of warm steam from the potatoes. After they had been crushed, I saw my imbecile of a boy go up close to the servant, put his arms round her and rub his face against hers. This lasted only a moment; they separated and went on with the work. He went out to get water from the pond while she poured bran and flour from a big basket on to the sticky heap of potatoes; after that she mixed it all with the water which he brought. Then they embraced and kissed again. They went no further. When I saw them take down the lantern I made off quickly and got back to the house before they did.

I said nothing to Victoire, who would have been very upset by the incident. But the next morning, when we got up, I could not refrain from catching Jean in the barn and giving him a lecture.

"An old creature like that, and ugly too! You ought to be ashamed of yourself! Elsewhere you can do as you like, but at home, behave yourself, do you hear me?"

A little later, while attending to the pigs, I told Mélie, who was very upset, that I would throw her out without any explanation if I ever saw anything again. I believe the lesson was learnt, for I did not see them indulging in any underhand behaviour again.

Charles resembled me physically, but in character he was more like his mother. He was rather cold, a little "remote" as they say; he always seemed to be complaining about some injustice, wishing harm to us all. On his way to and from work he would linger behind on any excuse, so as not to mix with the common group. When he went to Mass on Sundays he was never ready like the others. And in the winter, when we happened to spend an evening at Balutière, Praulière or Le Plat-Mizot, he would not go with us, he would usually stay in the house and go out alone the next one. He seemed to be happy when he was acting in direct opposition to everyone else in everything, and he was not at all obliging. Not being cowman he was never willing to do the grooming under any circumstances. On

Sundays he would stay in all day and disappear just when the animals had to be fed.

Jean always returned late, although he knew that his brother was out and that I would have to do everything on my own, for the young servant was often out too. The thing that made me most angry was the fact that this cunning young devil, who was so disagreeable at home, was quite ready to talk pleasantly with the neighbours.

It did not seem to me that we had made any difference between him and his brother, or that he had any cause to tax us with injustice. From the age of seventeen I had given him as much money as the elder boy for his little pleasures. Victoire had always bought the same clothes for them at the same time. I could not understand what it was that made him so surly. Perhaps there was no special reason: perhaps it was his natural turn of mind which made him see the black side of things, nothing more. Perhaps the childhood teasing he had suffered at the hands of the little bourgeois had helped to sour his spirit. And perhaps he was jealous of the slight supremacy which Jean enjoyed as a cowman.

* * *

Clémentine, the youngest, who was often affectionate and hard-working, sometimes difficult too, was more amiable when we were ready to satisfy her caprices. Like all young girls she had a mania for fine clothes. At that time we certainly had no conception yet of present-day luxury, but we had already moved a long way from the simplicity of my younger days. The lace bonnets in fashion at the time were very expensive and needed constant ironing. And dresses were starting to be complicated. The dressmakers in Bourbon, who kept up with fashion, even imagined that they could make their customers adopt the crinoline, which made them look as fat as barrels!

The town girls were soon supplied with them and it was not long before the country girls started to adopt the fashion. Clémentine insisted on having one; but I backed her mother in a firm refusal.

"Certainly not! I don't want to see you dressed like an actress! Just fancy, getting inside a hoop!"

In vain did I try to ridicule that crinoline which she desperately wanted. She returned to the charge a hundred times and when we persisted in our refusal she sulked for several weeks.

Sometimes we gave her permission to go to dances in the daytime, but she was not allowed to go out at night to fêtes and parties, even in the company of her brothers or the maidservant. But after Victoire had given in and gone with her two or three times in the evening the girl saw these occasions as precedents. So when an evening ball was in prospect Clémentine would start a fortnight in advance:

"*Maman*, say we'll go." And then she would try to coax her: "Please, dear *maman!*"

"Don't bother me! We'll see when the day comes!"

When the day did come, nine times out of ten her mother was not inclined to go; then the girl would quiver with fury, restraining her tears with difficulty. During the days that followed she was always in an impossible temper, not uttering a word and doing her work in a sulk. I remember a batch of bread which she ruined the day after an evening dance at Le Plat-Mizot: her mother had not been able to take her because of an attack of neuralgia. Clémentine denied having spoiled the dough on purpose but her bad humour certainly had something to do with it.

However, we often saw the other Clémentine, hardworking, affectionate and gentle. After a short period she spent apprenticed to a dressmaker in Franchesse she was good with her hands and could make our shirts and smocks and iron them. Then, too, she would hurry to fasten our cravats when we went out, to brush our clothes, to bandage our fingers when we tore or cut them, and to take thorns out of them. And if one of us had a cough, she was always the first to make a *tisane*—an infusion of lime-flowers, marshmallow, or blackberry leaves. She was much loved for all these little attentions. Even Charles became more expansive in his sister's company, and sometimes I would see them talking to each other in confidence and laughing like children.

Unhappily the poor child was not strong. When we had to send her into the fields in the summer, although we tried to save her from the hardest tasks, she used to get so thin that it was quite pitiful.

XXXVII

1870 came, and the great war, again one of those years one never forgets.

The harvest had been got in early; we were ready to put up the last rick when, on the twentieth of July, towards ten o'clock in the morning, Monsieur Lavallée came to tell us that the government of Badinguet had declared war against Prussia. He took me aside to tell me that Jean would be called up before long. This confidence truly upset me! Jean was just at the end of his twenty-third year; I had bought him out at the drawing of lots and he was engaged to the daughter of Mathonat of Praulière; the banns were fixed for the first Sunday in August and the wedding for the end of September. So they would really have the effrontery to take him, in spite of the money which I had paid to save him from the service! Alas! it was not long before that was settled: five or six days later he received his summons, and on the thirtieth of July he went away.

I shall always remember the incidents of that morning, the memory of which is one of the saddest in my life. I can see us all, silent round the table for the last meal, with Jean dressed in his travelling clothes. He had returned pale and red-eyed from Praulière, where he had been to say farewell to his sweetheart; he made a great effort not to weep, he even tried to eat; but the mouthfuls which he swallowed seemed to tear his throat. I could eat nothing either; and Charles and the servant were in the same state. On the kneading trough, Victoire and Clémentine were preparing the conscript's little pack, a few clothes and some food. Each moment we could hear their great sighs which were really strangled sobs.

"I have put in three pairs of stockings," said my wife, in a strangled voice. "I don't know if you'll be able to get them into your soldiers' boots," she continued.

"Oh! the boots they give are big," he replied, with an effort. Hanging on the wall near the chimney there was a wooden salt box, the colour of tobacco juice. I looked at it mechanically; some flies were moving on the lid. Jean tapped with the handle of his knife on the edge of his plate, on which was a potato omelette. Mice running about on the beam made some half-crushed grain fall down: the omelette was sprinkled with it. A cat mewed, the servant threw it a spoonful of soup on the floor. In the yard the cock flew on to the closed wicket gate: he was a fine fire-coloured sultan, with a large vermilion crest; he cackled, clucked, and appeared to be coming inside, as he often did, to pick up crumbs. But Clémentine chased him away roughly. Victoire went on in the same hoarse voice:

"I have put in a piece of ham, two hard-boiled eggs, four goats' cheeses – no bread – you can buy that on the way."

He nodded his head for "yes," and the painful silence began again. When the package was at last tied, Clémentine and her mother sat down beside the bread trough, leaned their elbow on it, their heads on their hands, and sobbed violently. We, the four men, remained round the table, sad and embarrassed, before us the almost untouched food, which no one could eat. The situation became so painful that I took it on myself to hasten things. Jean was to meet at Bourbon five or six others who were also going, and whom he knew. The appointment was for midday, and nine o'clock had only just struck. Nevertheless I said:

"Well, my boy, we must go; you'll keep your companions waiting."

"Yes, time's getting on," he answered.

He got up and everybody did the same. The servant had come back from taking care of the sheep: she was a little girl of fifteen whom we had taken on in place of 'Mélie; he kissed her:

"Good-bye, Francine."

He kissed the hired man good-bye, also his brother Charles; his eyes were swollen and his eyelashes damp.

He went over to Clémentine:

"Good-bye, little sister."

"Not yet! Let me go with you part of the way," she said. She and her mother each took one of her brother's arms. I walked behind, with the packets. It was in this order that we crossed the yard, that we came on to the Bourbon road, which had been made several years before. Not one word was said.

A rather strong west wind was blowing, making the leaves of the oaks curl, and twisting the tops of the high poplars; it had rained the preceding days and the pale sun did not yet signify really fine weather. At Baluftière and further, at the entrance to two or three farms, some washing was drying, touching with white the green hedges, which looked dark in the distance. In the fields we saw oxen grazing; a blackbird whistled; we heard a quail cry four times over his invitation to good financial behaviour: "Pay your debts!"

After we had gone about a hundred yards on the road, we came to a turning:

"Let's go back, let him go on alone," I said brusquely.

We stopped, and in turn the two women embraced the departing Jean with tears and cries:

"Oh! my boy, my poor boy, they're going to take you away, the scoundrels! I shall never see you again, never –"

"Jean, my brother, let us have news of you. Oh! why don't we know how to write! Above all, don't get killed, – dear Jean! –"

He, altogether unmanned, wept hot tears also; and I felt that in a moment I should do the same. I pushed my wife and daughter away and embraced the conscript in my turn.

"Go on, my boy, you *must* leave us, let's hope it will not be for long."

I gave him the little bundle. Then brusquely he disengaged himself from the dear embraces and after a last handshake strode away without turning his head. I had to drag the women away; but for me, they would have followed him, I believe.

"Poor child, I shall never see him again; I shall never see him again," repeated Victoire obstinately.

For three days she ate scarcely anything. I was afraid that she was going to be quite ill. However, little by little, in the ordinary course of things, her great grief changed into a latent sadness. And Clémentine soon began to smile once more.

We began work again as though nothing had happened; we got the oats in, the threshing machines whistled and grated; we started the manuring, then the ploughing.

Nevertheless there was a new occasion for grief when Jean told us, in a short letter, that he was being sent to Algeria, on the other side of the "big river". More than ever his mother believed him to be lost. But another letter told us that the passage had been good, that he was not unhappy, and that his companions were all from our own district.

Monsieur Lavallée had left for Paris with his family, and it was said that he had put on his officer's uniform again to go to the war.

We did not know much about the war, except that things were not going at all well for France. Roubaud, the keeper-steward, took a newspaper, and we often went to see him in order to hear the news. His house was always full of people in the evenings – they came from the six farms belonging to the property and even from other more distant places. Early in September the newspaper announced that Napoleon was a prisoner following a great battle which had been lost. His government had been overthrown in Paris and a Republic had been proclaimed.

Soon after there were reactions to this in our region. At Franchesse the *maire* had been replaced by Henri Clostre, the draper, who was a Red. In Bourbon Dr Fauconnet was *maire*, an office he had coveted for a long time. The Prussians however were advancing on Paris. And there was talk of calling up the young men aged between eighteen and twenty. That touched me closely, because Charles and the hired man were both likely to be involved. Things developed quickly and they left in the first days of October. That event caused a lamentable repetition of the scene which had taken place when the eldest had gone; a profound desolation followed.

I remained alone with the women on this big farm of sixty hectares – until I managed to get hold of old Forichon again, and I hired him from week to week until the end. With the aid of Clémentine and Francine, who were often with us in the fields, I succeeded all the same in sowing my corn and lifting the potatoes before the first heavy frosts.

The *métayers* on the other farms were nearly all in the same position. Everywhere you could see women in the fields, exhausting themselves doing men's work.

At the war things went from bad to worse. They said that the great generals had sold themselves to the Prussians, and that one of them, called Bazaine, had handed over an entire army. And the Prussians were still advancing; they beseiged Paris and spread into the *départements*. Roubaud's newspaper announced that they were successively in Moulins, Souvigny, Le Veurdre. Inaccurate news which helped to increase the anxiety we all felt. Wild ideas came into people's minds; some hid all their treasures in deep ditches and hollow oak trees, and one old miser buried his money under a heap of manure in a field; another proposed to take all the local young girls to Auvergne and hide them under a bridge.

In certain communes they organized national guards to attempt to resist the Prussians, should they appear. At Bourbon Dr Fauconnet got a stock of old guns together, and twice a week he called together for practice all fit men, from eighteen to sixty years old. An old exciseman, who had been a sergeant in the regular army, was given command of the militia with the title of captain; he had as assistants two ex-corporals; the old soldiers were heads of companies or squads. At the first meetings about a hundred were present, who were taught to march in step and in line, to carry a gun and to fire. At the end of the practice, the little troop crossed the town in good order, led by the *garde champêtre* banging on a drum, the trumpeter of the fire company, and a band of enthusiastic children. The doctor was delighted; he gave them wine – a litre between three – and some white bread. But he conceived the odd idea of placing a permanent guard of ten men at the *mairie*, to be ready for possible eventualities. The sergeant, Colardon, a carpenter, chief of the post, deserted first, because he was called to make a coffin.

"Urgent work!" he explained, quite reasonably.

The others were not long in escaping in their turn under different pretexts and after a few hours the *mairie* was abandoned. The doctor was furious and asked the old exciseman-captain to punish the culprits severely; but the good old man laughed in his face, saying he could do nothing, and the permanent guard was not renewed. The attendance at the practices became smaller and smaller. At the fourth meeting they had no more than fifty, at the fifth eighteen. At the eighth there were only Monsieur Fauconnet and the captain. Such is the story of the national guard of Bourbon, which entertained everyone for a long time.

* * *

In addition to the terror caused by the possible arrival of the Prussians, there were other very real scourges. First, the cold weather came early and became more and more severe. Then followed an epidemic of smallpox, which claimed many victims. The disease raged so violently in our neighbour's house at Praulière that at Christmas it caused the death of Louise, Jean's fiancée; her young sister was disfigured, and wept bitterly for her lost beauty, regretting that she had not died too.

When the Mathonats were all stricken and there was hardly one able to take care of the others, Victoire and Clémentine said they intended to go and nurse them, if they needed it. But that terrible malady was said to be so contagious that I was not at all willing to let them go. I said that we had enough trouble of our own, that, after all, the Mathonats were nothing to us, that they had relatives not far off, whose duty it was to look after them. As the women persisted in spite of what I said, I thought of making out that I was ill, so I began to be very sullen and miserable, eating nothing and pretending to be feverish. I only had a cold and was in poor shape, but I exaggerated it all. They took pity on me and only went to Praulière after the death of Louise, when the malady was on the wane. We had the good fortune to escape.

As though to add a sense of divine punishment to all these evils, the sky was often speckled with red marblings, at times it even became a uniform purple on one side of the horizon, as though covered with a bloody shroud. These were only unimportant atmospheric phenomena of which we should normally have taken no notice; but in those days of woe, of disaster and misery, they gave us lugubrious notions. The red sky announced deadly battles; it was the blood of the dead and wounded which stained it. The terror grew; we spoke of the end of the world as quite likely. Besides, every Sunday the priest enlarged on the idea of divine vengeance and horrible calamities; he seemed pleased at the universal misery and was delighted when he saw the women with anguished faces, and when they abandoned their over-fine dresses of the past few years.

"Your pride is lowered," he said as though inspired, "but it will be lowered still more; your humiliation shall become deeper!"

And before the threat of these other imminent scourges everyone bent their heads sadly.

At long intervals letters arrived from Jean or Charles. The elder, still under the African sun, was fairly happy. But Charles, who was with Bourbaki, in the army of the Loire, suffered a great deal from cold and often from hunger. He said he was badly clothed, and that they had to make long marches in the snow, wearing boots with cardboard soles. In the Côte-d'Or he was in a battle, and was nearly taken prisoner. Afterwards he was stranded in the Jura Mountains, where winter was even worse than here.

When the postman brought a letter, Victoire and Clémentine would run to Roubaud's house to have it read. But the steward often found it difficult to decipher it, he was not very expert in reading handwriting, and the letter was usually written on crumpled and stained paper by an obliging comrade, who scribbled for Charles a few lines with a pencil which hardly marked. Each of those letters bore signs of the circumstances under which it had been written, and of the extent of the writer's education. One day a long one arrived, which gave such heartrending details that everybody wept. Several, written by practical jokers contained coarse jokes, almost insults.

Roubaud did not undertake the replies, pretending that he was too busy, but it was chiefly because of his want of skill. Clémentine used to go to Franchesse to the grocer's daughter, who knew how to write; she had to go on a week-day, because on Sundays the grocer's customers were so numerous, each with the same motive of pestering the young girl to write their letters.

Ignorance seemed a great hardship during those months, because it bothered us more than usual.

A troubled spring succeeded that sad winter. The war with

Germany had come to an end, but there was still war: Paris, in revolt, struggled against the army. While nature, rejoicing in her annual reawakening, spread out her gifts lavishly, blood still flowed!

Paris was conquered, the rebels were massacred or imprisoned by hundreds, by thousands, and our children were returned to us. They returned, except all the latest conscripts, whom they kept for their term of service – and Charles was one of them – and except, alas! those who were dead, and those who had disappeared, of whom no one knew anything. The husband of a young wife at Saint-Plaisir was one of those. No news of him had come since November and he did not return with the spring. Three or four years later, the young widow married again. But afterwards people told her that there were always soldiers of the '70 arriving; they were those who had been taken prisoner, and condemned to several years more for having tried to escape; we saw them again only at the end of their term of imprisonment. So the poor woman lived in constant terror of seeing her first husband return. He never came back. Nevertheless, there was a rumour on this subject, which with time became a legend. Some people declared that they had seen him at Bourbon, and were assured that he was determined to disappear without showing himself, so as not to create difficulties for his former wife.

XXXVIII

Jean returned early in June, in time for the haymaking. His experience during his sojourn in Algiers had made him happy-go-lucky. Fearing that it would grieve him, we had refrained from telling him of the death of his fiancée. He took the sad tidings very quietly.

"Poor little Louise, I did not expect that," he said simply.

But it did not make him lose a meal nor an outing, and less than a year after his return, he married Rosalie, a daughter of Couzon, at the Carnival of 1872.

Two months later, at Easter, it was Clémentine's turn; she married François Moulin, of Le Plat-Mizot, the sixth of a family of nine.

The daughter-in-law and the son-in-law both came to live with us at La Creuserie, and this enabled us to do without the servant and the man whom we usually kept. But it made three families, and when there are three families in one house, things never go on long without some friction.

Rosalie was a little blonde, but no beauty: her neck was sunk in her shoulders, and she had freckles all over her face. But she was resolute, energetic and bold, talked a great deal, and worked to match. Clémentine was less robust, especially as she became pregnant at once and suffered from a kind of languor which left her with no appetite; she would make herself *tisanes* and little dainties, and she ceased to help with the washing. Rosalie did not hesitate to talk sarcastically about ladies who were ill if they put their hands into cold water, and who were obliged to take care of their little health by eating nice little tit-bits.

On baking days they took it in turns to knead and to attend to the oven. But one day the bread which Rosalie had kneaded was not a success, and she said it was Clémentine's fault for having lit the oven too late. The next time, my daughter, in her turn, declared that the crust of the bread was burnt, and that it was her sister-in-law's fault, because she had over-heated the oven. By common consent, they decided that one should do it all, so that they could not blame each other for defective work. From this arrangement Rosalie came out very well, for she was stronger, despite Clémentine's violent efforts to work conscientiously.

We had just provided ourselves, with the master's consent, with a donkey and a little carriage. During August friction between the two young families increased. Clémentine had spoken first of taking the carriage and going with her husband to the fête of the Patron Saint at Ygrande, for Moulin had an uncle in that commune. Then Jean and his wife expressed their intention of going to Augy, for the same fête day, to see a brother of Rosalie's who lived there; they also wanted the donkey and the carriage.

The two women argued, Rosalie telling my daughter that an invalid, a good for nothing, ought not to go out driving; Moulin interfered and called Rosalie a nasty creature. A real quarrel developed and threatened to last a long time. Victoire was much distressed. But I put a stop to things by declaring that Clémentine should have the carriage because she had asked first. Jean's wife was furious at my decision and gave me black looks for several weeks. After that the two sisters-in-law hardly spoke except to mock and criticize each other.

Besides, Moulin did little to make himself liked. He had a mania for giving advice on every subject; he even took upon himself to give advice about the grooming of the animals to *me*, who was considered one of the best animal-tenders in the country. That did not go down very well, and Jean did not hesitate to let him know that he irritated us. The resulting tension made our daily intimacy unpleasant.

XXXIX

Victoire had never been able to reconcile herself to Charles' absence. She would fret if a letter was delayed a few days; or if a letter made any allusion to night watches in the cold, or painful marches under the hot sun of summer. She would fret if she had a dream in which he appeared to her suffering and ill, and she imagined him dying perhaps, in a hospital, without tenderness and care. The end of his term drew near, however; but some late manoeuvres kept him away from the end of September to the end of October. As the days of waiting became fewer, Victoire's agitation and fears increased. She had fattened ten chickens; she wanted to kill the best one to celebrate the return of her son. Behind the barn there was a vine arbour, which I had planted at the beginning of our stay at La Creuserie, it was very productive at that time; it was well-situated, and that year it bore some superb golden grapes.

"Oh, dear!" my wife said one day as she looked at them, "if only I could manage to keep them till he comes back!"

During the next meal she said to us:

"Listen, I forbid you to touch the grapes in front of the barn; they're precious, I'm keeping them for Charles."

We all promised to leave them alone; only Moulin remarked that before the arrival of the soldier, the insects would no doubt have destroyed them all. Victoire watched, and soon saw that her son-in-law was right. Because they were in a good position and sweeter than the others, the hornets and wasps buzzed round all day, vying with each other in extracting the juice from the finest berries; some of the branches were almost bare, having only hard unwanted fruit and the flabby, dried skins left on them. In this way the poor soldier would run the risk of not even tasting the fine grapes that had been specially reserved for him. Maternal love makes women ingenious: my wife searched in her rag drawer, and with pieces of old linen, worn thin enough to allow the air to penetrate and resistant enough to keep the greedy insects off, she made some bags with a running string near the top. Clémentine and Rosalie, who were not in her confidence, watched her making these, and were puzzled. When thirty were tacked together, she placed a ladder against the wall of the barn, climbed to the height of the grapes, and enclosed thirty of the finest bunches in the protective bags.

* * *

Towards the middle of October, little Marthe Sivat, a dressmaker in the town, came to get some chickens for her sister's wedding breakfast.

"Goodness! are those grapes you've got up there?" she exclaimed, looking at the trellis. "What a clever way to protect them. Now I think of it, they told me to get some for dessert; will you sell them to me, Madame Bertin?"

My wife would not hear of selling the grapes.

"No, my girl, no! I wouldn't sell them even if I was offered much more than they're worth: I'm keeping them for my boy Charles."

"Ah! your son's coming back this year? You're quite right. You must take care of them; we'll find something else for the wedding dessert."

And laughing, little Marthe skipped lightly away.

* * *

A few days later a poor woman, whose husband was ill, came. He complained constantly of his stomach, he was feverish and had no appetite:

"I've been cooking eggs for him for several days," she explained, "but now he won't look at them. I took him a bit of meat yesterday; he didn't touch it. His only wish is for grapes: I've come to you to buy some."

Victoire was sorry for her, and gave her three bunches, saying she would give her those for her invalid; but she was careful to repeat:

"They're not for sale, you see: I'm keeping them for Charles, who's coming back from the army."

The whole of that year the Lavallées had not appeared. Mathilde had been married in the spring, and the parents stayed on in Paris until August, for Monsieur Ludovic was taking some examinations. Just then they were in Savoy, the country of the chimney-sweeps; they were at a thermal establishment where the waters were supposed to have the singular virtue of making the women thin and their husbands fat. Afterwards they had stayed with friends, and it was only during October that they came to La Buffère to spend the latter part of autumn.

The evening before Charles was expected to return they paid their first visit to us. Contrary to her usual custom Madame Lavallée came with her husband. Having grown stouter in growing older she had become still more listless and walked with very short steps, her fat body continually swaying from side to side. She looked like one of the old towers of Bourbon walking along. Her husband was still slender and alert. His angular face emphasized his quickly-changing expressions and his overcoat hung loosely on him.

After the first obsequious bows I took Monsieur Lavallée to visit the cowsheds, where some minor repairs were essential. During that time his wife, who had not wanted to sit in the house, walked slowly round the yard with Victoire. Chance decreed that she caught sight of the vine and its little white bags through which the fine bunches of grapes could be seen.

"What, Victoire, grapes still! Do you know they're very scarce? We haven't a single one at the château, and they are my favourite fruit. Why have you taken so many precautions to keep them till now?"

Victoire hesitated a moment, then with a strained smile she said:

"Madame, it was so that I might have the pleasure of offering them to you."

"Oh! Thank you! What a charming thought! You must bring me some this evening."

Victoire cried:

"Rosalie, get the little basket at once and fetch the ladder from the barn, gather those grapes and take them to Madame's house."

At supper that evening our daughter-in-law returned to the incident:

"It wasn't worthwhile taking such care of the grapes; my brother-in-law won't get much good from them."

For once Moulin agreed:

"What a miserable business it is; we're just as much slaves as they used to be in olden times."

I was silent, realizing how true those remarks were. I seemed to hear the explicit answers of Victoire to Marthe, and to the poor woman with the sick husband:

"No, no, I don't want to sell them! I'm keeping them for my son Charles."

And a little cry of admiration from the lady had been enough to make her offer them very humbly!"

"It's quite true," I thought, "we are still slaves."

Victoire certainly felt a little remorse for this action, but on the other hand, she felt a certain pride in having been able to pay court to the proprietor's wife, of having made her look favourably on us through offering her a gift which pleased her. Aware of all this, she replied in a conciliatory tone:

"Don't say any more about it: it isn't my fault; I had to please the lady."

XL

After twenty years at La Creuserie I was hardly any better off than when we went there; I had just been able to pay back the thousand francs that I still owed for my share of the lease of cattle. It had been a prosperous period during which more fortunate people had made a good deal. But Monsieur Parent's hesitations, the hail of '61, and Sébert's rascalities had made my first years too difficult; and then when I was afloat again, and in a fair way to make something – although Monsieur Lavallée had raised my annual rent by two hundred francs – there had come that new disaster, the war.

Afterwards, thanks to a succession of good harvests, I had finally been able to make some little profit; and after the deaths of my wife's parents, which happened with a month's interval in the winter of 1874, I found myself in possession of about four thousand francs.

Now, it was very worrying to keep this money in the cupboard; to begin with, it did not gain any interest there, and then I was afraid of thieves, for in the summer, the house was often left unoccupied. The notary at Bourbon did not know just then of any advantageous investment, so I thought of Monsieur Cerbony.

Monsieur Cerbony was one of the big businessmen of that district. He had three farms, and was a grain and wine merchant; he dealt also in manures and seed. In fact, he monopolized all the rural businesses. He was still a young man, with a smiling face, and was very likeable. Unlike most of the farmers-general, who were arrogant and vain, he was homely and jovial, shook hands with everybody, spoke to us peasants in patois and stood a lot of drinks.

He had built large shops and a one-storied house with balconies and arabesques, which made a grand show. He lived in fine style, travelled a great deal and kept a mistress in Moulins, they said, even though he was married, and had a family. He also went frequently to Paris, or the south. We knew nothing of his origins, but he was reputed to be very rich, and it was said that he did all this business from choice rather than from necessity.

I had heard that Monsieur Cerbony received money in the same way as a banker, simply giving a note with his signature as a guarantee. As I had confidence in him, I went to see him one Sunday morning after the first Mass, on the pretext of selling him my small quantity of oats. Having found him alone, I said timidly:

"Monsieur Cerbony, I have a little money at my disposal, I want to place it somewhere: will you take it?"

"How much have you?" he asked, screwing up his mouth.

"About four thousand francs, monsieur."

"It's not much. However I could use ten thousand at the end of the month. See your neighbours and friends; make it ten thousand francs among you."

"Monsieur, I don't know anyone who – Yes, though – I have a neighbour who ought to have about two thousand francs."

This was Dumont of La Jarry d'en bas: he had told me about it one day when we were both cutting the boundary hedge.

"All right, that's settled, bring me the six thousand francs at the end of the month, I'll manage to find the rest elsewhere. I'd like to please you, however, seeing you're a good customer. You know that I pay five per cent, like everybody else. Good-bye!"

The same evening I went to see Dumont of La Jarry to tell him about the arrangement; to my great astonishment he showed no enthusiasm:

"Cerbony, Cerbony," he said, "he's a man who does a lot of business, but we don't know if he's rich: suppose this should turn out badly?"

"But, stupid, he makes masses of money. If I had his earnings for one year, I should live at ease for the rest of my life."

"Fiddlesticks! If he earns a lot, he spends a lot; you know that as well as I do. Look here, Tiennon, I should like to lend you my two thousand francs, but on condition that I deal only with you; let us go to the notary together to make out a bill. I shall only ask four and a half per cent interest; Cerbony will pay you five, you will have a half per cent for your trouble."

I was on the point of taking Dumont's money on those terms, but Victoire and the two boys, dissuaded me.

At the appointed time I carried my four thousand francs to the busy brewer, explaining to him that my neighbour had lent his money elsewhere just before I went to see him; I added hypocritically that he was very sorry to miss such an opportunity. Cerbony had an outburst of bad temper:

"It would serve you right if I sent you about your business. However, hand over what you've got; but mind, it's only to please you."

He emphasized those words, and his face again wore its usual genial smile, while he spread out my gold coins and felt my banknotes. I was delighted at his friendliness.

Alas! my delight did not last long.

On the first of March the following year, that is to say, three months later, when we were loading wood in one of our fields beside the road, the Franchesse postman arrived from Bourbon, where he went each morning to get the mail; he stopped to talk:

"Have you heard the news?"

"What news?"

"Cerbony – the famous Cerbony – bolted three days ago. At the beginning of February his wife went with a lot of luggage: since then he has been continually sending things away; the servants understood nothing; the house was more or less empty and the shop too. On Tuesday he set off early to Moulins and he hasn't been seen since. But yesterday he wrote to the *maire* from Switzerland saying he would not be back again. They say his affairs are in a terrible muddle; he owes money to everybody!"

I was on the wagon piling up long branches from the pruned trees; I felt a sudden faintness, then a kind of giddiness which made me stagger. Jean saw it and gave me an anxious look, while he tried to hide his concern and to answer the postman.

At Bourbon, where I went the same evening, everybody confirmed the news of the disaster. I did not want to go to the notary, who would probably have laughed at my misfortune, being given that way, especially about money invested outside his office. But I went to see the magistrate's clerk to whom all the country people brought their difficulties. Almost in tears, I told him my business. While attempting to comfort me he said he could do nothing to help me.

"There's nothing to be done at present; you will be called with the other creditors; you can only give your documents to the receiver."

At home there were endless lamentations from Victoire.

"After all the trouble we've taken to save a few sous, and then we lose everything at one go! My God, what a misfortune! And the little bit of money which came from my parents! That makes it worse! ..."

Everyone was sad and very worried. Charles alone showed himself a philosopher, and tried to console us.

"What can you do? Don't think any more about it: it's lost, and that's it! It won't change anything in your way of living; you won't work any more or less than you did before ..."

I had moreover the consolation of knowing that there were plenty of fools like me. I congratulated myself above all on having taken Victoire's advice about Dumont's money. The good Cerbony had made a practice of taking as much as possible from his victims. A poor old gardener had borrowed from a third person several thousand francs in order to supply the gentleman with the sum he demanded. Stripped of his savings, and unable to repay his creditor, one night the old man climbed the rock on which stood the towers of the old château and threw himself into the lake below. Early next morning the washerwomen found his body on the shore.

I had to do many irritating things and make several trips to Moulins, for six of us creditors had got together in order to consult a solicitor. After two years, when all was settled, they gave us five per cent. I received two hundred francs. In various expenses, including travel, I had spent that amount.

XLI

While in the army, Charles had lost his surliness; he was pleasant to everybody now and expressed himself better than we did. At first he even laughed because we talked so badly.

"I think it's stupid to talk like that," he said; "when we go among people who talk properly we feel awkward, and can find nothing to say, or else we say silly things in a way which makes them laugh at us. I don't see why, because we are peasants, we should talk nonsense."

"It would be funny," said Rosalie, "if we began to talk like the lady at the château. It would soon be noticed; everybody would say: 'Listen to them trying to cause trouble!' "

"Nobody but a fool would say that," Charles answered; "and if we know that we have some intelligence we ought to despise the opinion of fools. I don't ask you to adopt the manners of Madame Lavallée: all I want is that we should murder our words less."

No doubt what Charles said was reasonable enough, but he did not manage to get us into the habit of talking any differently; on the contrary, it was he who, little by little, reverted almost entirely to his former way of speaking. It's difficult to go against the ways in which you were brought up. Even trying to do so can be asking for trouble.

XLII

My son-in-law and my two boys were in their prime; I still held my own and we four might easily have made the farm profitable. But the strife between the two young families continued, and Moulin was obliged to go. Thanks to the efforts of his relatives and to mine, he was able to rent the little holding of Les Fouinats from Monsieur Lavallée, and Roubaud, the steward, promised to employ him as often as possible at the château, as assistant to the gardener and general handyman.

In spite of that, the parting with our daughter was a great grief to Victoire and to me. We feared that she would be unhappy. She had only been married five years, and already she was pregnant for the third time. Her health still gave us a good deal of anxiety; she became thinner and paler and always looked depressed.

The first winter Clémentine found life in the little house tedious, and often used to come with her babies to spend the afternoon with us. She would take back with her a bottle of milk, sometimes even a basket which her mother would fill with cheese, butter, fruit and, on baking days, some *galette*. However, because of her state of health it was not long before the poor child paid us fewer visits and finally, owing to her condition, she stopped coming altogether. My wife however continued to take some provisions to her house. But one fine day Rosalie intervened. It happened when the cows were nearing their time, and there was so little milk that we had to do without ourselves. Even then my wife wanted to take some to her daughter, but our daughter-in-law seized the opportunity to say that she had had enough of it, working and killing herself for others, that she would go if things went on in that way. Victoire having answered gently that a few half-pounds of butter, a few cheeses and a little milk was not a great deal, she replied in a sharp tone that it was enough to keep the family in groceries and haberdashery, and that it was hateful to see Clémentine enjoying as much as she wanted of those things while those who had the trouble of preparing them had to go without.

"There's no point in working," she added, "if all that comes in at the door is to go out of the window; we shan't even make ends meet!"

This unkind opposition of Rosalie's, which recurred on every occasion, made my wife very unhappy; she complained when we were alone; we discussed it at length during the night. We gave each of our children an annual wage, so they had no part share in the business. But we recognized, nevertheless, that they had certain rights of control and criticism. They contributed to the prosperity of the household, they co-operated in work which they would continue on their own account later. We had to admit that they might consider themselves defrauded if the products of the combined work went out without bringing in any profit. It is only fair to say that Charles did not trouble himself; he even approved of the gifts being made to his sister. But the elder, goaded by his wife, supported her objections.

Therefore we had to give no more presents to Clémentine, at least openly. We became cunning. I often carried to her, hidden under my smock, little packages of provisions and food. But Rosalie's sharp eyes were everywhere, and it was difficult for Victoire to send the smallest thing without her knowledge; and there were too many bitter or violent scenes.

But a more important event occurred, which relegated our family troubles to second place.

XLII

Without boasting, I may say that the farm had gained in value a good deal since I began to work it. I had taken as much trouble as if it had been my own, or, as if I had been assured of spending my life there. I had cleared out the stones entirely from some parts, rooted out the brambles from others, thinned out the hedges that were overgrown, and dug ponds where there had been no water. After the gardener at the château had agreed to give me some lessons in grafting, all the wild fruit trees in the hedges had yielded good crops. I had been intent on making passable the lane which led to the road – neither Monsieur Lavallée nor his uncle had wanted to do so. All the fields had been limed a second time and gave good harvests; the meadows produced double, thanks to compost and manure; and my animals were almost always the best among those of the six farms. Business continued to be fairly good, and I would soon find myself in possession of a sum equal to that which I had lost.

But one day Roubaud came to see me, looking very sheepish:

"The master wants to raise the rent three hundred francs, to date from next Martinmas."

This news shattered me. Ten years before I had been obliged to resign myself to a first increase of two hundred francs which was justified to some extent by the rise in the price of cattle. But I could see no reason for this new increase, which would have raised my annual rates to nine hundred francs a year, and meant that the master, apart from half the produce and excluding my rent in kind, wanted a further nine hundred francs from me. Agricultural prices were not higher than they had been ten years previously. Profits had only gone up because of the shared outlay and also because of our toil and sweat.

I swore by God and the devil that I would not accept any increase.

"Think it over", said Roubaud. "You don't have to give a definite answer today."

"I *have* thought it over!" I replied.

And I repeated my oath: this injustice sickened me!

However, after talking it over with Victoire and the boys I offered an advance of one hundred francs. Roubaud transmitted my reply to the master, who was in Paris. But he, far from wishing to compromise, indicated shortly afterwards that those *métayers* who had not already agreed to the new conditions must find themselves another place. This was a definite dismissal to the tenants of Le Plat-Mizot and Praulière, and to us.

I should never have believed that the thin, restless Lavallée concealed such perfidy beneath his affable exterior. Later, Roubaud passed on to me something he had said:

"*Métayers* are like domestic servants: in time they become too bold; you have to change them now and then."

XLIV

A great weariness, physical and mental, overcame me. At every age there are periods of vexation when everyday miseries seem more intense, when everything conspires to sadden you, when you're weary of the life you lead. But in our declining years these impressions are more bitter and more painful. I was approaching my fifty-fifth year and my face was losing its last colour; the white hairs multiplied in my beard and it had snowed heavily on my temples. I could no longer work so hard.

The blow was a brutal one. On this farm of La Creuserie I had spent twenty-five years of my life, the best years of my full maturity, and I was identified with the place. To the neighbours, to all who knew me well, was I not "Tiennon of La Creuserie", and to others "Old Bertin of La Creuserie?" Long custom had made my person and the farm seem inseparable. Was I not linked to this house which had been my home for so long? To this barn where I had heaped up such stores of fodder, to the cowsheds where I had tended so many animals; to the fields whose smallest veins I knew – the seams of red, black or yellow clay, the flinty and stony parts, as well as the free and deep soil; to the meadows I had mowed twenty-five times; to the hedges I had cut, the trees I had pruned, under which I had taken shelter from the rain, or sought shade in the hot weather. Yes, all the fibres of my being clung to this land and this old house from which a gentleman was driving me away for no other reason beyond greed and the fact that he was the master.

Things I had never thought about before now passed through my mind. I began to reflect on life, which I found cruelly stupid and dull for poor people like us, condemned to forced labour for ever.

The first fine days come: quickly, let's sow the oats, harrow the ground for the wheat, plough and dig.

April comes with its mild weather; the buds open, the birds sing, the peach trees are pink and the cherry trees white: quick, we must sow the barley and plant the potatoes, quick, into the garden!

The "merry month of May is often dull and rainy, but the young green shoots are always a pleasant sight: take the plough onto the fallow land, clean the ditches, weed and hoe!

June, the hedgerows are full of wild roses, the acacias heavy with white clusters, flowers and nests everywhere: – we get up at three o'clock in the morning to do the mowing, the work's so hard as the sun gets up, so terrible at noon, we work without stopping until nine or ten in the evening.

July with its days of warm languor. Sweet siestas on soft sofas in closed drawing-rooms ... The delight of cool shade in a leafy garden, in meadows where the second crop is sprouting: – but there can't be any siestas ... In great haste we must get the hay in; the cereal crops are ripening. Quick, let's cut the rye and tread it out, we need the straw to bind up the wheat which is nearly ready. Courage! Into the wheat fields! Let's cut down the dry stalks in great swathes! Let's bind the burning sheaves, prickly with thistles or cammocks. Build the heavy sheaves up into stacks. I'm exhausted, but I must rally the others:

"Work keeps you going! Moving about will give us air. Courage, lads, courage!"

Or else, by way of variation:

"Let's hurry and get the wheat in. In this heat the oats will ripen quickly; we'll get behind."

August is just as hot. Season of holidays, season of rest. The oats are in, or soon will be. The threshing machines are at work. The neighbours help each other; we have to thresh the oats from eight farms. But when we return covered with dirt and dust, we must get on quickly with the work that had been interrupted! We must start on the big manure heap, cut it up into equal cubes which we line up symmetrically on the carts and transport to the fields while the paths are dry.

September, holidays still, walks, good shooting-parties. All our fallow land to be divided up, the potatoes to be lifted, always too much to do.

October and its mists: – The days are getting shorter, we must make them longer. We can gain an hour in the morning, an hour in the evening. Let's speed up the sowing, take advantage of the fine weather – rain may come. Courage lads!

Here's November at last, winter, and calm. We still have to go over the stubble fields, tidy up the meadows, trim the hedges. Now all the animals are in the cowshed. We have to get up at five o'clock all the same: let's do the grooming in the dark, we shall be ready earlier for work in the fields, – and we shall come back covered with mud, dirty up to our thighs. The evening is just right for cutting the root-fodder for the oxen and the fat sheep, and for cooking the potatoes for the pigs.

"Courage, lads! let's not sit idly by the fire."

The fire doesn't give out much warmth; the wood's damp, the chimney smokes, we might get stiff; it does us good to move about. Only snow can sometimes give us half a day of rest. It's the time when we make new fences for the fields, hay-rakes, too, when we repair our tools. There's too much to do in summer to waste time on such trifles.

Yes, there it is, the farmer's year. Has he the right to complain about it? Perhaps not. All poor people are in the same position and work all the days that God made. But in their shops, factories or workshops city-dwellers do not have to contend with the elements – or at least very little. In *our* lives it is the weather which plays the greatest part, and the weather delights in thwarting us. Here comes the rain, and the rain doesn't stop: the land is soaked, to shift the soil would be folly; the grass grows in the cornfields and we cannot clean them out; the ploughing and sowing are late and they go badly. Then there is the drought, which lasts for weeks and months, the vegetation fades; we have to go a long way to water the animals – and if we persist in trying to plough we tire the oxen, we wear ourselves out, we risk breaking the plough at any moment. A shower follows, a very brief one, but during hay-time it can upset the whole plan for the day . . . Here's a storm and we tremble in fear. Here's the snow which lasts several weeks, hindering outdoor work, causing a delay which it's hard to make good again. Here is frost without snow, with sunshine during the day which destroys the roots of winter cereals. Then the weather in autumn is too fine and no frost comes to kill the insects which attack the wheat as it sprouts; but it comes in May to spoil our young plants and destroy the buds on our vines. For one reason or another there is always something to complain about.

But the harvests are not all. We do some breeding; each year seven cows give us calves. As soon as each cow nears the time of calving you have to watch her day and night, and when the time comes you have to take care of the mother and the calf – we are the slaves of our animals. And they suffer from all kinds of ills: the calves get diarrhoea, the sheep get fluke-worm or tuberculosis, the pigs get paralysis – a whole herd of cows can get foot and mouth disease.

We go to get the vet or the *guérisseur*; we use our own experience and do our best; we look after the animals as though they were human beings. And in spite of all that they die.

We go to the fair to sell, the prices are low as though by chance, or simply, the merchants are crafty and take advantage of us. If, on the other hand, we're buying, our lack of experiences leads us to pay too dearly and we're not very successful.

After the threshing we sell the small amount of grain that we have over at a low price, because we find ourselves short of money. The rich proprietors and big farmers, who have capital and convenient storage, wait till later and often profit from a considerable rise in price.

* * *

And all the time we have to be there, wearing the same patched and dirty clothes, with the animals' hairs sticking to them; we live in the same old, ugly, dark houses surrounded with ruts, mud and manure – we are prisoners in the same setting. In other districts there is land different from ours, more hilly, or flatter; there are rivers much wider than the one at Moulins; there are mountains, there are seas. We shall never see anything of all that!

And we shall never see the big cities, their strange buildings, their promenades, their public parks, we shall enjoy none of the attractions or the pleasures they offer. Not for us do the shops go to great expense in their displays; the white bread with the golden crust is not for us, nor the fine joints of meat; our meat is the pork which we salt down each year and a piece of it, more or less rancid, goes into our daily stew. The pork butchers prepare some fine appetizing things from pig-meat: sausage for slicing, brawn covered with jelly, tempting knuckles of ham. But these products are too refined and expensive for us. On Sundays the pastrycooks' shops smell good when we pass by: *brioches*, succulent pasties, tempting tarts and gâteaux. There's no danger that these dainties will ever give toothache to poor country people!

And yet there are some things from which we ought to draw benefit: the produce of the poultry-yard and the dairy, for instance. But we have the trouble and others the enjoyment! We take more or less everything to the townspeople, along with the best of the vegetables and fruit. We must take a little money off them, they make us pay fairly dearly for what we have to get from them: clothes, shoes, headgear, or groceries and haberdashery.

The doctors, because we are a long way from the towns, charge us high fees for their visits – and the chemists ask a lot for their medicines and the priests for their prayers. As for the lawyer, if we need his services, he relieves us of a twenty-franc piece for doing nothing. Perhaps it's their right, good heavens! They need to earn money to live decently, to enjoy the pleasures which we do without, to educate their children. The tax-man also asks us for more and more taxes, for the government wants to provide its officers with an honourable existence, an existence fit for men – the producers remain only mercenaries, plebeians, yokels!

On top of this we have to deal too often with imbeciles like Parent, rogues like Sébert, skinflints like Lavallée. And if we do manage to save up a little we take our savings to scoundrels like Cerbony, who run away with them!

And yet for all that we are very happy. Monsieur Lavallée told me one day that this had been affirmed a long time ago by a man called Virgil, and that we ought to share that man's opinion.

For several weeks, months perhaps, these thoughts, true perhaps but discouraging, haunted my mind. It's not good to think too much about your fate: it doesn't change anything and it makes you more unhappy.

XLV

I negotiated with Monsieur Noris, a landowner of Saint-Aubin, for his farm of Clermoux, which consisted of seventy hectares. Monsieur Noris was a tall man with white hair and a white beard, an oily manner and a nasal voice. He called himself an "agriculturist", meaning that he managed his two farms himself. He lived with his two daughters near Saint-Aubin in an old, one-storeyed house where a covering of ivy only partly concealed the cracks in the grey walls.

He was a typical member of the local bourgeoisie, with rigid habits, tiresome eccentricities – and he was fiendishly mean.

He economized on everything and preferred to sell animals in bad condition rather than spend money to improve them. Neither could one ever mention fertilizers to him:

"No, no, don't talk to me about phosphates and nitrates! Farm-yard manure should be enough."

And he would shake his old bird-like head in terror.

He rarely decided to sell merchandise at the first fair it was taken to. His preliminary estimate was always too high and he would never go back on it. We would bring our animals home and then a few days later take them to a second fair with the same result. At the third fair, tired of arguments, we would sell, and often at a lower price than that quoted the first time.

Monsieur Noris needed a lot of persuading moreover before he would settle the accounts at the end of the year. The accounts for his other farm had not been made up for fifteen years. When the *métayers* demanded money he would give it to them with an arrogant air, and always less than the sum they asked. Once, at Bourbon fair, my predecessor at Clermoux had insisted on being paid a hundred francs, and this village gentleman had merely scattered round him ten hundred-sou coins, muttering in his nasal voice:

"There's some money then! There you are! Pick it up."

And the other man had to pick it up from the mud, to the great indignation of decent people and the delight of the foolish ones.

I wanted to avoid such scenes and settle at Martinmas as was proper. Charles had an idea which I thought worth trying.

At the appropriate time I went to see the master at his house.

"Monsieur Noris, I want to settle up, I'm in great need of money."

"You've hardly any to take, Bertin; the profits aren't much this year."

"I believe you owe me about twelve hundred francs, monsieur." (I knew that was at least double the amount.)

"Never in this world! Never in this world!"

He leapt up to consult his account book.

"I owe you five hundred and thirty-six francs, neither more nor less."

I pretended to be surprised, and then, after deep thought, to have forgotten the purchase of sheep, and insisted on having my money. He grumbled, gave me four hundred-franc notes and said he could pay no more for lack of change. I was obliged to pay myself the rest during the winter out of the sale of some bulls of mine – he was displeased, but did not dare show any anger.

Every year after that I had to resort to some new stratagem in order to be paid. And there was often a hitch.

We had a big bay mare which we used for breeding. Generally, farmers who have a mare use her for going to fairs and to do their errands, and sometimes for work in the fields. But ours was exempt from all heavy work.

"Work spoils a mare and tells on the foals," Monsieur Noris would say.

But the real reason was that he did not want his *métayers* to have the means of riding in a carriage, which seemed to him an unsuitable and superfluous luxury. He took the young foals home as soon as they were weaned and had them trained for shows and remounts. He paid us very little for them, although he always made a good profit out of them.

Despite his great age Monsieur Noris still had a passion for hunting. There was plenty of game on the farm, especially rabbits. As he walked round he liked to see them scampering off down the furrows at the approach of his big greyhound, but he did not want many of them killed. Round one small copse on our land there were so many of them that they destroyed our cereal crops as they sprouted – but all complaints were useless.

Poachers hardly dared come that way, because of his gamekeeper, a crafty, hirsute man, who kept watch with excessive vigilance. If any stranger happened to walk idly across any part of the property the keeper would arrest him. There would be no legal proceedings in this case, but the alleged delinquent would have to appear before the master and receive a lecture, in addition to paying out a hundred sous. If there was any evidence of hunting, the man would be prosecuted. Our neighbour Pinel, who ploughed the land next to ours, was once fined eighty francs because a snare was discovered in the boundary hedge. The good Pinel had always sworn to me that he did not know the trap was there and that as far as he was concerned he never set them anywhere.

Republicans, like poachers, also earned the implacable hatred of Monsieur Noris. He wanted both groups to suffer exemplary punishments, severe torture. He would have liked to see them all in prison, condemned to forced labour, or banished to distant colonies. Just as the destruction of a brood of young rabbits or a partridge's nest, or even the firing of a gun on his land made him fret and fume, the mere word *"République"* stirred him to great nervous shudders and made him shake his fist in impotent rage. In Bourbon a gang of boys, bribed by some practical joker, would often follow him, shouting: *"Vive la République"*, singing verses from *La Marseillaise*, or even hooting into his ears a continuous chant:

"Blique, blique, blique! Blique, blique, blique!"

On each occasion he nearly went out of his mind.

In 1877, when he was suffering from an attack of bronchitis which had nearly killed him, someone had come to announce that the result of an election had been favourable to the Republicans; he rose up in bed with a sudden bound and in a breathless whisper exhaled the deep hatred in his heart:

"The wretches! – So there's no more room at Cayenne!"

And he fell back on his pillow, helpless, fainting.

Four years later, he came to our house at election time. He saw some bills and newspapers that had been sent by Dr Fauconnet, the Republican candidate.

"Don't have those devilish papers here. Throw them in the fire! The wicked pamphlets! Throw the nasty things in the fire! You will bring some evil on yourselves if you keep them here."

I objected that no one could read.

"Their very presence is dangerous!" he said.

And he himself threw them in the fire; then he concluded:

"The keeper will meet you on polling day at the door to the mairie and give you the ballot paper to put in the ballot-box, you understand?"

Workmen, tradespeople, contractors of every kind were carefully chosen outside the Red party; and he made us boycott all those who held opinions which he regarded as subversive.

That was his way of revenging himself on the Republic.

XLVI

The two ladies kept a special watch on our religious conduct. It gave us all trouble enough to do as they wished.

As far as I was concerned, I used to go formerly to Mass almost every other Sunday, that is to say, I had kept the habit of my youth. When I went to Bourbon or Franchesse on Sundays, I seldom missed going to Mass, and I did not approve of those who spent their time at the inn instead of going to church.

I was far from believing all the priests' tales, or their theories about Paradise and Hell, confession and fast days. I looked on all that as nonsense. It seems to me that the true duty of each person lies in this very simple line of conduct: to work honestly, to cause sorrow to none, to help when we have a chance, and to come to the aid of the poor and suffering. If we conform to that as nearly as possible, I believe we need fear nothing either here or elsewhere. But as to that precious eternal life which is to come after this, the priests talk a great deal about it without knowing anything. I have noticed, like everyone else, that, while they expect this celestial joy, the priests do not turn their noses up at earthly pleasures; they drink good wine, they don't disdain choice food, and they know how to screw money out of the faithful. As to their creed, whether they believe in it or not, that is with regard to the question of the future of the soul, I have often thought that the shrewdest person in the world, even the Pope himself, knows no more than I do, for no one has come back to say what is going on there. Therefore, I thought seldom of death and never of eternal salvation, and I had quite given up going to confession since my marriage. I know some who were faithful to that custom and were not any better for it. Victoire confessed, and so did Rosalie; neither the one nor the other was kinder as a result. They acted exactly the same the day after as they had done the day before. My wife continued to be cold and ill-tempered, my daughter-in-law snappish and rude.

I said to myself, "So what's the use?"

All the same, I firmly believed in the existence of a Supreme Being who governed all, who ruled the course of the seasons, who sent the rain and the sun, the frost and the hail; and as the farmer's work is only done well if the weather is favourable, I tried to please the Master of the Elements, who held a good part of our interests in His hands. For that reason I seldom missed the ceremonies when the success of the crops was the subject, and I clung faithfully to all the little pious traditions which we practice in the countryside on various occasions. I always went to Mass on Palm Sunday, with a big bunch of boxwood, fragments of which I placed afterwards behind the doors, beside small crosses of osier which were blessed in May, the hawthorn of the Rogation days and the bouquets containing the three varieties of the herbs of Saint Roch, which keep the animals from illness. I joined the procession of Saint Mark, who cares for the good things of the earth, and some days after I went to the Mass of Saint Athanasius, the preserver from the hail. I never failed to sprinkle the haylofts with holy water before storing the fodder. On beginning to cut a field of wheat I made the sign of the cross with the first sheaf, and I also made it when vitriolizing the seed corn, and again on each loaf of bread before cutting it, and on the backs of the cows with their first milk after calving. I did not think it ridiculous to see a candle lighted during a thunder-storm. I raised my hat before the wayside calvaries, and each morning and evening said a bit of a prayer. A good deal of this I did from habit – I had always followed those practices and they seemed natural to me. But I could not see that missing Mass on a Sunday or failing to fast on a Friday ought to bring endless punishment, any more than it seemed right to attribute to the priest the power to absolve all sins at confession.

My boys shared my views, more or less. Jean attended Mass fairly regularly once a fortnight, as I did. Since his return from the regiment, Charles went scarcely once a month. It was he who found it specially hard to have to go regularly.

"A pretty business it is," he said, "to have the priest under one's feet all the time."

One Sunday he went to Bourbon in the morning and never set foot in the church. But the next day, while we were in the fields, the women had a visit from Mesdemoiselles Yvonne and Valentine Noris.

"Victoire," they said, "your young son was not at Mass yesterday."

"He went to Bourbon, mesdemoiselles, he must have gone to Mass there."

"We don't believe a word of that. Charles ought to come every Sunday to Mass at Saint-Aubin, as you all do; he can go to Bourbon or elsewhere afterwards, if he thinks fit. Tell him clearly that he cannot neglect that duty which is imposed on us although we don't know why. And if he persists in disobeying, you will all suffer for it."

He was obliged to yield. He was even forced, as I was, to go to confession at Easter. It was the only way to have peace and quiet; for I believe those ladies had us spied on by their keeper and their servants.

But that was not all: swearing was strictly forbidden. But Charles had got into the habit of swearing in the army; as soon as something went wrong, he would let out a "Good God," or a "Bloody hell!" adorned with various preliminaries. I tried to persuade him to get out of the habit, or at least to restrain himself in the presence of spies. But it was difficult for him, and one day he allowed a great oath to escape and the keeper heard it. The two old maids set to without delay.

"Victoire, your son continues to swear horribly; we will not have that here."

They went so far as to reprove me for saying bad words, because they had heard me use the expression "Devil take it! Good heavens!" I told them squarely that the expression was as necessary to me as my pinches of snuff and that I could not promise not to use it. In fact, those words came to my lips unconsciously, and it was the same with Charles and his oaths.

And indeed, although they were always in church, at the confessional, at the holy table; although they had an exaggerated horror of swearing, they were not any better for that, the two old trouts! They were as hard as rocks and as malicious as their father.

The winter of 1879–'80 was very hard. At night we could hear the cracking of the trees made brittle by the frost. The sparrows, green finches, wrens and robins sought refuge in the cowsheds. It was quite easy to catch them, they were so exhausted; every morning we used to find, near the outbuildings, some of those poor little birds frozen to death. Flocks of crows stayed close to the farms, cawing harshly, even daring, in their hunger, to come pecking at the manure heap. There was great suffering everywhere in nature.

Among poor people too, unfortunately. Day labourers, who were out of work, wandered about the countryside looking for dead wood, and some were mistaken enough to fell whole trees during the night. A great maple disappeared from one of our fields at Les Perches. Monsieur Noris and his daughters had come to enquire about the theft, and I heard Mademoiselle Yvonne's furious instructions to the keeper:

"You must make frequent rounds in the night, and if you happen to see any of those wretches, don't hesitate: shoot at him – you have the right to do it."

That is how those bigots practised the forgiveness of sins. As for their charity, it was exercised in petty revenge, in treacherous blows aimed at those who were so unfortunate as me to displease them. They gave a sou once a fortnight to the poor of the commune, and on Friday some dry crusts to wayfarers: on the other days nothing at all. It was we, the poor working people, who fed the vagabonds.

If there is a paradise, Mlles. Yvonne and Valentine ought to have some trouble in obtaining admission, in spite of all their genuflexions.

XLVII

My godfather's wife was dead, and I had to take my sister Marinette under my care, for the dead woman's daughter-in-law did not want to keep her.

"You've never had her," said my godfather; "it's certainly your turn: besides, you're the only one who can afford it."

I might have objected that he would not have afforded to take her when she was young and less of an imbecile, if she had not been useful. But I preferred to say nothing, and to consent with a good grace to take my poor sister into my home.

There, at the news, Victoire and Rosalie, in their different ways, said that we had no need of this poor imbecile girl, that we had enough work already. Silence is always the best remedy against scenes of that kind. But when, on the appointed day, I went to fetch Marinette, my wife and daughter-in-law submitted readily enough, nor would I have put up with it if they had been unkind to her.

The fact is that the poor woman's company was no pleasure to anyone. Her brain was so weak now that it held scarcely any trace of reason. She uttered words devoid of meaning, she often moaned in a kind of plaintive chant, which bothered everyone and frightened the children, then, suddenly, without any motive she would begin to laugh stridently and painfully. She was not at all useful; for a long time it had been impossible to trust her with the animals.

Her presence in our house caused some gossip in the neighbourhood at first; people talked all over Saint-Aubin about the poor idiot who never went out, and who cried out a great deal: she was the mystery, the ulcer of our home.

However, I never regretted having taken her. We must accept elementary duties, however painful they may be. In saying that I was the only one able to take charge of her, my godfather was quite right, for I had more resources than my two elder brothers, although my position was not brilliant.

My godfather had never been able to scrape as much as four sous together. He was then at Autry, in a poor farm, whose owners, formerly rich, wanted to appear so still. The life of those people was ridiculous, and they were laughed at by everyone in the whole commune. The husband, a great simpleton, who had been dissipated, and had allowed himself to be drawn into unfortunate speculations, was partly the cause of their precarious condition at that time. His wife had taken the management of the household into her own hands and made him pay heavily for his past mistakes. She kept the money and even did not give him enough to go the café once a week. The consequence was, that the bored listless man prowled about the village of Autry, not knowing how to kill the hours of the day. He would go to the carpenter's shop, to the farrier's, would accost the peasants and help the *garde-champêtre* sweep the little square or post bills on the church walls. Sometimes someone would say in an ironical tone, knowing that he was penniless:

"Will you stand a drink, Monsieur Gouin?"

"It's impossible, I must get back: they're waiting for me at home."

"Ah! But come all the same: I'll pay."

At that he would discover they were no longer waiting for him at home. He was so fond of drink, that he would shamelessly accept the contemptuous hospitality of hornyhanded workmen.

In his own home, all the satisfactions of a gourmand were refused to him. Madame Gouin – Agathe, as everybody usually called her – kept the key of the cellar in her pocket, and also that of the sideboard in which the spirits were kept, and she only opened those sanctuaries on grand occasions. At meals a bottle of wine would appear on the table, but only in an honorary capacity; all the week it remained intact, unless some visitor appeared at the wrong moment. Otherwise, the bottle was emptied only on Sundays.

Agathe was niggardly about the smallest things; she was like the wives of the poorest day labourers: grudging about lights and heating, butter, soap, even pepper and salt. The servant had no white bread; she helped herself to some of the third-class loaf which was the dog's food; if she had not done that, she would not have had enough to eat. Three servants in a row left that house suffering from anaemia.

Yet the Gouins wanted to go on putting up a good show in the local world of prosperous squires. They went visiting at various châteaux, sometimes even dining there. When it was necessary to return those dinners, the house was turned upside down for a fortnight.

"Do it well and spend little, that is the end to attain," said Agathe, naïvely.

Expenses were heavy all the same, and a heartrending time followed; for several weeks the employers condemned themselves to onion soup and poor quality bread, and the bottle of wine was only emptied when it was in a condition to dress the salad. In the course of one of those days, Monsieur Gouin called at my godfather's house during a meal time. They offered him some cooked dried pears, which he had looked at covetously: he ate half a dish of them.

Of their former splendour they still retained a carriage of passable appearance which they called the victoria. From time to time the lady would decide to go to Moulins to make purchases or even to pay visits, or in good weather simply to take an airing. Then she would send the servant to tell my godfather that he was to take the old mare from the farm. At the appointed hour, he harnessed the horse and climbed onto the seat, for he had to act as coachman. The turnout was truly comic, and gave rise to jokes without end. Even now I can see that old mare with its rough, dirty white coat, often bespattered with mud from the pastures, dragging along, slowly, heavily, the once fine carriage; the old countryman in smock and *sabots* turned into a coachman, huddled on his seat, awkwardly handling the whip; and in the depths of the carriage, lolling proudly on the faded cushions, that couple of hungry *bourgeois*.

It was said that the Gouins collected in their granary the skins of the *métayers* whom they had flayed alive. Very few of them stayed longer than two or three years under their yoke. And, having arrived usually very poor, they always left more destitute than when they had come.

My godfather had certainly not found the road to fortune there.

All workers dream of making a fortune. My brother Louis believed at one time that he had succeeded. In the twelve years between 1860 and 1872 he had managed to save eight thousand francs. Then the devil tempted him to buy a farm at Montilly, for fifteen thousand francs. So he settled in, rode a horse, had a spring carriage, and a goat skin jacket, and went to the fairs looking like a big farmer. He played cards every Sunday for high stakes, and had good meals with his friends. They made him a municipal councillor, and he was very proud of that. When we met at Bourbon, he used to look at me from a great height as though embarrassed to talk to me.

His wife Claudine was even prouder than he was; she wore jackets made in the fashion of the day, bonnets with a double row of lace, and a gold chain round her neck. She indulged in dainties to eat, bought a lot of coffee, and sugar by the half loaf. Victoire, who could not stand her, said to me one day:

"Claudine plays the great lady, I wonder how long it will last?"

It only lasted five or six years. The former proprietor of the holding, who had been paid half the amount required, had taken a mortgage for the sum still owing to him. Louis paid him interest at five per cent, and thus gave him a sum nearly equal to what he would have paid in rent, Besides, having done some repairs, he was in debt elsewhere; he could then only go down-hill quickly. When he realized that he was in trouble he tried to struggle against it: he sold his carriage, went less to the café and set to work again; but it was too late, the harm couldn't be mended. The former owner to whom he owed three years' interest, repossessed his holding, paying just enough to pay the other creditors. Left without any means, my poor brother was reduced to living in a miserable hovel, and to working here and there as a day labourer. He died two years later of congestion of the lungs, one very cold day when he was breaking stones on the road to Moulins.

Claudine, who knew so well how to play the fine lady, had to take in washing and beg for charity at funerals. Her career had a very sad end.

XLVIII

In the autumn of 1880, we were visited at Clermoux by Georges Gaussin and his wife. Georges was the son of my sister Catherine. He had just married, and he took advantage of this occasion to renew his acquaintance with his Bourbon relatives; for he had never been back since the time when his parents had brought him as a boy. My sister and her husband, having only this one child, had kept him at school until he was eighteen. He went into the Army for a year as a volunteer, and he had since occupied a position as an accountant in a great business house.

Georges and his wife had decided to make our house their head-quarters, one of my nieces at Autry having written to them to say that I was best able to accommodate them. When the letter arrived announcing their coming, Rosalie exclaimed:

"Parisians! What a nuisance they're going to be! They will talk fine, my friends."

Victoire, very worried, wondered where she would put them to sleep, and even what food she could prepare for them. They discussed it, and finally it was decided that we should give our guests the bed in the room in which Charles and little Tiennon, Jean and Rosalie's child, slept: they would use the shepherd's bed in the kitchen, he having consented to make up a bed for himself with some blankets in the hayloft.

The day came; Charles borrowed a donkey from a roadman in the neighbourhood, harnessed it to our little carriage, which we had kept, although we had no use for it on that farm. He went to meet the Gaussins, who were to arrive at Bourbon by coach from Moulins about five o'clock in the evening.

They reached our house a little before dark. I was busy carting manure: I came with an empty cart into the main road, from a very steep side road about two hundred yards from home, and appeared right in front of them. Georges and his wife walked in front arm in arm: Charles led the donkey by the bridle; the baggage was piled up in the carriage; there was a big trunk, two bags, and a hat-box.

I cried "Woa!" to my oxen, and stopped them. Charles introduced me:

"This is my father."

The two young people exclaimed together:

"Ah! It's uncle! Good evening, uncle."

They threw themselves on me to kiss me.

"Poor uncle, we are very glad to see you."

"So am I, nephew, so am I, niece," I stammered.

I let my goad fall from my hand and allowed them to kiss me.

"I'm not in a nice state to receive you," I said, with some embarrassment.

In fact, my *sabots* were nearly worn out, blunted at the toes, and my grey linen trousers, torn at the knees, my blue check shirt, even my old straw hat frayed at the edges, were hardly respectable, and all smelt of manure; my feet were bare in their *sabots*, and I had not shaved since Sunday, so that my face, this being Friday, was hirsute and prickly. I wondered what impression I was making on the elegant little Parisienne, so fragile and dainty, whose black hair smelt so nice. To touch her seemed a profanation. She wore a plain blue dress, a big straw hat trimmed only with a bunch of daisies, and her fine varnished boots creaked at every step.

"Those boots are too fine for our roads, niece."

"Yes, indeed, uncle, your roads are rather rough; they certainly do need levelling."

She smiled gently, and that smile corrected the somewhat serious expression of her face; it was a long face with a thin nose, pale cheeks, and big, deep, black eyes.

Though thirty years old, Georges looked rather baby-faced, despite a slight red-blonde moustache and a scanty beard of the same colour cut to a point at the chin. He was dressed in fancy black and white check trousers, black jacket and round, soft hat; a loose black bow was spread out above his waistcoat, emphasising the whiteness of his stiff collar.

I shouted to the oxen to make them go on again, and I walked beside Georges, who took his wife's arm. He gave me news of his parents, who were still in the same house, in the service of an old lady of seventy-five. They did not want to leave her, as they counted on being remembered in her will.

"So, uncle, you are just getting back from the fields with your cart," Georges said, after a silence.

I answered a little absent-mindedly:

"Yes, mons –" (I nearly said "monsieur." Heavens! he was like a gentleman, that nephew).

"Yes, nephew, we're manuring the fallow lands before ploughing them.

"Oh, yes, the manuring;" he appeared to reflect; "the manure from your animals, the product of the dung and the cowshed litter?"

"Yes," I answered, with a rather mocking smile. It seemed a stupid question.

His wife asked for other explanations, which drew from me the answer that I was taking the manure to where we sowed the wheat.

"Oh, how horrible!" said she, with a little cry. "The wheat our bread is made of, does it come like that – in the manure?"

"Mixed with the soil," said Charles, "the manure is not seen again."

Georges went on: "Does that surprise you, Berthe? The earth would exhaust itself, you see, if we ceased to provide it with fertilizing matter."

"Is your cart comfortable, uncle?" asked Berthe. "My cousin's was not very nice; I got into it for a little while on the road. I was shaken so much, I felt sick."

We arrived in the yard. Victoire, Jean, his wife, and the little one came forward to meet the Parisians: everyone embraced. Georges and his wife kissed even Marinette, whom we had dressed in clean clothes on purpose. She submitted unwillingly, and then began her usual plaintive chant, which seemed to upset our pretty niece.

Victoire had wondered uneasily if our nephew and niece were accustomed to fast on Fridays.

"Pooh! Do you think townspeople pay any attention to that!" Rosalie had exclaimed. "They don't trouble much about forbidden days; they have no religion."

My wife had prepared milk soup, some French beans with butter, a roast chicken and a salad with nut oil. This meal was only for the guests. To have cooked extra for everybody would have been too costly. She served them on a little table in the bedroom. But Berthe was troubled:

"But what about yourselves? Oh! no, we don't want to dine alone; we have come to be with the family."

I told her that we had our meal afterwards, at eight o'clock, when it was too dark to work any longer out of doors.

"But, indeed, uncle, at least you will come and keep us company, you and my little cousin."

And she made little Jean sit near her.

Victoire, seeing that they meant it, said to me:

"Well, yes, Tiennon, you had better dine with our nephew and niece."

I changed my trousers and *sabots*, put on a clean smock and took my place beside them. They ate with pleasure, but very small quantities. They declared the milk soup excellent, and regaled themselves with the beans, which were very tender, and on which Victoire had not stinted the butter. On the other hand, they ate very little of the chicken: that was more common for them perhaps than the milk and fresh vegetables. I noticed that they were full of little attentions to each other.

"See, Georges" or "Isn't it, Georges?" she would say all the time.

And he:

"See, Berthe, that'll make you ill, my darling; you are eating too many beans —"

For dessert they had some big black plums.

"Those plums aren't good for you; don't eat too many, little one."

I thought such ways rather silly. In the country, if wives and husbands spoke like that, everyone would laugh at them. At bottom we love each other just as much, but we are never so liberal with tender words.

From time to time, when Victoire came to serve them, Georges and Berthe complained gently again because she had prepared two dinners, and forbade her to do it in the future, seeing that they were quite ready to wait till a little later. At his mother's request, Charles had brought a *couronne* of white bread from Bourbon, for our household bread was eight days old and was already hard: nevertheless, they had a fancy to eat that.

"We want to be just like country people, Uncle," they said.

They asked me endless questions about everything, how many

sheep we had, how many cows, and how we did the milking.
"I shall come to see all the animals tomorrow," said Berthe. "Let
me see, you get up very early – at six o'clock?"

"Oh, niece! by six o'clock we've already been at work for two
hours."

"You get up at four o'clock! Really! Oh! Uncle, we are lazy;
Georges goes to his office at nine o'clock; we get up at eight, never
earlier. But here, we're going to get up at dawn, you'll see."

When the meal was finished, we had to return to the communal
room, where the others were having their supper. After they had
swallowed their soup, they crumbled as usual some bread in the
great red earthenware dishes and steeped it in a big spoonful of
skimmed milk. Berthe was astonished at that:

"But that's another soup – Do you eat two soups at dinner?"

She realized at that moment, no doubt, that this second dinner
had not taken much time to cook. I proposed that we should take
a turn in the fresh air, for I saw that their presence bothered the
women who were about to do the washing up. Jean and Charles
joined us, and we went together round the meadow near the house.
The moon gave a little light, but the sky was dark and the wind
fresh. Georges, having felt his wife shiver, repeated at every moment, although she denied that she was cold: "You'll catch cold, my
darling, I'm sure of it: we must not stay out long."

Thanks to Charles, who talked well enough, the conversation did
not languish so much; but for my part, I said very little, because
I felt it ridiculous to talk so badly alongside those who talked so
well, and also because I dared not ask questions about the town,
seeing that my questions would have been at least as simple as theirs
about the country.

When we returned to the house, before saying "Good-night,"
Victoire asked the young people what they would take in the
morning.

"Don't make anything special for us, aunt," they said together,
"we will eat soup, like everybody else."

They did not understand that the morning meal at eight o'clock
was the most important of our meals, when we would have bacon
and vegetable stew. Of course my wife took no notice of their reply
and made coffee for them.

But they said so much again in the morning about not wanting
to eat apart from us, that they wished to eat with us and as we did
at the midday meal, that we felt obliged to satisfy them. For that

reason we sat down to table at twelve o'clock, a whole hour earlier than usual. And there were a lot of unusual things: to begin with, wine, then a juicy omelette made with fresh eggs, some beefsteak, cream cheese sprinkled with sugar, and pears from an espalier in the garden: we could have sold twenty-five of these for at least twenty sous at Bourbon market, but Victoire had a fancy to have a dish at each end of the table. The dishes at the end nearest to the visitors contained food which was like the other in appearance only, for our omelette was made with potatoes, the steaks were pieces of grilled bacon; the cheese had hardly any cream and no sugar; the pears alone were the same, but my wife gave the servant boy an angry look when he dared to take one:

"You ought to be able to find enough in the fields," she told him quietly; "fallen ones are not scarce just now."

Then the members of the family knew that the fine ones were only for ornament, and no one presumed to touch them.

At the evening meal Victoire made no more attempts to save appearances. There was milk soup for everybody, as usual, and the Parisians had a vermicelli soup with a *purée* of potatoes and a piece of roast veal. Berthe appeared to have a marvellous knowledge of how to prepare those small fine dishes, and helped Victoire with her advice.

The following days our guests accepted the superior fare without protest. I believe they were quite simply astonished to see that we lived so simply, and yet our fare was quite better than usual.

"We don't want them to be too sorry for us," I had said to my wife.

Georges and his wife slept late in the mornings as they did when in Paris. On their account we closed the old, dilapidated shutters, which had always been open; Jean and his wife slept in the same room, and made the least possible noise when they got up, and the young couple stayed in bed till seven o'clock and later. Rosalie said this was the only quiet time of the day, since they were not on our backs.

As soon as they got up, Berthe, in a dressing-gown and slippers, would run here and there, crying out with astonishment, like a child. She made a tour of the garden, and went into the hen-house to hunt for new-laid eggs. She liked to see the little ducks and the young chickens feeding. She even went into the cow-shed when the cows were being milked, but between the badly joined stones there were holes full of liquid manure, which she had a lot of trouble avoiding; once she lost one of her slippers in a hole; some dirty drops stained the bottom of her light dressing-gown with brown spots, and, what with her bother about the accident, she almost got in the way of a cow's droppings. She was afraid, too, of calves; she uttered piercing cries when we loosed them and they dashed off to be suckled. For these various reasons she did not stay long, and did not want to cross the threshold of that dangerous place again. When she was tired of running about outside, she busied herself with embroidery, lace-making, and little accomplishments which she seemed well up in.

Georges came to join us in the fields, tried his hand with the plough, and then went to the ponds to catch frogs. The young man never went out of the house without kissing his wife's forehead and saying "au revoir" to her. On returning he would embrace her again: she would say, coyly:

"Have you had a good walk? And your fishing? Let's see if you've had any luck, Georges dear."

She herself would open the little thread bag in which he always brought home some frogs. No one knew how to cook them, so our nephew was obliged to do it himself.

Rosalie said: "I don't know how any one can eat such filth: they're too much like toads!"

Rosalie's remarks, and her words, free from all hypocrisy, amused Georges and Berthe a great deal. But they were saddened when Marinette would look at them fixedly, with big eyes like an animal's, pointing at them with her thin finger and laughing her foolish laugh; or when she uttered her endless chant, piercing and mournful.

On Sunday Charles hired a horse and spring cart from the grocer in the town, in order to give our visitors an outing. After a long ride through the forest they decided to go to Bourbon, where they lingered a little. Climbing up the towers of the old château exhausted them without providing enough entertainment. But they were interested in the warm spring and its great pool where in the past invalids would come from afar to bathe unashamedly in public, the day before Holy Cross day.

Our visitors returned at nightfall, delighted with their outing. But it rained on Tuesday, and the day was dreary and dull.

Georges could not go out, and was very bored: he smoked cigarette after cigarette, and wrote letters – after he had been to the town to buy ink, for we had none. The rain ceased in the afternoon and he felt like going out, and Berthe wanted to go too. But there was too much water and mud for her to go out in her boots; she therefore put on Rosalie's Sunday *sabots*, but her feet soon turned in them, for she had no idea how to wear them; she went a hundred yards and then returned, fearing she would sprain her ankle. In the evening she was nervous and did not attempt to disguise her chagrin.

Our guests stayed till the Saturday, eight full days. I don't know if they took away with them a good impression of their stay amongst us, although they had had the satisfaction of drinking big bowls of fresh milk which they liked very much. I think it bothered them to see that we had gone out of our way for their meals. Also, I think they were sorry for us, for working so hard, for having so few pleasures, and for being so backward. They must have lost many of their illusions about the countryside.

"Niece," I said to Berthe, on the morning of their departure, "admit you would find the days long if you had to stay here always?"

'It's true, uncle, I should not find it easy to become a farmer's wife. To be happy I should want to have a comfortable house, a garden with gravel paths, with flowers and shady places, and a horse and carriage to go out in."

"I," said Georges, "would like the country for six months in summer, to hunt, fish, and wander in the fields, and to cultivate the garden."

I thought to myself:

"All townspeople must be like that; they see only the *pleasures* that the country can give; they dream about the meadows, the trees, the birds, the flowers, the milk, the butter, the vegetables and fruit. But they have not the least idea of the sufferings of those who work there, the peasants. And we are in exactly the same position, when we speak of the advantages of the town, and the pleasures it offers, we give no thought to the conditions of the workers who live from day to day on work which is often hard and unpleasant.

Our young people had been very nice but we felt a sensation of relief, such as prisoners must feel when they find themselves in the open air again. Their presence had inevitably caused some inconvenience. It is always difficult to live with people of different character and manners, even when they are our kin. When there are no ideas in common, the position is sure to be uncomfortable.

The shepherd was the only person to regret their departure. The same evening I heard him say to the servant:

"I shouldn't have been sorry if those Parisians had stayed longer: we had better food!"

XLIX

We were very worried about our poor Clémentine, who was ill and short of money. She had just had a fourth child, Moulin had quarrelled with the gardener at the château and was out of work. Their diminished means did not assure even necessities for the larger family. They were behind with their rent, owed for two sacks of flour to our successors at La Creuserie and for fabrics to a shop in the town.

Our daughter did not even go to Mass any more, because of the children, for their father did not want to take care of them, and she had no suitable clothes. But the worst trouble was the state of her health; she was getting weaker. One of the nuns from Franchesse, who sold a few medicines and understood a little about illness, told Clémentine that she was suffering from chronic anaemia.

"You must have rest, nourishing food and good wine," the nun had said.

That was a cruel irony for her, for with four children on her hands, all needing clothes, and who, she was afraid, might be in want of food too, how could she care for herself?

"She is pitifully thin and so weak she can't stand", Victoire said, weeping, one day when she had been to see her daughter, during October, 1890.

On All Saints' Day I went myself to Les Fouinats. My heart was wrung by the impression of misery the poor cottage gave, and by the only too obvious decline in Clémentine. She looked old, exhausted and pale as death, suckling the youngest child, who was pulling greedily at her dry breasts. She smiled, however, when she saw me come in. And as I asked her about her health, the memory came back to me of another scene which had been enacted in that house one summer morning, years ago, when I had gone to ask the woman who was living there for a drink of water . . .

"I'm not too well, father," she said. "I need care which I can't provide for myself."

She was short of breath; her sentences faded away and were

almost inaudible. I comforted her as best I could, gave her some money and suggested I should send the doctor to see her, but she did not want that.

"No, father, no. The nun has given me a tonic – that's all I need. I'm not ill enough to need the doctor, and besides, it's too expensive for us!"

That's something we say very often where we live. We make *tisane* and treat ourselves. And the sight of the doctor's carriage in our old country lanes strikes many people as a premonition of death.

Alas, that was indeed the case with Clémentine. A few days after my visit she became so much worse that she was unable to get up. Then her husband went to Bourbon to find Dr Picaud: Fauconnet, a Councillor-General and a Deputy now, had ceased to practise. Monsieur Picaud found her very ill, stating that jaundice had developed on top of the anaemia and ordered that her baby must be weaned at once. One of Moulin's sisters took him, and one of the brothers took the elder boy, who was already grown up. We took charge of the younger, a little girl of six, and the third, a boy of four. Rosalie made a face as usual, when these children arrived, but she soon became fond of them and later was quite devoted to them.

Victoire installed herself at Les Fouinats to take care of her daughter. To no avail, alas! Within a few weeks her illness became so much worse that Clémentine died at the end of November, on a day of frost and dense fog. She was thirty-one.

This loss caused the postponement until the spring of Charles' marriage with Madeleine, the Noris' servant.

L

Ever since I had worked for his father, and especially since he had come to La Creuserie to set my broken leg, Doctor Fauconnet had been kind to me. When he met me at Bourbon during the summer holidays, he never failed to speak of "that old *chouan** Noris, who ought to be sent to jail."

As Councillor-General and Deputy Monsieur Fauconnet was an influential man: he could obtain a favour, get a conscript out of the army or intervene in legal proceedings. So during the summer

*The 'Chouans' of La Vendée in western France, had risen several times against the Republic and continue to represent last-ditch "white" reaction.

holidays the Château d' Agonges, where he had lived since the death of his father, was besieged by people asking for help.

But the former uncompromising Republican who had formerly offered such fierce opposition to the Empire had become a good bourgeois; he supported the Government and felt fear and contempt for extremes, from both Left and Right. When Monsieur Noris died his daughters hastened to let the two farms to a popular farmer-general who dismissed us. I was indifferent enough about that, for I had intended for a long time to leave the joint management to Jean and Charles while Victoire and I would retire to some smallholding. I had the opportunity now to carry out this plan.

I wanted to help the two boys to find a new farm. Knowing that Dr Fauconnet had one available I took the opportunity of his New Year's Day holiday to go and see him.

He received me cordially, as I had hoped, and before his departure for Paris the business was settled. The conditions moreover were not much different from those imposed by the other great landowners, his political enemies. He, to whom the happiness of ordinary people used to matter so much, fleeced his poor farmworkers like any other vulgar Gouin. What a difference there always is between words and deeds!

For myself I was able to rent at Le Chat-Huant – or "Chavant", at Saint-Aubin, a smallholding big enough for three cows, about the same size as the one where I had started out on Les Craux at Bourbon. The rent was rather high, but with the interest on my small savings – for which the notary had found me a good investment – I reckoned I should be able to manage fairly well.

LI

I found it strange, and so did Victoire, to be living in such a small house again – and so few people! Marguerite, poor Clémentine's little daughter, had stayed with her uncles. But we had kept her brother Francis, who was now starting to go to school, and also Marinette, for I was afraid she would be unhappy anywhere else.

I had more leisure and less anxiety than at Clermoux, but it is often very difficult when you have to do everything yourself. Once more I had to do all the heavy work which the boys had taken off my hands when we were together. In summer I was soon obliged to take a labourer to help me sometimes.

And often I had hours heavy with discouragement and weariness, as did my wife, who was still as weakly and complaining as ever.

But outside school hours our little Francis was good company for us. During the winter evenings his childish liveliness brought a ray of happiness into our dull, elderly household; thanks to him the transition was less painful for us.

Besides, he was a good-natured child, bright, active, lively, and very sharp, and he was good-natured. We spoiled him. Victoire made milk soup for the little gentleman, because he did not like bacon soup; she gave him big pieces of bread and butter; and the best fruit in the garden was kept for him.

Francis would often beg me to tell him stories; he remembered having heard me tell them to his sister and his cousin, and he wanted to get to know them too.

I knew some of the old stories which we hand down on the farms from generation to generation. I knew "The Green Mountain," "The White Dog," "Tom Thumb," "The Devil's Bag of Gold," and "The Beast with Seven Heads." After a show of resistance I would give in with a good grace:

"Once upon a time there was a great beast with seven heads who wanted to eat the king's daughter. The king proclaimed throughout his realm that he would give his daughter to the man who would kill the beast: but no one dared to undertake the adventure. Now there came a young peasant, bold and brave . . . who went resolutely to the forest to meet the big beast, and he succeeded in killing it. He put the monster's seven tongues into his pocket and returned to his village, where he had left his mother very ill: he wanted news of her before going to the palace. Now a wicked wood-cutter had watched from afar the killing of the beast; when he saw that the good young man did not go up to the palace at once, he went and cut off the monster's seven heads and carried them to the king, pretending that he was the victor. The king did him great honour, and commanded his daughter to fix the date of the wedding. But she distrusted the wicked wood-cutter, and found ways of delaying the ceremony under various pretexts. In the end, however, she had to name the day, for her father was angry. That same day, at the very moment when they were forming the procession, the good young man returned from his village. When he came into the capital he was astonished to see green arches and paper garlands in all the streets, and from all the windows flags and streamers floating in the wind. He asked what happy event had caused the town to be decorated, and they answered that it was in honour of the wedding of the king's daughter to the slayer of the beast with seven heads. Then he ran to the palace and approached the king, near whom stood the betrothed couple.

" 'That man is a liar,' he said, pointing to him. 'It is I who killed the beast with seven heads.'

"The wood-cutter was very haughty, and reminded him that he had brought the seven heads, and the king threatened to have the young man hanged. But without moving, he said:

" 'He has been able, Sire, to bring you the heads, but not the tongues, for the tongues are here.'

"And opening a package he carried he showed the beast's seven tongues preserved in a jar of spirit. The king sent for the heads, and satisfied himself that they had no tongues. Then he had the wicked wood-cutter hanged, and gave his daughter to the good young man."

Francis was all ears: as soon as that tale was done, he wanted another, and he made me exhaust my repertoire each time. Monsters, devils, fairies marched past by the dozen; and also princes and princesses of Dreamland, princesses who wore dresses the colour of gold, silver and azure, and who had started out by guarding turkeys. There were also shepherds whose fairy godmothers had endowed them with supernatural powers, who hewed down whole forests in one night, and the next day constructed magnificent palaces, thanks to which they became mighty lords.

When I had finished, the boy demanded explanations which I found embarrassing. He seemed to believe that all those things had really happened, and he wanted to know the "why" and the "how" of each episode. I preferred him to have a taste for riddles:

"Look here, sonny, what is white when we throw it up and yellow when it falls down?"

He would think, then:

"I don't know, grandfather."

"An egg, stupid."

"Oh! yes, ask me something else."

"All right; what is it that travels without making a shadow?"

He remembered having heard that one.

"The sound of the bells, grandfather."

"What is it that every morning takes a turn around the house and then hides in a corner?"

"The broom."

"What has an eye at the end of its tail?"

"The frying-pan."

"What is it that neither wants to drink nor lets you drink?"

"The bramble."

"In a big black field are some little red cows –"

He did not allow me to finish.

"The oven when we heat it; the embers are the little red cows."

"There are four looking at the sky, four treading upon the dew, four carrying the breakfast; and they all make one. What is it?"

This time, embarrassed silence.

"I don't know, grandfather."

"It is a cow, not one of those in the oven, a real cow; her horns and her ears look at the sky; her four feet tread on the dew; her four udders are full of milk – carry the breakfast. There."

When Francis began to work at problems, I puzzled him very much by asking him about the number of sheep the shepherdess had.

"Look here, sonny, see if you can find the solution to this problem. A gentleman was passing a shepherdess; he asked her how many sheep she had. She answered: 'If I had as many more plus half as many, plus a quarter as many, plus one, that would make a hundred.' How many had she?"

After puzzling a long time, he was obliged to give it up, and I had to tell him that the number of sheep was thirty-six.

On days when I wanted to make him laugh, I told him stories of Father Bergeon. Father Bergeon, dead a long time ago, had had the reputation of being a practical joker and an expert liar. His 'tallest' stories were still quoted.

"Now, Francis, open your ears:

"Once Father Bergeon lost his sow. Three whole days he searched for it; he scoured the canton without success, and returned home very disconsolate. But when he went into his garden to gather some sorrel, he heard a grunting that seemed to come from an enormous gourd at the end of a bed of kidney beans. He hurried up to it: the sow was hidden there, in the inside of a great pumpkin; she had had her piglets there, eight of them, pink and white and very lively, and there was still some room left.

"One morning in August he went to his potato field; he was much puzzled to see the soil raised in places. At first he thought it was due to the working of moles underground, but not at all: he dug with his hoe, just to see, and found it was simply that the potatoes had grown with such unheard-of rapidity, that they had made these abnormal swellings."

Father Bergeon had been a poacher, like everybody else and his sporting tales were more extraordinary still.

"One day, in winter, having fired at some starlings on a service tree, he killed so many that he took home several sacks quite full, and during the whole week the dead birds kept falling from the tree."

"Another time, passing by the edge of a lake, he saw some wild ducks swimming quietly on the surface of the calm water. He had no gun, so he conceived the idea of throwing them a cork attached to a long thread, the other end of which he held. Ducks are very greedy and digest quickly: one threw itself on the cork, which it swallowed and passed five minutes later; another immediately swallowed it in its turn, and thus from beak to beak, the cork passed through the bodies of twenty-four ducks, which, because of the thread, found themselves impaled. All Father Bergeon had to do was to pull them out of the water and carry them off."

But it was not long before Francis knew my collection of stories and riddles and funny tales as well as I did, and I was no longer able to amuse him. He then began to tell me the things he was learning at school. He talked of kings and queens, of Joan of Arc, Bayard, Richelieu, Robespierre, of crusades and wars and massacres. He seemed to know all that had happened down the centuries. Of course I listened with only half an ear and was too old to remember all those things when he asked me afterwards in what year such and such a battle took place, at what time such and such a king had reigned, and what had been the exploits of such and such a famous man, I would make stupid mistakes, even to the extent of being a thousand years out. With geography it was the same thing. I confused the names of countries, seas, *départements* and towns – which made him laugh a good deal.

There were times when I felt a little vexed to find myself getting lessons from this child; however, I was happy to know that he had some taste for his school-work. When I went to the fairs at Bourbon, I always brought him a newspaper, and he would read it aloud in the evenings. I found a pleasure in listening to him, in spite of the fact that there were many things which neither of us understood.

Unfortunately Marinette often interrupted the reading with a burst of laughter or lamentation, which upset the little lad a great deal.

When he was bigger, he began himself to buy a paper every Sunday at the shop of Father Armand, tailor and tobacconist. This paper contained stories and coloured pictures; in it we saw the portraits of celebrated men, plumed generals, soldiers with haversacks and guns, and pictures of accidents and crimes. Francis pasted the illustrations he liked best on all the empty spaces on the walls.

When the time came, however, for him to try working with his hands I regained my superiority and did my best to advise and guide him, and that gave me great pleasure.

LII

One Sunday I got the idea of going to Meillers, to see once again the farm at Le Garibier, where I had been brought up, and which I had left nearly fifty years before. The road alongside the small wood, where the pines with the resinous scent grew, looked just the same. When I turned aside into the yard, the dogs rushed at me, barking just as Médor used to do in bygone days, when strangers came. It was I who was a stranger in the place which had been so familiar to me long ago! The old barn, low and dilapidated, had disappeared; there was now a fine new one with high, rough-cast walls, and the roof-tiles still kept a little of their new red colour.

On the other hand, the house, such as it was, very old even in my time, still stood unrestored. The farmers-general naturally tried to get the proprietors to provide good quarters for their beasts, of which they owned half, but the houses of the *métayers* mattered little. They had, however, provided something which was very useful for the people: a well, quite near the door. There were still rushes growing in the yard and the pond surrounded by willows was the same, except that they had made a sloping bank of stones on one side for the animals, so that they could drink more easily. The willows had aged greatly and rotten débris escaped from their unsteady trunks.

I did not know the people who were living at the farm, so I had no reason for going to the house. I only passed by, therefore, gazing at everything a long time, and then I rambled along the lane to La Breure. It was still the same sunken lane, still narrow in places, still enclosed between high, quick-set hedges, whose leaves September had yellowed; the same oaks towered over the banks, with their roots protruding and their branches thick with leaves, but some had been cut down, although their stumps were still visible. Some of the deepest ruts had been levelled; the water had created new ones; these were the only changes to be seen in the Rue Creuse. But at the end I did not find my familiar Breure: they had cleared it; it had been transformed into an honest cultivated field, where only some grey stones still showed their noses, recalling the old state of things. Without much emotion I wandered about this plot of land, now much too civilized, contenting myself with scratching the surface here and there with the end of my stick, or the tip of my *sabots*, to see what the nature of the soil was, and if it seemed productive. I saw once more the horizon I had so often contemplated, the fertile valley, and the naked, distant hillock which rose in front of the forest of Messarges. And memories, memories of the time when I was a shepherd there assailed me so sharply that, for a moment, I forgot the rest of my existence; I felt myself again the little lad of long ago, open to everything, whom a mere nothing amused, whom a mere nothing grieved. It was a passing illusion, quick as a flash.

I roamed about some of the fields of the farm, which I also found unchanged, save for some trees hewn down and some brushwood cleared. I went into the meadow at Suippières, beside the spring from which we used to get our water: it was abandoned; the oxen in the pasture came there to drink, and their feet had sent the soil from the edges into the bed of the stream. I went along a boggy ditch, the home of some green frogs, where I used to gather yellow irises in the spring: the same thread of clear water ran along the bottom on the same grey mud. I followed the way to Fontivier along which I had gone, carrying on my back Barret, stricken to death; that memory gave me a pang of anguish. Finally, after a round of three hours, I regained, passing by Suippières, the little lane from Meillers.

After the village, I passed the mill on the way to Saint-Aubin, I found myself face to face with Boulois of Le Parizet, who was returning from Mass. Since my marriage we had been bitter enemies; Boulois had never been able to forgive me for having abused his confidence in marrying Victoire, whom he coveted. When we happened to meet at fairs, he gave me furious looks, and I made as though I had not seen him. So this unforeseen encounter took us both by surprise. Boulois looked at me without anger.

"Hullo! you here?" he said, stopping.

"Yes, I wanted to see my old home."

"Ah!"

He was silent for a moment, visibly embarrassed as to what line to take. Then he held out his hand:

"And how are you, old man?"

"Oh! very well, thank you: and you?"

"Like other old folk, one time ill, another time well, more often ill than well. Tiennon," said he, after a short silence, "I forgive you for that dirty trick you played. I have sulked long enough; we can surely be friends again."

"It really was mean of me; I quite realize that – only, you know, I had no situation."

"Yes, that marriage must have done you a real good turn; perhaps without it you might have been a day labourer all your life, which is not much fun, indeed it isn't. As for me, I married another of whom I have no cause to complain. So let's say no more about it."

We stopped a moment to talk, passing in review the chief events of our lives. He had never left Le Parizet: at the death of his father the management of the farm had come to him. He had worked well, brought up five children, played some good games of cards, and drunk a good deal. The proprietor was one of those decent rich men of whom there are not many; he held Boulois in great esteem and had just built for his use a new room in which he reckoned he would grow old and die: naturally his eldest son would succeed him on the farm.

He had, indeed, a great many things to say, and yet, after just a quarter of an hour's talk, we found we came up short. The past is a pit where our impressions of the moment are endlessly accumulated, layer by layer, the more recent obscuring the others which in time become a formless mass, where it is difficult to find anything clear.

The mill was not working. I looked at the tall brick chimney, its blackened top standing out against the clear sky. Boulois contemplated the vast pond which the slight breeze moved gently and on which the sun made reflections like melting ore. He suddenly broke the reverie in which we were both plunged.

"Tiennon," he said suddenly, "come and have some soup with me."

I refused at first, but he insisted, and I ended by accepting. When we arrived at Le Parizet, towards three o'clock, the women were just about to grate some quinces to make cordial.

"Wife," said Boulois, "I have brought my old communion comrade; it is owing to him that I married you, you know; you ought to like him for that. We're hungry; give us something to eat and drink."

She was a short, stout woman, troubled with asthma: she had a simple smile.

"There is nothing very grand, you are too late; we had our meal two hours ago."

She brought the remains of the thick soup which had been kept warm, quickly fried some eggs, and took a whole goat's cheese from the sideboard. Boulois pressed me to drink all the time and his hand trembled with happy excitement.

"Do have something to drink – do eat something; do you remember the time when we went to catechism?"

We stayed at table a long time: we had to taste three different kinds of liqueurs. Memories of the past came to us more easily and we kept finding things to say. To please him I had to go and see the garden afterwards, then the animals, and it was night before I left. Victoire had been anxious about my long abscence and she made a scene, but it was not in her power to annoy me. I was satisfied with my day, happy at this reconciliation: and drinking had contributed also to my rose-coloured thoughts, so much so that I felt myself as light as a young man, and carried away by joy.

*   *   *

Alas! misfortunes follow closely on the good days. During the week we had a letter from Paris announcing the death of my sister Catherine. She had remained at work till the end: death had struck her before the old mistress, from whom she had expected to inherit something.

LIII

The narrow-gauge railway with which Fauconnet had endowed us passed right at the end of one of our fields, and crossed the road nearly level with the ground, at a hundred yards from our house. Its construction had caused endless recriminations. Certain small proprietors, although they had received ten times the value of their land, grumbled continually about the great damage it had caused.

Others criticized the track which certainly made a lot of curves for which no one could demonstrate the necessity. They said that the contractor, sure of a good profit, had deliberately increased the mileage. They declared that Dr Fauconnet and the other gentleman of the Council-general, consciously or not, had idly squandered the rate-payers' money. When election-time came, the council's opponents did not fail to make this clear. If they had been in power they would not have been more successful in pleasing everybody. But it is quite normal to criticize those who are in charge.

In spite of its curves, and in spite of all the various complaints, the little railway worked: every day we heard its whistlings and rumblings, and it entertained us to see the train pass by. At first we feared for our animals, for the level-crossing could be dangerous, and when they were out in the pasture they might break through the fence and come down onto the line. We all complained about these "mad inventions" which would remove all peace and quiet from the poor country people. My wife, as usual, looked on the black side and said that we could no longer have any goats, pigs or fowls. On the other hand I tried to be optimistic. In fact the railway only claimed three stupid goslings.

But Marinette was the one most upset by the train. The sound of it made her tremble convulsively, and when it came in sight she would gaze at it fixedly with her empty eyes, shaking her fist at it until it disappeared – and it would always start off her clumsy monologue.

I too always looked up to see the train go by. Each day there were two fairly long goods trains, consisting mainly of open trucks full of lime on the up journey and full of coal on the return. But the trains were much longer still on the days of Cosnes fair – then there was a long line of closed wagons containing grunting pigs, or frightened cows too closely packed; through the shutters we could only see their uneasy heads. The regular passenger-trains usually consisted of two or three coaches, often only one. It looked almost like a toy, the little engine with its low furnace towing the long brown coach, taking it slowly and carefully through fields, meadows and woods. I got to know all the men in the blue smocks soiled with grease and coal, who drove the trains; also the others, those who wore gilt-edged caps and black tunics with gold buttons, who usually stood on one of the platforms. I even got to know a good many of the passengers, at least the regulars: small bourgeois, big farmers, businessmen, and priests. Except on fair days, there were hardly any peasants or workmen: you need money and leisure to go for outings in trains.

Those are clever types, thought I, who manage to do well at the expense of the producer, and who, on top of that, don't give a damn about him.

In fact, there were times when some of the people looking out through the carriage windows, seemed to smile ironically at me, the old labouring peasant.

LIV

I had a lease of six years; when it expired in 1890, I hesitated a good deal about renewing it, because I was seventy years old and felt it. Victoire, although three years younger, was more decrepit than I. Francis was nearly thirteen and could now manage on his own. However, in the end, especially on account of Marinette, I took out a new lease. How could I take her to my sons' house, seeing that they were unaccustomed to her presence now and she was becoming more and more difficult? I prayed that Victoire and I might survive her, for I wanted to guarantee her the necessities of life, and Victoire was kind to her, although she complained constantly of having to put up with her.

But alas, that did not come to pass. My poor wife was carried off suddenly the next summer, and I had the great grief of feeling that in a measure I was to blame for her death.

A neighbour generally helped me to bring in my wheat, and one day when rain threatened he was absent; I had to call Victoire who didn't much like the job, to pack some sheaves, which we had bound the evening before, onto the cart; she got very hot at first, and then she got soaked with rain and started to shiver. That night she vomited blood; two days after she was dead.

I had to hire an old deaf widow to take care of my house. She was not very good in the dairy, so, for the first time in my life, I had to make the butter and the cheese, working with her. Marinette, who could not stand her, played endless tricks on her: she would put the fire out, turn the saucepan upside down, hide the kitchen utensils; then she would laugh to see her worried. The old woman told me she would not come again if that kind of thing was to go on. I was obliged to stay in the house for several days in a row to take care of the poor idiot. When she was about to do some stupid thing, I used to take hold of her wrists very firmly, and fix her with a threatening look; I managed to terrorize her in that way and make her quiet. On the other hand, knowing that she was very fond of haricot salad and fritters, I used to tell the servant to prepare one of these dishes as often as she could; thus, vanquished and satisfied, Marinette ceased to pursue her with hatred.

Before very long, new anxieties arose. I had to hand their mother's property over to my children, and for that I was obliged to recover my investment. I had to go several times to Bourbon, and I found myself once more, awkward and embarrassed, in the notary's office: I felt affronted by the disdainful way in which the head clerk shrugged his shoulders. He was a great scented fop, who, if I did not immediately understand his explanations, seemed anxious to let out what he was thinking: "What an imbecile this man is!"

For a long time I kept in the house two thousand francs which remained to me after all was settled. They were in the drawer of the cupboard, and I used to hide the key in a hole in the cowshed wall. When the servant wanted to put away the linen, she would ask me for the key with a sulky air, as though accusing me of being suspicious. In the end, I gave up and took my two thousand francs to the bank at Bourbon.

And my life went on, monotonously, between these two old women, one deaf, the other an idiot. Francis, who was working on a nearby farm, came sometimes on Sundays, and his visits always gave me a little happiness. But they became less and less frequent as he grew up, for he began to go out more: the company of young lads of his own age seemed more attractive to him than that of his old grandfather among his dull surroundings.

One day I took the train and went to Saint-Menoux, where my godfather, who was eighty-one, had returned to live. Cancer was consuming his face. It had begun by an itch on the left of his nose to which he had hardly paid any attention; it became purple, then a wound formed which little by little increased in size. The day on which I visited him, he took off the linen and dressings which hid the wound, and showed it to me, bloody and repulsive. His nose was simply a mass of flesh from which oozed a red fluid, and his eye was in danger.

The poor old man suffered without respite and he spent long nights without sleep. And he suffered also in his mind, for he felt he was an object of loathing to all. He was not allowed to sit at the table: they poured his soup on his bread in a special bowl, which remained unwashed for weeks; they no longer allowed his grandchildren to come near him; the servant had refused to wash the cloths which he wrapped round his face; and he had heard his daughter-in-law say one day as she set herself to do this sickening task:

"Will he never die, then, the disgusting old man!"

He told me this in a voice strangled with fury and tears. "I often want to kill myself! I think of hanging myself from a tree, or a beam in the barn, or even throwing myself into the water. Up to now I've had the courage or the cowardice not to do it, but I can't be sure: resignation has its limits. Oh, my God!"

I longed to try and comfort him, but I found nothing to say, so much did I realize that the deep despair in his heart was as incurable as the cancer which gnawed his face.

LV

After ten years my boys left Monsieur Fauconnet's estate, not being able to get on with him any longer. As he aged, the doctor became eccentric, surly and tyrannical. He was no longer a Deputy: He was too old, and his Republicanism too faded. For the old red ox-blood was now only a pale rose colour. He was all for order and propriety, and hated 'advanced' thinking. He almost imitated Mousieur Noris, whom he had mocked so much in the old days: the cry of "Long live Socialism!" made him livid with anger.

The last year that my lads were with him, they were using the threshing machine one day of great heat, and a wind of revolt ran through the exhausted workers. The doctor had come to see them towards three o'clock in the afternoon, at the most trying moment; a young servant perched on a rick shouted defiantly "Long live Socialism!" and the others responded. Mousieur Fauconnet looked at the shouters in turn and was about to get into a passion. But he saw there were too many of them, and that he was powerless against this disrespect shown him, so he restrained his anger and took Jean aside, commanding him not to tolerate that outcry. That is how people in authority act when they are no longer masters of the situation: they put responsibility onto their inferiors, who can do nothing. The doctor went away, leaving the workers to their misery and malice. When, in the evening, they took his share of grain to his house, he thought he could take his revenge easily by not offering even one miserable glass of wine to those of the threshers who had gone with the drover to take the sacks up to the granary. They went away very discontented indeed, shouting meaningfully: "Long live Socialism!" and they returned in the warm night after supper with friends: for an hour they made a tour of the château, giving enough and to spare of the prohibited cry, which they alternated with the still worse one of "Down with the bourgeois!"

* * *

My lads took another farm, in Bourbon, at Puy-Brot, between the Ygrande and the Saint-Plaisir roads. The master, a certain Mousieur Duverdon, was a young farmer-general, with a long, light auburn moustache, and an arrogant air. He passed for being a good business man, and he was renowned for Martinmas valuations of stock over an area of at least thirty kilometres.

In the agreement, he introduced a new clause, stipulating that the nursing cows should not on any account be milked: consequently the women could not sell either milk or butter without incurring a fine of fifty francs. The rest was in keeping. Duverdon, cunning upstart, took from his *métayers* the few advantages they had kept so far.

"And you've accepted all that without resistance?" I said to Charles on the day that he announced that the lease was signed.

"What can we do? If we had not accepted, several others were ready to do so, and in this district it would be hard enough to find another vacant farm."

LVI

In 1893, on Easter Sunday, having arrived early in the town to attend High Mass, I had a chat with old Daumier, an old man of my own age. We were in the square in front of the church. Some young girls, fresh and pretty, in fine new dresses, brushed past us.

I said to Daumier:

"If they could come back, the women of the old days, those who've been dead fifty years, wouldn't they be astonished to see those dresses?"

"They would think they were in another world, old man. Indeed, Saint-Aubin follows the Paris fashions, but who knows if we won't go back after all this advance?"

"Oh no! now it is started it will go on whatever happens; the Bourbon caps, like the lace bonnets, will never be seen again."

"Do you think that's a good thing?"

"Consequence of the times; what can you do? It's good for trade."

The bells rang joyfully, calling us to Mass. The weather was bright and the sky serene; the spring sunshine was tempered by a fresh breeze. The blackbirds piped gaily in a big meadow near by, where the tender green mingled with the yellow of primroses. The swelling buds were bursting on the old elms in front of us in the square. The distant bells of Bourbon and Ygrande mingled their peals with the shrill vibrations of ours.

On the walls of the church and on the tree-trunks were spread big green, yellow and red posters, separated by long streamers stuck on askew:

"Look!" said Daumier, "there you are, those who can read have something to amuse them. That means that we are going to vote for Deputies soon; it seems even that one of the candidates is going to speak here after Mass."

"Ah! which of them?"

"Renaud the Socialist."

A neighbour joined us and told us that it was not Renaud, but one of his friends, who was working the small communes in his name.

"It doesn't matter; shall we hear what he has to say, Bertin?" said Daumier.

"My word, yes, if you like," I answered.

After Mass we went and sat down at the table in the inn where the orator was to hold his meeting. The room filled in ten minutes, and the potman had to improvise some tables outside. But the man they expected was not there. He arrived on a wretched bicycle, but not till nearly two o'clock. As he entered, everyone gazed at him as at a curious animal. He was a little dark man with an unhealthy complexion, and he walked with lowered eyes and a timid air. At the end of the room they had reserved a small, narrow table for him, and from behind this he began to talk among the hubbub of persistent talk. He spoke at first slowly, as though with difficulty, seeking his words; then, having won attention, he gained confidence, his eyes shone, and his voice became firm. He described the poverty of the workers, to whom everything was promised and for whom nothing was ever done; he attacked the bourgeoisie, and the priests,

whom he accused of being accomplices in fooling the people.
At his left a drunken fellow of fifty or so with a congested face
got up frequently and called out:

"Unhappy farm workers, bent by endless toil, whom everybody
fleeces, you don't have the right to call yourselves men. You are no
more than slaves! We have had four revolutions in less than a
century, but in vain: you remain ignorant, sneered at, poverty-
stricken! The true revolution will be the one that makes the people
sovereign. Work to this end, comrades. Your ballot paper will say
that this is what you want. Do not allow yourselves to be represented any longer by the bourgeoisie, who look after their own interests
before anything else. Monarchists, Bonapartists, Republicans,
quarrel to make a show, but they all get together in order to get the
better of *you*. Show them that you've had enough of them. Be
represented by one of your own kind: vote for the Socialist candidate, Citizen Renaud! Then, think about getting together, stand
up for your rights. Like this you will be strong. And the new dawn
will bring light . . . The day will come when as farmworkers you will
own your own fields, just as the miners will own their own mines,
and the factory-workers their factories. Then there will be no more
parasitic middlemen, no more masters nor serfs; there will only be
the great mass of humanity in touch with the riches of nature. It is
for you, comrades, to hasten the coming of the new time –"

"He is a *partageux**!" a man beside me said in a low voice.

Another went on:

"His name is Laronde; I know his father, he's my brother-in-
law's cousin; his father is a ploughman at Couleuvre; but he left
him, no doubt because he was too lazy to work on the land."

"In any case, he has a good mind," said a third.

Laronde had ceased speaking; he wiped his face, which was
covered with sweat. Some of the young people applauded and cried:
"Long live Socialism!" "Down with the bourgeoisie!" In the middle of the room the drunkard stood gesticulating, railing all the time
against the freemasons; some *métayers* took themselves off fearfully,
afraid of compromising themselves in this revolutionary assembly.
Daumier seemed embarrassed.

"They ought not to let men talk like that. It only makes dissen-
sion in the world, making people believe things that can never
happen."

*Socialist (or Communist) who wants to divide up property.

"How do you know it won't happen?" I said. "Think of all the changes we have seen in the course of our lives, of all the greater comfort that we have now."

"We are not happier nor richer for it; when we have that, we want something else; and comfort does not prevent us from getting old."

"Growing old is not everything; we must think a little of the pleasures we can enjoy while life lasts, surely!"

Laronde crossed the room, bowing to right and left and smiling. He went out and mounted his bicycle, stared at by a lot of women who had come to the door of the inn to look at him. He went on to Ygrande, where he was to speak in the evening. After he had gone, everybody began to discuss what he had said; some approved, some criticized.

A master quarreyman, who was a glib talker, had heard my replies to Daumier, and now came up.

"Of course," he said, "we shall continue to go forward, because we shall make new discoveries which will make work easier. But only science can produce improvement. Politics are powerless and ineffective. The deputies will never really make the laws for the people. The rich bourgeois, whom we tend to ignore at election time, none the less conserve all their influence, believe you me. As to Renaud, Laronde and their like, they're only ambitious men who want to take the places of others and become bourgeois in their turn. 'Get out of there and let me in': it's always the same story. The opposition, as long as they haven't got the responsibility of power, tell themselves that they can do wonders – after which they hasten to imitate the others. If the Socialists succeed in having a majority you'll see how little of their programme they'll achieve. Then people who are more advanced than they are will arrive on the scene and try to turn them out of office: it's in the nature of things. Politics! It's all rubbish!"

Several people approved noisily the diatribe of this man without illusions. But a merchant, a friend of the retiring Deputy, Monsieur Gouget, replied:

"We mustn't exaggerate, politics are important. Didn't the Republic provide us with free schools and reduce the length of military service? If we had a majority of good Republicans like Monsieur Gouget we should soon have a tax on income which would fall on the rich, and there would be pensions for old workers. At last the State will break with the Church; the priests will cease to be office-holders; those who want their services can pay for them.

That's the programme of all true Republicans; it is that of Monsieur Gouget, who has always supported it with his vote; unfortunately, up to now the majority remain hostile to these principles. And many electors, who understand nothing, withdraw their confidence from Monsieur Gouget under the pretext that he can't bring about the reforms he preaches. As if he was the only one!"

I began to talk too. I had been accustomed to vote for Monsieur Gouget and I meant to remain faithful to him. Nevertheless, addressing the master quarryman, I proclaimed myself more or less a Socialist: "Listen, it's hard to make sense out of this . . . There will always be the strong and the weak, the sly and the fleeced . . . There'll always be some to live off the work of others. The men who go in for politics are often humbugs, or ambitious rogues. But since we have nothing to fear, since all our income is at the end of our arms, we can take the chance of voting for the most radical candidates, if only to trouble the bourgeois who've troubled us so much!"

Then the quarryman replied: "You believe in division, Father Bertin; you want to have your holding without paying rent. But if they sent you to such and such a place" – he mentioned some bad holdings, badly situated – "what would you say? It's not easy to divide things right."

"We can't change things that have always existed," said old Daumier.

"No, I'm not a *partageux*! All that's a lot of silliness. But I would like to see land owned by the commune rather than by some gentlemen from Paris or elsewhere. The commune would rent it to peasants on good terms and use the revenue for improvements, which would benefit everyone, and help the old and poor too. Wouldn't that be as good and rather better than what we see now? Do you think it just that one individual should own a whole commune, while so many others, by selling their labour, can hardly drag their bread out of it from day to day? Do you think it natural to see old men die of hunger and poverty, while idle revellers waste money in an unheard-of manner, spending, they say, in one night what would feed several poor families for a whole year?"

"As to your objection," I said, turning to old Daumier, "it doesn't hold water, you know. My late grandmother could remember the time when the priests went into the fields to collect their tithes, when the masters had all kinds of privileges and exorbitant rights. At that time there were, no doubt, people who maintained that these things, having always existed, could not be suppressed. They were suppressed, however, and now it seems to us amazing that they could have lasted so long. The same will happen to many laws and customs of our day and our descendants will be astonished, perhaps, that they have lasted so long. To speak of the things that concern us closely, do you think we could no longer live if there were no more farmer-generals? That should be quite possible, now that the young know how to read and write. And we should have to feed fewer big-bellies who do nothing, that's all!"

"Well said!" exclaimed the quarryman, rising to go and join a client, who was signalling to him.

"Bravo, Father Tiennon. Long live Socialism!" exclaimed three young people who had heard me.

And they offered me coffee. But I felt myself a little giddy with the noise in the room and the heat and smoke. I looked at the clock.

"No, my friends, no; it's time for me to go and look after my cows."

Daumier interposed:

"Come along, let's have some coffee with the young lads, old Socialist."

"No, really; I have a bit of a headache, and I would certainly say stupid things; that's always what happens when you stay too long at the inn. Good-bye!"

I shook hands with everyone and went, leaving old Daumier, who got abominably drunk. It is the only time in my life that I have talked politics so much.

*   *   *

The elections were quickly forgotten, and the discussions and the dreams of social improvement which they had aroused, in the great disaster which came upon us that year: all the spring, all the summer without rain; a constant sunshine which burnt the plants down to the roots; a ridiculous crop of hay; an indifferent crop of corn; pastures dried up; ponds empty; the value of the animals fallen away to nothing; what a wretched state of affairs! I was obliged to go to the wood and rake up dry leaves, for the cows' litter, and to buy fodder from the South that a merchant sent to Saint-Aubin in trucks; I realized that year that the railway could in fact help peasants.

LVII

During the great heat of 1893 my poor martyr of a brother was carried off by the death he had so longed for.

At the end of that same year my old servant left me to go to the service of a priest, hoping to have a quieter time than with us. I hired another, a big woman with a masculine voice, unkind and unreasonable, who pestered me with the constant repetition of the same tales, got offended at every turn and upset my sister when she played her pranks. Later, I discovered that she made a profit on the sale of my provisions at the market at Saint-Hilaire, and that she drank cups of coffee and sweet wine at my expense. I kept her though, preferring to bear all that, rather than to change again, knowing that I should never find the ideal housekeeper.

During the late and hard winter of 1895, Marinette and I had influenza, and Madeleine, Charles' wife, had to come from Puy-Brot to take care of us. That attack carried off Marinette, who had been failing for some time. For myself, I believed that I, too, was near the end, I felt so weak, so wasted by the fever, and exhausted by a horrible cough, which tore my stomach. I recovered, however, very slowly, to tell the truth, after being languid and stiff for several months; but I had only a small part of the vigour that I had kept till then.

Then I looked forward to the day when, my lease having expired, I might return among my children.

During that time my thoughts were often melancholy. I thought of how I was left alone, like an old tree, forgotten in a copse, in the midst of the young growth. One by one, those whom I had known had gone. Dead, my grandmother, of the brown shawl and the Bourbon cap. Dead, Uncle Toinot, who had served under the great Emperor and who had killed his Russian. Dead, my father and my mother, he kind and weak, she often ill-natured and harsh from having been so unhappy. Dead, the Girauds and their son the soldier from Africa, and their son-in-law the glass-blower, who always talked of pushing up the daisies. Dead, Victoire, the good partner of my life, whose faults I hardly noticed by the end, as she must scarcely have noticed mine under the effect of habit. Dead, my little Clémentine, gentle and rebellious. Dead, my niece, Berthe, delicate Parisian flower, after a painful confinement. Dead, the Fauconnets, father and son; Boutry, Gorlier, Parent, Lavallée, Noris. Dead, all those who had played a part in my life, including Thérèse, my first sweetheart. I saw them often; they filed past together in my dreams at night, in my daytime memories. In the night they lived again for me; but by day it seemed to me that I walked in a line of spectres.

And the idea of death had now no terrors for me. Ah! my first melancholy emotions in La Billette, at the death of my grandmother! The tightening of my heart at the appearance of the great long box in which they placed her, and my sharp, sincere grief when I heard the shovelfuls of earth fall upon the coffin down in the grave! I had seen too many such scenes since, and my heart was now hard and resolute. At each new funeral my indifference increased, so much so that I was frightened at it myself. However, it would soon be my turn, it would be me they would nail in such a box, that they would lower on the side with ropes to the bottom of a yawning hole and upon which they would throw by shovelfuls the great heap of earth lying, like the infinite barrier separating the dead from the living! But even that thought did not move me.

Besides, apart from those moments of weakening and morbid fancies, I was interested in all the energetic growth which expanded around me. My sons were serious men, the elderly men of the present day. My grandsons represented the future; they appeared to believe that it would never end. Nevertheless, behind *them*, infancy prattled, grew....

LVIII

It is now five years since I have come back among my children. They are not bad to me. Rosalie, even, shows me tokens of affection that astonish me. Madeleine is very devoted, very loving, and allows her sister-in-law to rule. Harmony reigns in the household and I am very content. In spite of that, a separation is imminent; they are becoming too numerous to remain together.

The reason is that there is a third family. My grandson, the son of Jean and Rosalie, who returned from military service three years ago, was married last Martinmas. I have a granddaughter-in-law: I shall soon have a great grandchild. And Charles has two daughters who are likely to marry also. It is getting urgent that my two boys should each have their farm. Duverdon, who likes them, has promised to place the one who goes out in another of his farms. As for me, I am the old man!

I do little services for one and another. The daughters-in-law say to me:

"Father, if you don't mind, could you ..."

And to please them, I supply the kitchen with the wood which is necessary; I feed the rabbits; I look after the geese.

In summer my lads often beg me to do one thing or another, when time is scarce. And I take the cows and the sheep to the fields, I even take care of the pigs, as though it was seventy years ago. I end as I began; old age and childhood have their analogies; extremes often meet. When we make hay, I still toss and rake. When we load, I preach prudence; I urge them to make the carts lighter; good advice which they don't always take. The young like to be daring, to risk all for all, to be knowing. But fatal to rashness is the experience which age gives. And I am old!

My strength declines more and more, my limbs stiffen; the blood does not seem to circulate in them. Every night in winter Rosalie puts a warm brick wrapped in a cloth in my bed; but for that I would never get warm or sleep. I am bent; in vain I try to straighten myself, to look in the front of me as in former days: no, it is the points of my *sabots* that I examine in spite of all! The soil that I have handled so much seems to fascinate me, it seems to rise towards me to defy me, it seems to be saying that it will soon have its turn. I see things enlarged and I shake a little; I make gashes on my face when I shave: it happens that when I go to Mass I don't recognize people whom I know quite well; I even did not know my little Francis when he came to see me after his term of service! I am always a little hard of hearing, and at times very deaf, especially in the winter. At such times I can't follow the conversation; when people address me, I have to make them repeat what they have said several times, and in spite of that, I understand badly and answer wrongly, which makes them laugh at me. When I have eaten, if I remain seated, I go to sleep, and in the night, on the contrary, I am often unable to get to sleep at all. I have absurd lapses of memory. I remember very well the striking incidents of my youth, but the things which happened the day before escape me. I suppose my mind has been so fatigued by the events which have occupied it through three quarters of a century, that it finds itself powerless to grasp new subjects. The result is that I am too fond of talking about things of former days which I recall, and which interest no one else, and I show an artlessness about new things that makes people laugh at me. I appear a little ridiculous. On my grandchildren's faces I often read the phrase from the language of today:

"What a bore the old man is!"

Oh, yes, I'm the old man! It is well to recognize the fact with a good grace. My body has had its day; it longs for the great rest.

And truly one sees many astonishing things. In my youth everybody travelled on horseback because carriages could not go along the bad roads. Now there are carriages that have no need of horses. I was taking care of the pigs this summer in one of the fields which is bounded by the main road. I would often hear a noise, shrill and disagreeable, which got louder and louder, and the motor-car, carrying men dressed like savages and wearing goggles like stone-breakers, would tear past, raising a cloud of dust and smoke and leaving a disgusting smell of petrol.

One day one of the young servants from a neighbouring farm was taking a herd of cattle to a meadow which was separated from the road by a fence. From the direction of Bourbon one of those carriages came at full speed, and the animals began to run. The driver sounded his horn, and that frightened the cows more. Two of them went down a side road to the left; two others jumped over the hedge and went through a field of oats; the other three continued running. I joined the poor weeping child on the road; she said she could see them a very long way off, still fleeing before the car, which moved at the same rapid rate. I sent the child to tell her master. A man set out to find the three runaway cows; he returned a long time after, bringing two only, the other had died of fatigue at the side of a ditch; he had got a butcher at Ygrande to take it away.

In talking of the incident at our house, I remember saying:

"Ah! we were wrong when we complained about the railway; the train has its own road and passes at stated hours: with care we can avoid it. But these motor-cars really are the instruments of the devil, invading the roads, upsetting us and doing us mischief."

That's what I said at first, but afterwards I thought that I had no need to trouble about such things. A man from a bygone age, a grandfather with a nodding head, it was not for me to pass judgment. The young people will get used to these new vehicles; they will hate the rich people even more for causing them annoyances every day, and sometimes accidents, through thoughtlessness or sport. Moreover, the animals themselves will get used to them.

For me, what does it matter? I ask only one thing – to remain in fair health to the end. So long as I can help my children they will keep me easily. They will still be kind, I have no doubt, when I become good-for-nothing. But I dread being a trouble to them, becoming paralysed or blind or falling into dotage, or suffering from some lingering illness. It would be too painful to know that I was an encumbrance which they would wish to see disappear. I remember how I saw my grandfather like that a long time ago, and more recently my poor godfather: that would be dreadful. Let death come; it does not frighten me; I think about it at times, without bitterness or fear. Death! Death, but not the horrible downfall of becoming a burden to the young, to the healthy, to the ordinary life of the family. Let it strike me whilst still at work, so that they can say:

"Old Tiennon's kicked the bucket; he was very old, very worn-out; but he wasn't a burden; he worked right to the end."

I hope my epitaph won't be:

"Old Bertin's dead: poor old man! In his condition it was a happy release for him and a blessing for his family."

From life I have nothing to hope, but I have still something to fear. That I may escape this last calamity is my one desire.

Ygrande, 1901–1902